AND THEN YOU DYE

This Large Print Book carries the
Seal of Approval of N.A.V.H.

A NEEDLECRAFT MYSTERY

AND THEN YOU DYE

MONICA FERRIS

THORNDIKE PRESS
A part of Gale, Cengage Learning

GALE
CENGAGE Learning®

Detroit • New York • San Francisco • New Haven, Conn • Waterville, Maine • London

LIBRARY OF CONGRESS CATALOGING-IN-PUBLICATION DATA

Ferris, Monica.
    And then you dye / by Monica Ferris.
      pages ; cm. — (Thorndike Press large print mystery) (A needlecraft mystery)
    ISBN-13: 978-1-4104-5602-1 (hardcover)
    ISBN-10: 1-4104-5602-1 (hardcover)
    1. Devonshire, Betsy (Fictitious character)—Fiction. 2. Needleworkers—Fiction. 3. Women detectives—Minnesota—Fiction. 4. Large type books. I. Title.
PS3566.U47A83 2013
813'.54—dc23   2012043725

Published in 2013 by arrangement with The Berkley Publishing Group, a member of Penguin Group (USA) Inc.

Printed in the United States of America
1 2 3 4 5 6 7 17 16 15 14 13

AND THEN YOU DYE

ONE

It was a Wednesday evening in early May, close to seven thirty. The surface of the library table in the Crewel World needlework shop was thickly layered with newspaper over a sturdy plastic sheet. A big kettle and a large, long-handled stainless steel pot were simmering on a hot plate in the middle of the table, and there was a smell in the moist air as of some unpopular green vegetable cooking.

All eight seats at the table were taken, and two women were standing, all attentive to a handsome dark-haired woman in her middle fifties. She was enveloped in a white smock generously spattered with soft colors, some faded almost to invisibility.

"In dyeing there are two kinds of fibers," she was saying, waving an arm over the pot, "protein fibers and plant fibers. Protein fibers come from animals: wool, silk, alpaca, dog and cat, yak, et cetera."

A standing woman's hand went up. "I beg your pardon," she said. "Silk is animal protein?"

"Certainly. It comes from the silkworm. And worms — they're moth larvae, actually — are animals."

"Oh, the silkworm. Well, yes, I guess they are." But her nose was wrinkled in distaste.

"Cotton, linen, soy, bamboo, and corn are some of the plant fibers." She paused, waiting for someone to question that, but no one did.

Betsy Devonshire, the other standee and owner of Crewel World, thought that might be because the speaker was Hailey Brent, whose hand-spun and hand-dyed yarns, made of all the aforementioned fibers and more, were familiar to these people, who were customers of Betsy's shop.

Hailey looked at the smaller pot on the hot plate. The liquid in it was thick with wilted pinkish lavender flower heads. She picked up a foot-long wooden dowel to stir the mixture. "Just a little longer," she said.

Four small glass bottles stood in an irregular cluster on the table, each containing a powder: one white, one gray-green, and two gray. Each carried a white stick-on label with uncial lettering: TIN, COPPER, IRON, ALUM.

"Now, mordants." Hailey gestured at the bottles. "Mordants are chemical or metal salts such as these, dissolved in water. The word comes from the Latin for *bite,* because they cause the dye to penetrate the fiber. Any fibers you are going to dye should first be soaked in one of these mordants. They change the way color from the dye bath affects the fibers. They may also brighten, dull, or strengthen a color, and they all serve to make the dye more colorfast. All the metallic ones are poisonous, which is the main reason why, if you decide to try dyeing, you should *absolutely never* use a pot or pan or bowl that you use in ordinary cooking. Not even careful washing is guaranteed to restore it to a condition safe for food use. I hope that is clear?" Hailey's genial tone had turned serious, and everyone solemnly nodded back at her. Those who had been taking notes were seen writing this down.

Betsy, who had been thinking that dyeing might be an interesting way to spend an afternoon, changed her mind.

"Good. Now, let's strain out the vegetable matter from our dye bath."

Hailey reached under the table for yet another stainless steel pot, this one large with two pouring spouts. Atop it was a big, deep strainer. She slowly poured the flower heads and the liquid, the color of thin tea, into the strainer, using the dowel to poke the last of the flowers out.

"Ms. Brent," asked one of the observers seated at the table, "is that brown the color we're going to get on the wool?"

"Possibly. I'm not sure," Hailey replied. "One of the more interesting things about vegetable dyeing is that when you try a new variety, you're never quite sure what color you're going to get. But I don't think we're going to get pink or lavender."

"Oh," said someone else in a disappointed voice, "I was hoping for a nice, bright pink."

"For a nice, bright pink, I'm afraid you need to go to the aniline dyes — chemical dyes. Natural dyes tend to be softer in color."

"But wasn't there a red dye back in the eighteenth century?" asked another woman. "The British used it on their soldiers' uniforms. That's why they were called redcoats, right? And that was before aniline dyes."

"There is a natural dye that gives a true red, but it comes from an insect found on Mexican cactus plants: cochineal. It was a very expensive dye — still is, in fact. The British were showing off, using it for ordinary soldiers' uniforms. The closest red you'll get from a vegetable dye is orange. There is actually a local flower that will give you a nice, rich orange when mordanted in tin, but it isn't fast — it fades in sunlight and after a couple of washings."

"What flower is that?" asked the woman.

"A new variety of marigold. You'll probably notice, when we dye our samples, that the wool mordanted in tin gives us the brightest color."

Also on the table was a low stack of fabric cut into four-inch squares, each with five short lengths of white yarn slipknotted through slits cut down one side. Beside each slip of yarn was printed on the fabric with permanent marker ALUM, COPPER, IRON, TIN and NONE.

Hailey picked up the squares, counted the number of people present (including herself), and pulled a dozen squares off the stack. Setting them aside, she lifted the strainer off the big pot and dumped the flowers into a wastebasket lined with a plastic bag, then poured the liquid back into the pot and returned it to the burner.

"Now let's try dyeing some of our wool." She took the dozen squares and dropped them into the pot, poking at them with the dowel. She checked her watch, and half the members of her audience checked theirs, too. "We'll give it five minutes," she said.

Meanwhile, she lifted the kettle off the hot plate and poured its steaming contents into a stainless steel dishpan. "Rinse water," she explained.

She reached under the table and came up with a twin to the pot currently holding the squares. "Betsy, could you fill this about halfway with hot water?"

"Certainly," said Betsy, taking the pot with her into the back room, where — having been forewarned — she had earlier filled the electric teakettle and plugged it in.

Hailey Brent had come into Crewel World several months ago to see if Betsy would be interested in carrying her hand-dyed and hand-spun knitting yarns. Betsy was pleased to add them to her stock, and some of her customers were willing to pay the higher prices for the yarns. It was a natural progression for Betsy to invite Hailey to spend an evening in the shop giving a demonstration on dyeing.

So here they were on a Thursday evening in early May, learning some of the basics.

Betsy poured hot water into the pot and brought it back to the table.

Hailey was lifting one of the squares out with her dowel, checking its progress.

Already one of the slips of yarn was a dark brown color, one was a bright yellow, one was palest cream, and one was olive green. The last one, marked NONE, was not visibly affected. It was an interesting, seemingly magical effect to see fibers coming out different colors from the same dye pot. The square itself had turned a pale olive.

"None of them is tea colored," said one of the seated women, surprised.

"This is what I told you, you never know when you try some new vegetable dye what color you're going to get," said Hailey cheerfully.

"I was really hoping for something lavender," remarked another of the sitting women. "I don't see why lavender flowers don't produce a lavender dye."

"You know something?" said Hailey with a chuckle. "Neither do I."

"Maybe if we used the roots," persisted the woman. "You said earlier that roots can be a source of dye and that you don't always get the color of the roots when you use them as dye."

"But we don't have the roots," said Hailey. She added slyly, "Marge evidently didn't dig these up out of someone's garden — did you, Marge?"

Marge Schultz, who was standing beside

Betsy, turned pink. But she said, calmly enough, "I bought these flowers at the florist shop on Water Street."

"You didn't take them from your own gardens?" asked another woman.

"No, of course not. These are summer flowers; it's only May, too early in the year for them to bloom in my garden."

Marge owned a nursery called Green Gaia Gardens, which Hailey must have known about, since she called her so casually by name. Betsy also knew Hailey was herself a gardener, so she must be aware that lavender daisies wouldn't be blooming in the spring.

So why the crack about digging them out of someone's garden?

"Thanks," Hailey said as Betsy set the pot down. "This will do for a second rinse. You want to rinse and rinse again and again until the water runs clear." She lifted a square out of the dye, held it over the pot for a little while to let it drip and cool, then very gently squeezed it before putting it in the dishpan. "You want the rinse water to be the same temperature as the dye," she said. "And you don't want to agitate your fibers. Otherwise they may felt." Meaning turn into a solid mat.

She continued the process, lifting the

other squares one at a time and squeezing them. "There's one mordant I haven't mentioned yet: sugar. Sugar makes a great fixative — that's why if you spill a dollop of jam onto your white trousers, the stain is permanent." She looked up briefly. "Right, Marge? The stain is permanent." The sly tone was even more evident this time.

Though her face was still pink, Marge said in a tone bordering on indifference, "How would I know?"

One of the seated women offered, "I ruined a favorite blouse last year by spilling blueberry preserves down the front of it."

"Why is she picking on you?" murmured Betsy to Marge.

"I don't know," Marge said wearily.

Betsy asked Marge to stay after the demo was finished. "I lost some of my bleeding hearts over this winter," Betsy told her friend. "We used too much salt in the parking lot, I guess. I want to replace them — or maybe get something else that likes shade instead."

Betsy owned the old brick building in which her shop was located. It was two stories high, and consisted of three shops on the ground floor and three apartments on the second. Betsy lived in one of the apartments herself.

At the back of the building there was a small parking lot just big enough for four cars plus a Dumpster. The parking lot backed onto a steep, tree-filled rise; Betsy owned about two-thirds of it. The trees kept the ground in deep shade, and Betsy had thought of having some of them cut down so she could plant some sun-loving perennials back there. She especially envied Marge's collection of hydrangea shrubs. New to central Minnesota, and hardy, hers offered large round clusters of rich pink blooms from June to frost. But they needed lots of sunlight.

"I'm wondering what you'd suggest for the hill behind my parking lot," said Betsy. "Did you get a chance to look at it before the dyeing demo?"

"Yes, I did. Hostas would look nice, and they spread, so you could buy only a few to start with and then be patient."

"Yes, but everyone has hostas. What else is there?"

"Well, if you want something large and showy, you should just buy more bleeding hearts. But plant them on the margin of your wooded lot, they do need some sun. For deeper in, and if you want something hard to kill, lily of the valley is a good choice. They spread fast and are very aggressive at driving out other plants, which can be good or bad, depending."

They talked about how many plants Betsy should buy, and Betsy promised to visit Green Gaia sometime during the next several days.

Then Betsy asked, "Marge, what's the problem between you and Hailey Brent?"

"Oh, no problem. We just don't get along."

"You're neighbors, aren't you?"

"Yes. Maybe that's the problem. She has a very artistic temperament, you know."

"So?"

Marge shrugged uncomfortably. "Well, she has this attitude that anything that drives her artistic sensibilities is permitted. For example, she has come onto my property and stolen blooms. Not a lot, and not often, but when I get something she thinks would make a good dye, she'll just take it without asking. She knows it's wrong, because she sneaks. I mean, if she really thought it was all right, she'd just take them openly. I asked her one time what she would think if I came into her garden and took a plant I liked. And she said, 'If you needed it badly, I wouldn't say a word.' " Marge sighed. "One of these days maybe I will call the police on her."

"It's gotten that bad?"

Marge sighed again. "No, not really. But she's a terrible nuisance. And now she's got it into her head that I'm just looking for a chance to steal something from her garden — that's what the fuss was this evening. I'm sorry it happened. It must've been at least as aggravating to you as it was embarrassing to me. I only came because I've been thinking of setting up a little garden of plants useful to dyers and wanted a look at the skill set. And then she behaves like that! Honestly, sometimes I could just brain her!"

Marge laughed wryly, but Betsy was to remember this conversation in the weeks to come.

Two

Irene Potter was *inspired.* Well, sort of. She knew what she wanted to do next. That is, she mostly wanted something *different.* She was rich enough nowadays that she could pretty much stitch whatever inspired her and demand anything she wanted by way of art materials.

It was such fun being an artist. Especially a rich one. Famous, too. She'd always known she was artistic, but now she was also an *Artist.* Her picture had been in the newspapers more than once, there had even been an article about her in a national magazine, and, best of all, her work was in museums and art galleries.

Of course, not everyone agreed she was truly an Artist, but the people who thought she wasn't were wrong. It was because she used a needle instead of a paintbrush. But that made her unique, and being unique was a really big part of becoming a famous Artist. And having some "attitude" helped, too, though Irene wasn't sure exactly when she was showing "attitude" and when she was simply giving an opinion.

What she did know was that she wanted to start work on a new piece. (How glorious it was to be able to not work on a piece until the drive to do it was firmly established!) It was going to be a small one, after several years of increasingly larger ones. But dense, very dense. She closed her eyes and could almost see it. She knew it was going to be busy, with lots of overlapping detail in lots of fancy stitches. An abstract, of course. Done in shades of yellow, green, tan . . . and white? Maybe not white. And maybe some touches of blue. The vision was not yet clear. She needed to see the fibers she was going to use, touch them with her fingers, inhale their scent.

And where was she going to buy the wools and flosses to use on her piece?

She could call a cab — she had never learned to drive — and go to Stitchville USA over in Minnetonka, or Needlework Unlimited in Edina. But perhaps she should start at her favorite needlework supply store, Crewel World. They were right here in town and had been the ones who first recognized her amazing skills and encouraged her to present herself not just as a skilled stitcher but as a true Artist. They were among her oldest friends.

Irene rose onto her toes, swiveled a hundred and eighty degrees, then started walking swiftly down the sidewalk. She was a slender woman in her late forties with very curly black hair cropped short, dark shining eyes, and a slightly crooked smile. She wore a brightly patterned heavy cotton skirt that came nearly to her ankles, brown sandals over navy blue socks, and a white peasant blouse with a scoop neck and puffy short sleeves under a navy blue sweater vest she'd knit herself. Irene bought most of her clothes at secondhand stores, a holdover from her impoverished days, and she saw no reason to change, especially since a reporter had once described her dress habits as "endearingly eccentric."

So she sailed down the street with her head held high, looking forward to a pleasant, profitable visit with her good friend, Betsy Devonshire.

Meanwhile, Betsy and Godwin had their heads together at the library table. "I don't think this will be as difficult as you're thinking," Godwin said, gesturing at the legal-size pad with notes scrawled all over it.

"Have you ever run a contest?" asked Betsy.

"Well, no, but I know Margot did, and she said they weren't hard to do." Margot was Betsy's late sister, who founded Crewel World years ago. Godwin had worked for her before starting to work for Betsy.

Betsy remembered her sister as an incredibly organized and hardworking woman, traits more feebly present in herself. She said, "We'll want to keep this as simple as possible."

What had happened was that Alix Jordan, a steady customer of Betsy's shop, had been moving into pattern designing, and had come in ten days ago with an open chevron pattern of nine vertical rectangles outlined in black to be filled with — what? She had several ideas and brought them to the shop for opinions.

Betsy couldn't decide, and had offered to conduct a poll among the shop's customers. But Godwin had had a better idea.

"Hey, Alix, how about we offer just the template you've designed, and hold a contest for the best filler?" he'd said. "We could buy the template pattern from you, and sell it to customers with an offer of a prize for the best-designed filler."

Betsy had said, "But who will we get to be

22

the judge?"

Godwin had said, "Oh, neither of us. We'll get a committee to do it. And I think it would be better to offer several prizes."

"You mean first, second, and third?" Betsy had asked.

"How about Best Execution, Cleverest Use of Space, and Just Plain Wow?" Alix had suggested.

"Yes! I *like* it!" Godwin had cheered.

Now, Betsy and Godwin were discussing the rules and other parameters for the contest when the shop bell rang. Irene Potter walked in, and by the big smile on her face, it was clear that she was flush with some grand stitching idea.

Betsy's spirits rose at the sight of Irene, even as a tiny worry tempered her joy. Irene spent a lot of money on stitching materials, but she was picky, contentious, and demanding. Betsy was glad Godwin was working today; Irene respected his opinion more than hers.

"H'lo, Irene," said Godwin, the cheer in his voice also tempered by wariness. But he added with a smile, "How can we help you today?"

Irene hurried to the table, her dark eyes shining, the very curls on her head trembling with excitement. "I have this wonderful Idea!" she exclaimed. "And I just know you'll be able to guide me in realizing it!"

Betsy's heart sank. Irene in the grip of one of her *Ideas* could be very difficult. Still, she never complained about the prices Betsy charged. And, Betsy admitted to herself, Irene's art was never boring and often gave a fascinating glimpse into the mind of a person who perceived the world in a way very different from her own.

So, "What is it we can do for you, Irene?" she asked.

"It's time for my next project," Irene replied. "And I want to focus on the materials. You know, pay tribute to silk, or wool. Only maybe not them, but something else, something *different.* So I want to talk with you about how to do that."

"You mean, use both silk and wool as materials in the composition?"

"Something like that."

"But that's been done," said Godwin in a puzzled tone. "You've done things like that in many of your own pieces. Even more than two kinds — lots of stitchers use more than one kind of fiber in their needlepoint work. I've done it many times myself."

"Me, too," said Betsy, remembering a needlepoint canvas of part of a Christmas tree with lots of fancy ornaments. What fun

24

it had been selecting the wool, silk, metallic, cotton, and blends of floss for it!

"No, not used separately, but a blend," said Irene. "Like the silk-wool blends of yarn. Only I want an exotic blend. How about soy-bamboo? Or corn-soy? Wouldn't that be interesting?"

"I've never seen or heard of those blends," said Betsy.

"Yes, see? I haven't, either. I like the way soy-bamboo sounds, better than corn-soy. Soy-bamboo sort of bounces off the tongue, don't you think?" She made a bouncing gesture with one thin finger. "Yes, soy-bamboo, soy-bamboo, soy-bamboo. I want it specially made for me, for this project. Can you tell me where I might get it?"

Godwin said, "You're going to need only a limited quantity, so I doubt you'll get a factory to do it for you. What you need is someone who can spin it by hand."

Betsy said — reluctantly, because she wasn't sure she wanted to burden someone new with Irene — "I know someone."

"You mean the person who did that dyeing demo here Wednesday night, right?" said Godwin.

"Yes, because she spins, too."

"Hand-spun," said Irene in a thoughtful voice. "Is she local?"

"Yes, in fact she lives right here in Excelsior," said Betsy.

"Betsy . . ." warned Godwin.

But Betsy was thinking of the malicious way Hailey treated Marge at the dyeing demo. "Let me get you Hailey's phone number," she said.

THREE

Such a brilliant inspiration she'd had! Irene was sure she was blessed with a swift, clever imagination, and could be justly proud of it. A blend of exotic fibers! Yes! What an amazing and wonderful idea! She would make the stitchery a tribute to the blend, which would have been impossible — unthinkable, really — just a few years ago. Who back then would have thought bamboo could be made into embroidery floss or yarn? Or soy? Her fingers twitched as in her imagination she ran them across the amazingly soft and smooth fibers coaxed from woody bamboo.

Progress! That would be the exultant theme! She would make the piece an explosion of joy and triumph! Another success! More praise! Her fame would endure forever!

Hold on a bit, she thought. She seemed to have gone from a successful piece of Art to her own success. But what a delightful thought, her fame lasting forever!

Hold on again, maybe not forever. There were lots of Artists famous in their day whose names were forgotten. Perhaps her own name would vanish, too. Worse, it seemed most still-famous artists were unsung in their own day, discovered only after their deaths. So maybe it wasn't such a good thing that she had recognition now.

If she were offered the choice — fame while living *or* fame after death — which would she choose?

That was a difficult question, which Irene earnestly contemplated while walking in the brilliant spring sunshine, its warmth lightly soaking through her dark blue sweater vest onto her thin shoulders.

Distracted by the warmth, she was sidetracked into thinking about how much she liked the vest, with its complex pattern of welts and big knots, and a heavy but unnoted scatter of orts, tag ends of floss from various cross-stitch patterns she'd worked on. It was her lucky sweater, one she'd knit herself. She often wore it while working on a new project.

She wasn't going to work just yet on her newest creation, she decided. Instead, she was going to talk to Hailey Brent again.

Hailey was a very interesting woman, very artistic, like herself. Full of ideas and observations. And actually enthusiastic about the soy-bamboo blend Irene wanted for her new project. She had a few samples of it, which she'd given to Irene to try out. The samples had been smooth and easy to work with, so she'd ordered fifty yards. Only eleven days later, it was ready and Hailey was about to dye some of the completed yarn for her. Irene was going to go watch it happen. It was very intelligent of Betsy to put her and Hailey together. Betsy was a good friend.

Irene had initially thought to find someone to weave some fabric from the soy-bamboo blend, but it turned out that would take too long. Spinning and then weaving the fabric in a large enough piece would take months, and Irene's creative urge was screaming and yelling for her to *get on with it right now*. If she disobeyed, the project might never be completed. It had happened once before, when her sister was so sick with cancer and Irene had gone to stay with her. She had abandoned that project about birds during that difficult time, and when she finally came back home, all she wanted to do was throw away all those feathers she had collected, the project having somehow decayed in her absence. Even the smell of the feathers was sickening, and she couldn't get them out of the house fast enough. She'd lived with open windows — in December! — for two weeks to get rid of the smell, it was so awful. The cold coming in through the windows had frozen a pipe in her kitchen, but Irene hadn't minded. It was worth it, to cleanse the house of the feather smell. Her small nose wrinkled at the memory. She still couldn't stand to be around feathers.

Her agent had been very annoyed, but it was worth that, too. She had to do what her muse — what an interesting word! — wanted her to do.

Hailey, when told the story, had been amazingly sympathetic. Unlike everyone else, who thought Irene was insane. She wasn't insane, she was just being an Artist. Sensitive, that's what she was, Hailey had said. And Hailey, being an Artist, too, understood these things.

Hailey was wonderful, Hailey was going to be such a help. And she was going to see Hailey right now, see how far along she was with the dyed yarn.

If Irene had been the type, she would have burst into song at the prospect of finding that Hailey had dyed a usable amount of yarn. But she wasn't, so she merely smiled as she strode along in the lovely late afternoon sunshine.

Soon she came to Green Gaia Gardens — look, the tulips were at their peak — and just beyond it stood the white and green cottage that was Hailey's home. Set back from the street, it was further protected by three big trees, and two smaller ones that were densely covered with deep pink blooms. There was a faint hum coming from the trees — bees, there were hundreds of bees feasting on the sweet nectar. Irene paused to look and listen. She wondered if the honey they would be making was influenced by the kind of flowers they visited. Probably, probably. She had a vague childhood memory of eating a honey so dark it was almost black. Buckwheat honey, it was called. Was buckwheat a flower?

She went up the narrow old sidewalk, made uneven by the roots of a big tree, neared the offset front porch — it made the house look lopsided to not have the porch in the center, how could Hailey stand it? — and continued past it to the side entrance near the back of the house. There she pulled open the screen door and pushed on the dark green wooden door.

"Hailey?" she called, stepping into the middle of the small kitchen. The screen door slapped shut behind her. "Oh, HAY-leeee!"

No answer.

She was probably down in her basement, where she had set up a space in which to dye things, doing something exceedingly interesting. Like Irene, when Hailey was focused on her work, she became deaf to outside sounds.

Irene went to the narrow, dark stairway and took the steps down into the well-lighted basement.

"Hailey? Are you down here?"

Still no answer.

Then she saw her. Hailey was lying on the floor near the sink in the second kitchen. And there was a big black puddle of — Oh my God, it was blood, dried blood! And Hailey's face looked odd, her eyes all starey and kind of bulging. And she wasn't breathing.

Dead, she was dead.

Irene stood there for a few seconds, her heart pounding, her own breath stuck in her throat.

Then she remembered something she had done a few years ago when she'd found another dead body. Hadn't that been the right thing to do?

She tried to scream, but it was a pitiful effort. She threw her head back and that opened her chest so she was able to scream again and again with all her might.

Marge was standing with a customer at the far eastern border of her garden center. They were discussing the purchase of a young potted hydrangea bush.

"I have some nice pink ones over there. This one is a pure white," Marge was saying. "It's called a snowball hydrangea."

"Did you hear something?" asked the customer, looking around.

"Hear what?"

"I don't know — listen, there it goes again."

Marge heard it, too, very faintly, a high-pitched noise.

"Do you suppose it could be the steam whistle on the *Minnehaha*?" asked the customer.

"It could be, I suppose." The steamboat *Minnehaha* plied Lake Minnetonka in the summer, but the lake was nearly a mile away. Marge had never heard its whistle at this distance before. Anyway, she thought the *Minnehaha* didn't start up until Memorial Day.

The scream was suddenly much louder, and this time it came with words: *"Help,*

help, help! Murder, she's been *murdered!*"

Mike Malloy hated this kind of murder. Actually, he hated all murders. And he wasn't fond of murderers, for that matter. But he particularly hated this kind, done by an amateur, undoubtedly for amateur reasons. Hailey Brent was not a drug dealer or a gangbanger or a thief. She wasn't rumored to keep large sums of money in her house, and she didn't allow her home to be used by crooks as a safe house. She was a nice, if rather eccentric, older woman who liked to mash roots, leaves, and flowers and use the juice to color yarn.

So no snitch was going to come forward and tell him something useful, like who had done this.

What he did know gave him a slight frisson. Did the fact that there were skeins of yarn hanging on a clothesline mean that Betsy Devonshire might get involved?

He'd come to cautiously admire Ms. Devonshire for her sleuthing abilities. On the other hand, she was an amateur detective, and amateurs were not restrained by the rules that governed the building of an airtight case against the perp.

It didn't help that the person who discovered the body was Irene Potter. Irene was scatty and opinionated; you never knew what she was going to say or do. Worse, she was a big fan of Ms. Devonshire, and was already declaring that Mike could do worse than call her in for a consult. As if.

Irene claimed she hadn't disturbed the crime scene at all, but she had, of course. She'd entered by the only unlocked door on the premises, for one thing, laying her fingerprints over any others that might be on the handle of the screen door and the knob of the wooden door. And who knew what else she'd touched while standing in the basement making a spectacle of her emotions.

Malloy was a volatile Irishman, not a stoical Scandinavian like a whole lot of Minnesotans, but he didn't think female hysterics were very helpful in a crisis. It had taken him a considerable amount of time to bring Irene back down to earth, and he angrily suspected she enjoyed every minute of the attention.

The sheriff's department's forensics team had finished their work, and Hailey Brent's body had been removed to the custody of the Hennepin County Medical Examiner for autopsy.

Now that he was alone in the space, Mike realized that Irene had been right. What he had thought was a second kitchen in the basement was actually a setup for some other task. Irene had said Hailey Brent was a dyer, a statement it took him a minute or two to understand. It wasn't about D-I-E, it was about D-Y-E. This place down here was like an ordinary kitchen, in that it had a gas stove, and a refrigerator, and a double sink.

But on the stove were three pots, one much bigger than the others. The big one had a lid on it, and the liquid in it was a dark green. The other two had yarn floating in the colored liquid. One of the officers responding to the initial call had noticed that the gas burners beneath the pots had been turned on low, and he had shut them off. One of Malloy's first questions had been, who would want to cook yarn? Then Irene Potter had said this wasn't just a second kitchen, but a setup in which Ms. Brent had dyed things.

That hadn't seemed likely — and Irene wasn't exactly a reliable source — but there were numerous stainless steel pots and pans in one cabinet, and a big copper one, for example, but no glasses or silverware, no plates or cereal bowls. There were a number of wooden spoons, and, oddly, fat and short wooden dowels, most of them stained half-way up in various muted colors. There were measuring cups and spoons. So some kind of cooking was going on. There were two big glass bowls on the counter next to the stove, both containing a clear liquid. Soaking in one bowl was more yarn. Malloy, stepping carefully around the dark puddle on the floor, sniffed at the liquid, but it wasn't bleach. Next to the bowl were two small, dark brown glass apothecary jars with glass stoppers. A hand-printed label on one jar read ALUM, the other TIN. He unstoppered the Tin bottle and in it saw a rusty-looking powder.

Under the sink was a white plastic trash bin, clean and empty, though next to it was a box of plastic bags appropriate to use to line the bin.

Mike opened a cabinet door to find more stoppered glass bottles containing, according to the labels, such things as iron, salt, and copper. In another cabinet were big clear-plastic bags of yarns, most of them white or buff, but some colored yellow or green or blue. The yarns were mostly organized into skeins, though two of the bags were full of balls of yarn.

And there was a plastic-coated clothesline strung up over the counter that held the double sink. Hanging on the line were two loose bundles of thin yarn, one flecked a light and darker brown, one flecked orange. So all right, Irene was correct; clearly this was some kind of setup to do with coloring yarns.

But what was there about dyeing yarns that could arouse such anger that only shooting the dyer in the head would be a solution?

Mike's eyes narrowed, and his thin mouth pulled even thinner in his freckled face as he glanced at the dreadful mess the killer had made on the otherwise nice, clean floor. He would find out the answer to his question.

FOUR

"Thank you very much," said Marge, handing the customer her credit card receipt. "Remember, plenty of water the first week." She looked around and raised her voice. "Raymond, please help Mrs. Wacker with her tree."

"Sure," said an impressively tall and broad-shouldered young man in his late teens. He came over and took the handles of the wheelbarrow the tree was resting in. "Okay, which way?" he asked, and followed her out.

Marge shifted her attention from Raymond and the customer to the person who had been patiently waiting. She was dismayed to see it was a slender man of medium height with faded auburn hair and very pale blue eyes set in a face spattered with freckles: police detective Mike Malloy.

"Ms. Schultz?" he said in a tone she interpreted as gruff and unfriendly.

"Yes?" she replied, as if she didn't know who he was.

He produced a small leather folder and opened it to show her a gold badge and photo ID. Her heart sank. Obviously he wasn't here to buy a potted plant.

"I'm Sergeant Mike Malloy, and I'm here to talk with you about the death yesterday of your neighbor, Hailey Brent. Is there someplace private we can talk?"

The marrow in her bones turned to ice, and she struggled to maintain her composure. "Certainly," she said and called, "Beth, can you take over for me for a few minutes?"

"Yes, I'll be right there," replied a slim, middle-aged woman, who was leading a man carrying a bag of potting soil to the register.

Marge showed Malloy to the small, cluttered office at the back of her store. She invited him to sit at her desk and took the armless wooden chair beside it.

"That was a terrible thing that happened to Hailey," she said. "We were all very shocked and scared when we heard about it. Do you have any idea who would do that to her?"

Malloy produced a notebook from an inside pocket. "Nothing I can talk about as yet. How well did you know Ms. Brent?"

"She was a neighbor, of course, and so we knew *of* each other."

"So you weren't friends."

"We were friendly, but no, not friends."

"Did she buy any of her garden supplies from you?"

"Some, but not all. I think she bought a lot of things by mail order."

"What makes you think that?"

Marge hesitated, aware of the notebook in Mike's hand. "In the spring I would often see the FedEx truck stop by her place. Then not at all in the summer, but again in the fall. Not as often as in the spring. Bulbs, you know."

"Okay, I see. Very observant." Mike, smiling and nodding, made a note. "How did you get along with her?"

Again Marge hesitated. What did he know? Who had he already talked to? Hailey had been found late yesterday afternoon, so not a whole lot of people. "Well . . . we had kind of an ongoing problem. Hailey liked to experiment with natural dyes. I think most of her garden was taken up by plants she could use in dyeing. The problem was, she would sometimes see something in my inventory she didn't have in hers, and instead of buying the plant, she would sneak over and cut flowers off it. She wouldn't

41

permanently damage or destroy the plants, but it would hurt my chances of selling them until they bloomed again. I spoke with her about it, but she denied taking any flowers. She seemed to think her work was more important than my business."

"Did you ever report her to the police?"

"No, of course not. I never saw her do it, for one thing. And anyway it didn't rise to that level of lawbreaking. It was just annoying."

"How often would she steal flowers from you?"

"Oh, maybe four or five times a summer."

"Are we talking a lot of flowers or just a few?"

"More than a few, but it wasn't as if she stripped the plants bare."

"Would she steal flowers from other people's gardens?"

Marge, surprised at the idea, shrugged. "I don't know. I wouldn't put it past her."

"Could she have been doing it out of malice toward you?"

"Oh no, I don't think so. She was just very wrapped up in her experiments."

"Did you ever threaten her about these thefts?"

"With what? About the worst I ever said to her was that she wouldn't like it if I went into her garden and stole one of her plants. I know that made an impression, because she mentioned it the other day when I attended one of her demos on dyeing."

"Angrily?"

"No, she was teasing me about it, in a sarcastic way."

"Did you ever actually carry out your threat?"

"No, of course not."

"Can you tell me where you were yesterday afternoon?"

"I was here from about nine till we closed at eight."

"Long day."

"That's what the job calls for this time of year."

"You didn't take a break at all? Just worked straight through?"

She hesitated, trying to read his face, without success. "Well, yes, I went out for a couple of hours, had lunch, ran an errand."

"What time was that?"

"From a little past eleven to, I don't know, maybe one thirty?" She watched him write that down.

"What time did your employees arrive yesterday morning?"

She would have lied, but Green Gaia kept time sheets. "Ten or a little after."

"Did you murder Hailey Brent?"

That very direct question made Marge feel as if the floor had opened beneath her feet.

"No, I did not." She glanced around her office as if to reassure herself that it was still there. "I had no reason to murder her. Like I said, she was annoying once in a while, but that's all."

Mike finished making a note and closed his notebook. "All right, that's all I have for right now. Thank you for speaking with me."

"You're welcome."

With another sharp-eyed look at her, Mike rose and left the office, leaving Marge feeling weak and frightened.

Then a wave of indignation swept over her. How dare he seriously ask if she'd murdered Hailey! Did he really suspect her? No, of course not, he was probably asking everyone who knew her that dreadful question.

Right?

"She was not a nice person," said Marge the next day.

She had come to Crewel World right after it opened.

"Well, I'm sure you had reason to think so," said Betsy.

"Believe it. You saw her at the dyeing

demo. But the thing is, I'm not the only one who thinks that. If you check around, you'll find others."

"Mike is perfectly capable of doing that. In fact, I'm sure he is doing that."

"All right, but you've helped him out before, haven't you? You've found things he's missed."

"Yes, once or twice. But honestly, he's very skilled at investigations. Which is good, because that's his job. I'm sure he doesn't think you had anything to do with it."

"I hope you won't get angry if I disagree with you. I'm afraid he's looking very hard at me. I don't know who he's talked to, but he knows I was angry with her because she was stealing flowers from me."

Betsy sighed with exasperation. "Now, Marge, I hardly think being mad at her because she stole some flowers is a motive for murder."

"I agree! But he's been poking around, talking to my employees, and it's making me very nervous. Please, Betsy, can't you just take a quick look into this? Surely you can find proof it wasn't me. After all, what you are best at is helping people falsely accused of a crime, right?"

Betsy had her own business to run, plus

the contest to get off the ground. But Marge was looking desperate, with a sheen of earnest perspiration on her forehead. "Well, yes, that's generally how it turns out." Betsy didn't want to add that the falsely suspected were friends of hers or steady customers of Crewel World, neither of which described Marge. "I have to dig into the lives of people to find out what really happened and why. You may not like what I find out on my way to the truth."

Marge hesitated but said bravely, "All right, treat my life like an open book. I've got nothing to hide."

For once, Godwin wasn't enthusiastic. "I'm sure she's really grateful," he said, a little doubtfully when Betsy told him about Marge's visit later that day.

Betsy, remembering the beaming face with its tearful eyes, nodded. "She sure was."

Marge wasn't a stitcher; her forte was growing plants — trees, shrubs, vegetables, and flowers — for sale. Betsy knew her from working with her on the committee that put on the annual Art in the Park event. But Godwin didn't know her at all. He had no personal connection to her plight, which explained his lack of enthusiasm.

"So where do you begin?" he asked.

"I'm not sure. I think a lot of what I've got to do will be just repeating things Mike has done or is doing."

"I wish he trusted you enough to tell you what he's found out."

"Me, too." Betsy grimaced, then turned to another task. "Meanwhile, let's get set up for the template contest."

They were ready to offer it to their customers. Betsy had copied Alix's pattern and run fifty good-quality copies of it. The rules hadn't even suggested what size or even what kind of fabric the pattern should be stitched on. Betsy had stitched the model outline on 18-count Aida with two strands of DMC 310 — black — and put it in an inexpensive frame. Godwin had designed a poster describing the contest with its rules and a deadline — July fifteenth — to get the entries in. They put the poster on the mirror of the white chest of drawers near the entrance of the shop, where other announcements of interest to stitchers were posted. On top of the chest of drawers they put a stack of templates with the price, six dollars, penciled on the top right-hand corner of each.

Godwin had run a "tease" about the contest on Crewel World's web site and in its newsletter, and he had talked to customers about a forthcoming contest to raise funds for a local charity. Even so, it was wonderful how strong the response was by the next morning.

"Can I stitch it on canvas?" asked the first customer to bring the pattern to the checkout desk.

"Certainly," said Betsy. "I look forward to seeing what you come up with, Jenna," she added. Jenna Wilson was always willing to take a pattern as merely a suggestion from the designer and to change colors, stitches, even design elements in her work. With her as an entrant, the contest was off to a fine start.

They sold six more patterns that day. The purchasers seemed excited at the prospect of making up their own designs to fill the template.

"Who are the judges?" was the question most often asked.

"We're not saying," replied Godwin. "We don't want people who know them to design their projects around what they think they'll like."

"So, they are people we know, hmmm?" was a common, thoughtful reply.

"I'm not saying anything more," replied Godwin with one of his famous guileless smiles, and he didn't. Nor did Betsy.

On Sundays, Crewel World was closed. This Sunday, the twenty-second, was a beautiful day, sunny with a few scattered clouds, the temperature in the upper sixties. After church and breakfast, Betsy set off in her car for Green Gaia to look at shade-loving perennials. Spring, summer, and fall were prime selling periods for greenhouses, and Green Gaia was open on Sundays, except in the winter.

Once in the neighborhood, she began to look around for a parking spot. She nearly missed one just in front of a big SUV, and braked sharply beside a little Ford Focus ahead of it to parallel park. A car sounded its horn immediately behind her. She lifted her foot off the brake — and the car whipped around and cut in front of her, missing her front fender by a whisker. It pulled into the driveway of a private residence, leaving Betsy standing on her brakes and gasping for air.

In the driveway, the passenger door opened. The car's horn blared, and Betsy, hands trembling, quickly backed crookedly into the parking space. The passenger was shouting something, and Betsy lowered her passenger-side window to hear if it was an apology.

"I said, why don't you watch where you're going!" The shouter was a woman, short and slender, dressed all in black, with thick, straight, shoulder-length hair a pretty but improbable shade of blue-green.

Betsy got out of her car, pressed the button that locked it, and walked with careful deliberation toward the car and its annoyed passenger. The driver remained in her seat.

"What did you say?" asked Betsy quietly.

"I said, why don't you watch where you're going?" the young woman said, but much less angrily, having read something in Betsy's face.

"I agree, your driver should watch what she's doing," said Betsy, amazed at how calm she sounded. Her elbows and knees were still weak from the fright she'd received, her fingers tingly. It was all she could do to keep from bursting into angry tears. "You're lucky she didn't hit me."

"I wasn't talking to her," the woman said petulantly.

"Well, you couldn't be talking to me. I was driving in my own lane, and below the speed limit."

"You were driving so slowly, and Ruth was trying to pass you when I saw she was going to overshoot the driveway. I —" The woman hesitated, then confessed, "I guess I might've got a little bit excited when I told her to turn, turn right now." The deepening pink of her complexion combined with her blue-green hair to give her the look of a Pixar cartoon character.

"Is this Hailey Brent's house?" asked Betsy.

"Yes," the woman replied, seemingly confused now by the abrupt change in topic. She turned a little so she could look over her shoulder, as if perhaps to see whether Hailey's name was posted over the door.

"Do you know her? Who are you?" asked Betsy.

"If it's anything to you, I'm her daughter, Philadelphia Halverson."

"You are? Well, how do you do? I've been wondering how to get in touch with you. I'm very sorry for your loss. I'm Betsy Devonshire. Your mother gave a dyeing demonstration in my shop a little over two weeks ago."

"Die — ? Oh yes, she e-mailed me about that. She said you produced a good turnout." Her mouth turned down in a sad grimace. "She loved to show people how much fun it was to dye fibers."

The other car door opened and the driver stepped out. She was an attractive, middle-aged woman with short, dark hair streaked with gray, and very pale blue eyes. "Is the ruckus over?" she asked.

"Yes," said Philadelphia. "That is, I think so." She looked inquiringly at Betsy.

"Yes," agreed Betsy.

"I'm sorry for the scare I probably gave you. Philadelphia startled me."

"That's all right. I wasn't paying attention to cars around me." Betsy smiled, her fright dissipating like morning mist. "I'm Betsy Devonshire. I was on my way to the garden center right over there."

"I'm Ruth Ladwig," the driver said in a pleasant voice. "Philadelphia is the daughter of a friend of mine, Hailey Brent, who lived in this house." She gestured toward the house whose driveway they were in.

"Ruth Ladwig? I've heard of you. You work at the Science Museum in Saint Paul, right?"

"Part-time, yes. I work in the gift shop and give dyeing demos over there."

"So you knew Hailey Brent well, didn't you?"

"Yes." Ruth nodded.

"I just love the Science Museum," said Betsy. "Someday soon I'm going to use my day off to go to the King Tut exhibit over there."

"It's well worth your time," said Ruth. The exhibit, which came from Egypt, featured wonderful things, and was at the museum in Saint Paul for a limited time. "Is there something we can do for you besides apologize?"

"Maybe. I've been asked to look into Hailey's death, to see if I can figure out who killed her. I would like very much to see where the murder happened, and to talk to both of you about Hailey."

"Are you a private investigator?" asked Philadelphia.

"No, but I've been useful to the police before."

Philadelphia and Ruth exchanged glances. "What do you think, Philadelphia?" asked Ruth.

"I don't know. I don't know this lady," she said.

"I heard Hailey talk about her," Ruth said. "She told me that Betsy had actually helped the police arrest a murderer."

"Is that true?" Philadelphia's tone was sharp, her gaze intent on Betsy's face.

"Yes, it's happened more than once."

"Do you really think you could find out who murdered my mother?"

"I don't know. Perhaps. I certainly am going to try."

"If you do, I'll believe God sent you to me."

"Well, if He did want to arrange an introduction, He didn't need to scare the life out of me doing it," said Betsy.

"Come on," said Philadelphia. "I'll show you the whole house, and try to answer any questions you have."

FIVE

Betsy estimated the little house to be at least seventy-five years old. But on the first floor, instead of a series of rooms — kitchen, dining room, living room — typical of a house that old, there was one open space. The kitchen was marked off by a low, broad counter that was part breakfast bar and part desk, on which sat an outdated computer. The kitchen floor was covered with gray linoleum tile.

The floor of the small dining room was hardwood. Its severely plain oak table held a vase of dying lilacs. Only two chairs were drawn up to it. There were two windows on one wall and a tiny powder room opposite.

The living room was marked off by a light tan flat-weave carpet, and was furnished with a love seat and an upholstered chair in a matching tan shade, set off by brightly colored needlepoint pillows. An OttLite magnifying light sat beside the chair, along with a basket whose open lid revealed needlework materials, including a partly finished counted cross-stitch piece in a wooden stretcher. The heavy drapes were a rich brown. The room was well lit, with a big front window.

"I thought you told me this house is nearly eighty years old," Ruth Ladwig said.

"It is," said Philadelphia.

"But that big front window and an open floor plan like this make it seem much newer than that," Ruth said.

"It was remodeled about a dozen years ago. Mother had just finished paying off the new mortgage she took out to update the house when . . . this happened." Philadelphia turned her back on them with a painful sniff, then regained her composure. Her mother's death had occurred only a few days ago, and her emotions clearly were still very near the surface.

The rooms were in good order. The air smelled faintly of decaying lilacs and Clorox.

Upstairs were three pale green bedrooms and one bathroom. One bedroom was completely empty, without even curtains on the window. Another was used as a storage space, with chairs, suitcases, and taped cardboard boxes taking up most of the floor space. The third, although the largest, was modestly sized, and modestly furnished. A pinwheel quilt with badly faded colors looked to be equal in age to the old brass bed it lay upon, but well cared for. A long crocheted dresser scarf ornamented the top of the dresser. Betsy noted a very faint smell of lavender in the room. The bathroom was small but had modern floor tiling and fixtures.

"See anything helpful yet?" Philadelphia asked Betsy.

"I'm afraid not."

The place seemed to have belonged to a person much older than Hailey Brent, whom Betsy estimated had been in her middle fifties. Betsy hadn't seen crochet work topping a chest of drawers since she spent part of a childhood summer at her grandmother's house.

"Is this the house you grew up in?" Betsy asked Philadelphia.

"Yes," said Philadelphia, nodding. "In fact, my mother grew up here, too. She lived here until she married, and when she divorced Dad, she moved back in and we all — Mom, me, and my brother, JR — took care of Grandmom and Pop until they moved into a nursing home." She smiled sadly. "They both lived to be eighty-seven, and died a little over a year apart."

"That's a long family history at this address. So what are you going to do with the house?"

"Oh, sell it. Our current house is nicer than this one. Besides, I don't think I could bear to live here, or even let someone I know live here. So we'll clear it out and sell it." She looked around the hallway where they were standing and shrugged. "Some other family will love it, I'm sure, someone who doesn't have a connection to the terrible thing that happened here. Now, I suppose you'll want to see the — the basement. That's where it hap-happened."

She was looking more and more distressed. "You don't have to —" Betsy started.

"Oh no, I want to. It's all right, we cleaned . . . we cleaned it. Anyway, I agreed to show it to Ruth so she can tell me what's valuable in it."

"But if it's going to upset you —"

Philadelphia spoke fiercely. "I can endure anything that might help find out who did this."

There was a steep and very plain wooden staircase between the kitchen and dining room that led down to the basement, where the Clorox smell was stronger. Philadelphia led the way, descending into the dimly lit space, then flipping several switches, flooding the basement with light.

"Well, this is very nice," said Ruth, looking around at the finished half of the room. In contrast to the old-fashioned, cement-floored unfinished space, this half of the basement — which was by far better lit — was divided into a kitchen and a carpeted space with a real spinning wheel resting at the very center. A hard wooden chair with a thin pink seat cushion was pulled up to the wheel. Beside the chair was a low cabinet with two stainless steel bowls on top of it; fuzzy, off-white material half filled each bowl.

"I wonder if she was working on Irene Potter's floss," Betsy said.

"Yes, she was, and she was working hard on it," said Ruth. "I talked with her about her finding soy and bamboo fibers, unspun, a couple of weeks ago. It's very likely that's what's in the bowls over there."

"Could you tell for sure if it's soy and bamboo?" asked Betsy.

"Not me," said Philadelphia.

"I can make a good guess," said Ruth. She went to the bowls and lifted a small wad of fiber from one bowl. She rubbed it between thumb and fingers, then raised it to her nose for a gentle sniff. "I'm sure this is soy," she said, dropping the fibers back in the bowl. She did the same with a wad from the other bowl. "I can't say for sure, but feel and logic say this is bamboo."

"She was working on a blend," said Betsy to Ruth. "That's why she has both on the table." She went over to the spinning wheel to look at the spindle, which was about half full of a thin, very pale beige yarn. "This is probably the blend," she said. "Right?"

"Very likely," agreed Ruth.

"This was a special order," said Philadelphia. "When I talked with her on the phone she said it was coming along well, and that Ms. Potter had made a generous offer for the material. I'll have to talk to Ms. Potter about whether she should get a refund, or if Mom agreed to accept payment on delivery." Her face twisted; here was a project that would never be finished.

"Over here is where she did her dyeing — and where she died," continued Philadelphia with an effort, walking up to the border between the spinning wheel setup and the kitchen. "She was found on the floor near the sink." She made a truncated gesture in that direction. "JR came with me and we cleaned up the blood. I was shocked to find out that the police are not responsible for that job." Her lower lip began to tremble, but with an effort she stopped it. "The police said there are companies that will do it for you, but I felt I just couldn't let strangers down here. That was a mistake, I know now, because it was a nightmare, and the aftereffects have been horrible." She gave a little sigh. "We used just plain water at first, and emptied three buckets on her bed of lilies out back." She looked at Ruth and Betsy with worried eyes. "Do you think that was wrong, to do that? I just couldn't pour it down . . . the drain . . ."

Betsy said warmly, "I think that was very nice and really appropriate."

Ruth said, "I agree, very nice."

Philadelphia added, her voice still a little worried, "We used bleach at the end, to . . . disinfect and . . . deodorize."

"That must have been a terrible task," said Betsy, dismayed by the thought but clearly sympathetic.

"Yes, far worse than you can know." Philadelphia turned and walked over to the spinning wheel and stood there with her head down.

"Ms. Ladwig, what can you tell us about this setup?" asked Betsy, trying to distract Philadelphia.

"Please, call me Ruth. This is an excellent

setup for dyeing," she said. "I wish mine were as nice as this."

"Did your mother do this as a profession?" Betsy asked Philadelphia.

With her head still down, she replied, "It was more like a paying hobby. She went to work full-time at General Sportswear Company in Minnetonka after her divorce, then cut back to part-time a few years ago."

"Was it an amicable divorce?"

"No, there was a whole lot of shouting and screaming, and it left some hard feelings between the two of them."

"What happened to your father?"

"He remarried, then re-remarried, and took his newest family to Oregon. That was five years ago. He sends me and my brother Christmas cards."

"Does he know about your mother's death?"

"Yes, JR called him. He was very shocked but didn't come back for the funeral. He and his latest wife have three small children, so it would have been an expensive trip."

Ruth had gone into the kitchen to open cabinet doors. She remarked again, admiringly, on the completeness of the setup.

"Well, isn't this interesting," she said from the stove, gesturing at the three stainless steel pots on it, the lidded one much bigger than the others.

"What is it?" asked Betsy.

"She was dyeing some yarn; it's still in the pots. I wonder who turned the stove off."

Philadelphia said, "It must've been the police. Or maybe Mother turned it off before . . . they shot her."

"Maybe," said Ruth. "But it's a small window of time between shutting off the burner and lifting out the dyed stuff."

She looked at the clothesline hanging over the sink, with two skeins of dyed yarn draped over it, one a medium green with pale green flecks in it, the other a pale rust color with darker flecks in it. She went to touch the green yarn. "I wonder if these aren't also the soy-bamboo blend she was spinning. Soy and bamboo accept coloring differently, even with the same mordant. Blending the two might give you this effect." She touched them again, thrusting her fingers into the middle of each skein. "They're both bone dry." She looked back at the stove. "The dye in the pots doesn't match either of these skeins."

Philadelphia returned to the border between the two sections of the basement and said, "They were hanging there when I first came down here after — afterward. She just didn't get a chance to take out the rest from the dye pots."

"But there are no pots on the stove with no yarn in them," said Betsy, coming to take a look. The dye in the two smaller pots was pale brown and bright yellow. The yellow dye had something that looked like carrot tops in it. The pale brown dye held a much darker brown shade of yarn. She lifted the lid on the big pot and saw the liquid was a deep, almost opaque green. Something might be floating in the dye bath; it was hard to tell.

"It's possible she rinsed these skeins, hung them, then washed the pots and put them away," said Ruth, "meaning to take the other yarn out later. But didn't get the chance."

"Is that how you'd do it?" asked Betsy.

"No, but everyone has her own method." Her tone seemed to indicate she thought it possible, but eccentric.

"What's more likely?" Betsy asked.

"That she dyed stuff on two successive days," replied Ruth. "She dyed this stuff the day before she was killed, and was in the process of dyeing the yarn in the pots when she was interrupted. And see, here's some yarn being mordanted." She gestured at the big glass bowls with what looked like water in them. Floating in the water was more yarn, this of a near-white color. She picked up the glass-stoppered bottles beside them. "Tin and alum," she read aloud.

"What do the police think?" Betsy asked Philadelphia.

The woman lifted her shoulders until they touched her blue-green hair. "I don't know, they didn't tell me anything. But I couldn't tell them anything, either. I knit, crochet, and weave, but I don't dye."

Betsy wondered if another reason they didn't tell her anything was that they considered her a suspect. Probably. Murders like this were generally done by someone the victim knew, or even was related to.

"Do you and JR share the inheritance of this house?" asked Betsy.

"Yes, half and half, equal shares of everything."

"Does JR agree that you should sell it?"

"Yes — he and his wife live in Fridley with their two children, and their house could use some upgrades, which selling this house will help them afford. He's like me in that he doesn't want to own a house our mother was murdered in. Even worse than me, actually. He says I can have an extra thousand dollars from the sale if I'll arrange the estate sale and have it prepped."

Betsy wondered how badly JR's house

needed repair. And how far he might go to get the funds for it.

"Did the police ask the two of you for an alibi?" asked Betsy.

"Yes," said Philadelphia. "JR was at work, but I was home sleeping — I was working the night shift at HCMC." Betsy knew she was referring to Hennepin County Medical Center.

"Are you a nurse?"

"Yes."

Betsy wondered what a patient waking up after surgery would think on seeing someone with blue-green hair.

"It might be hard to sell a house with an extra kitchen in the basement — unless you can find a buyer who likes to dye fibers at home," said Ruth.

"I'm thinking the buyer could turn the other half of the basement into a bath and bedroom and make this a mother-in-law apartment," said Philadelphia.

Betsy walked back to stand near Philadelphia. "When do you plan to sell it?" she asked. "Right away?"

"As soon as I can find someone to advise me on staging it," said Philadelphia. She looked around the space and, frowning, gave a sad little sigh.

"When you hold the estate sale," said

Ruth, "please let me know. These stainless steel pots and the glass bowls would be very useful to any dyer."

"All right," said Philadelphia, her voice gone creaky and her mouth turned downward.

"I think maybe we've seen enough —" began Betsy.

"No, no, no!" said Philadelphia harshly. "Go on, look! Look at everything, don't miss anything! Mother's dead and gone, you can't hurt her anymore!" She caught her breath on a sob. "And what I want or feel doesn't matter."

"Yes, it does, and I'm terribly sorry to be bothering you with all this," said Betsy placatingly, patting the air between them with her hands.

"Please, ask me more questions." Her voice was sad, but her expression determined.

"All right." Betsy sighed then asked bluntly, "Who was angry with your mother?"

"No one. That's what's so awful about this. Who could be angry with a woman whose main occupation was to turn roots and flowers into dyes? She liked to spin, she liked to do handwork — embroidery and cross-stitch. She was a strong feminist, but

67

she liked all the old-fashioned womanly things. She was a dedicated folk artist. Who could hate someone like that?"

"Marge Schultz was angry with her," said Betsy.

"Oh, that! Once or twice Mother went over there and cut some flowers. So what? I'll bet Marge didn't notice most of the time when she did it."

"So she did it more than once or twice."

Philadelphia blinked at her self-contradiction. "All right, more than once or twice. She didn't destroy any plants, she didn't hurt Marge, it was almost a compliment when you think about it. She saw some flowers that would make a lovely dye and she took a few."

But Betsy remembered the large number of blooms Hailey had used in making a relatively small dye lot. If Hailey was dyeing a large amount of newly spun yarn, "a few" flowers wouldn't describe the number needed.

And she'd done this more than twice.

"I'm surprised Marge didn't do more than merely complain," Betsy said.

"Oh, I don't think Marge Schultz's hands were clean enough for her to go crying to the police."

Betsy felt her attention sharpen. "What do

you mean?"

"I don't know exactly what she did, but my mother said whatever it was, was illicit."

" 'Illicit'?"

"She used the word *illicit,* which is the same thing as illegal, isn't it? In fact, it sounds worse than illegal. Nastier."

"Do you know what she was referring to?"

"She kind of talked around it, without saying what it was. More hinting than telling."

"Hinting at what?"

"That Marge was a thief, too. But she never said what Marge stole, or who she stole it from."

Betsy remembered the hint Hailey dropped at the dyeing demonstration. "Still, if she actually saw your mother stealing a quantity of flowers, I don't think your mother knowing something about her would stop Marge from filing a complaint with the police." Unless we're talking blackmail here, thought Betsy.

"I don't think she ever actually caught Mom doing it," said Philadelphia. "Besides, like I said, it wasn't like Mom did any real harm."

"But Marge — and you — are sure it was her."

"Well, I don't think she confessed to it to Marge, but she said as much to me. She was very pleased with a color she got from some flowers she took from Marge's garden. She liked it so much she planted some of the same variety in her own garden the next year."

"So she wasn't very sneaky about it."

"Everyone knows artists are allowed almost anything if it furthers their work. I mean, read their biographies. They can get very crazy and determined about some things."

"Crazy and determined?"

"Certainly. I should know."

"Why," Betsy asked. "Are you an artist, too?"

"Oh yes."

"What kind?"

"I knit three-dimensional people." Her tone was faux nonchalant overlaid with an air of confessing an amusing misdemeanor. "My bestselling ones are the Red Hat Society women, though I like my fetus-in-the-womb one better. I'm in art galleries as far away as Chicago. Plus, I paint. Abstracts, mostly. But those don't sell like my people."

"I'd love to see some of your knitting art. But we're getting off topic. When did your mother start taking flowers from Marge's garden center?"

"I don't remember exactly, but more than

three years ago, four or even five. It started with a pretty yellow-orange dye some flowers made. She says you never know what color you're going to get. I mean, she said that." Reminded that her mother was no longer alive, she made a curious sound, stifling a sob.

"Here, this is getting to be too much for you," said Betsy, starting to feel really bad.

"No, no, please go on, ask me more questions."

"Actually, I don't have any more questions for you right now," Betsy lied.

"But I don't think I've helped you!" Having severely tested her own endurance, Philadelphia was probably upset that nothing helpful was being produced.

"I think maybe you have. You've given me a much clearer picture of your mother, and that is always helpful."

"I think we should go away now," said Ruth. "I agree with Betsy, you're becoming too upset for this to continue. I can come another time. This isn't something we have to do today." She was standing by the sink, out of Philadelphia's line of sight. She began making faces and moving her hands, gestures Betsy interpreted as meaning she would talk to Betsy later.

"Maybe she's right," said Philadelphia. "I

think I'm getting one of my headaches, anyway."

Ruth said, "Yes, then it's definitely time for this to stop. You've got my card. Why don't you call me in a day or two and I'll come look at your mother's spinning and dyeing equipment again. You don't even have to come along, if you don't want to. I should be able to give you a written estimate of its value. I know that spinning wheel is a good one, for instance, and the things in this kitchen are good quality, too."

"Thank you, Ruth."

The three of them went upstairs and out of the house. Betsy gave Philadelphia one of her business cards, and, as if in afterthought, she handed another one to Ruth.

Then Betsy continued on her original errand, to buy perennials for the wooded portion of her back lot.

Six

Godwin was a warm-weather person; any time the thermometer registered less than seventy degrees, he reached for a sweater. Today, with the thermometer unable to climb higher than sixty-three, even the sweater was not enough. But swinging at a half-size "warm-up" bucket of balls at the driving range warmed and loosened his joints a bit, and he stepped up to the first tee at Brookview Golf Course feeling confident. And hit his first ball so far to the right that it landed on the fairway of the second hole.

"Why did I agree to try playing this stupid game?" he demanded with a scowl, swinging his driver over his head, thinking that perhaps he should release it and let it fly into the little pond that guarded the tee box.

"Oh, *mi gorrion,* don't! You were just a little hasty." Rafael, medium-tall, with lots of dark, wavy hair surrounding a very handsome face, had been born in Madrid, and while his English was excellent, he had traces of an accent, and he sprinkled his language with Spanish words. *Gorrion* was Spanish for "sparrow," his nickname for Godwin, because he felt that, like the bird, Godwin was a small, bright, brave fellow.

"Why don't you hit another?" The two frequently permitted themselves to hit a second ball off the tee if the first went awry. There was time to try again because there wasn't another set of golfers waiting for them to tee off. The chill in the air was one reason they had the place to themselves. Also, it was a Monday morning — not the most popular time for a golf game.

Godwin said, "Who besides you thinks I'll do better if I try again?"

"You will do better if you take your time," counseled Rafael. "Now, set up your new ball on the tee. Look down the fairway to the place you want it to go. Then look at the ball and let your mind settle. Only then strike it."

Godwin wanted to grumble some more at that exceedingly basic advice, but he didn't. As advanced piano players practiced scales, so golfers needed reminders of the fundamentals.

He pulled another ball from his pocket

and balanced it on the little wooden tee. He put his driver next to the ball, then looked down the fairway, picking a spot he knew he could reach.

He drew back the club, keeping his left arm straight, deliberately cleared his mind of extraneous thoughts, then focused on the ball. He took a deep breath, cocked his wrists, and brought the club swiftly down, hearing it smack against the ball with a crisp, metallic *clink.* He followed through on his swing and watched as the ball flew in a beautiful arc farther and farther down the very center of the fairway to land right on target, bounce, and roll another ten yards.

"Sweeeeet," he sighed. Maybe he wouldn't throw his driver away just yet.

But that was his best drive of the game.

On the seventh hole, they caught up to the quartet ahead of them and had to wait while they holed out. Godwin turned to Rafael. "Is something on your mind?" he asked. "You've been kind of quiet this game."

"You know me too well, *gorrion.*" After a pause, he said, "I do not know how to begin this conversation," and Godwin felt his heart give an alarmed lurch.

"Have I done something wrong?"

Rafael smiled. "No, no, not at all. I've just

been thinking about you, and me, and us. You really like your work, don't you?"

Godwin, leaning on his club, frowned at him. "You know I do, and why not? I like my boss, the shop is humming along — and I'm a big part of that. What's not to like?"

"Do you think I'd be good at retail?"

Godwin considered him for a few moments. Was Rafael angling for a job at Crewel World? He'd taken up counted cross-stitch lately and seemed to enjoy it, but Godwin thought it was just a move on his part to share more in Godwin's life. Just like Godwin had taken up Rafael's passion, golf.

"You'd be all right, I guess. Maybe pretty good, in fact. Do you want to come to work at Crewel World?"

"No, no. But would you support me in a decision I'm thinking of making?"

"You know I would always support you," said Godwin, a little puzzled — then he grew alarmed again. Rafael had spent a lot of time lately communing with his computer. "You aren't thinking we should relocate, are you?"

"No, I don't believe we will need to move."

"Good, I'm glad to hear that. But then what is this decision?"

"I would like to open a store of my own."

Godwin almost laughed, but managed to choke it back. Rafael had never been so much as a sales clerk. "What kind of a store?"

"Collectible coins, of course." Rafael had not so long ago begun to collect coins. He tended to throw himself into new interests with a passion, and so quickly built a large and eclectic collection, ranging from ancient Roman and Greek coins to modern gold coins. He was especially proud of his medieval Spanish, French, and English hammered silver coins.

"You mean you want to sell your coin collection? You haven't had it very long."

"No, just some of the coins."

"You could do that without opening a store."

"I know. I have done a great deal of buying, selling, and trading from the start, you know. But I'm doing so much more of it lately that I want to make it official. I want to open a proper place away from home, where people can come in to see what I have, and bring me pieces to see in person. Make it into a real business, to buy and sell not just coins but tokens and perhaps paper money as well. Maybe help a customer begin a collection, or fill in some . . . gaps.

Is *gap* the right word?"

"Yes, *gaps* means holes or spaces." Godwin was thinking, squinting down the fairway at the golfers on the green. One made his putt and waved his putter in the air. Another pointed his at the man in a fencing pose, goofing off, further delaying the game. "What advice do you want from me?"

"Actually," said Rafael, sounding unusually diffident, "I want more than advice. I would like you to join me in the business, as a partner."

Godwin's heart sank into his shoes. "You *do*? Wow, Rafael, I'm honored that you ask me! But you know I wouldn't have time for that. To do it right would be a full-time job, and I already have a full-time job at Crewel World." Besides, Godwin's money was tied up in a trust he didn't have free access to, so he wouldn't be able to invest his share in Rafael's business.

"Yes, well . . ." Rafael fell silent.

Godwin stared at him. "You want me to *leave Crewel World*? Abandon *Betsy*?"

"No, of course not! Well, not all at once. Just back off a very little. She works you very hard, you know. Expects you to step up whenever she needs time off to sleuth. There are weeks when you actually work more than forty hours."

"What she's doing is important," Godwin pointed out.

"Not to you. And the pay isn't very good."

"Oh, Rafael, I thought you understood about me and Betsy. It's not about the money. I would rather die than disappoint her."

"I do understand. But I need you to help me. Think how we would be spending more time together."

Godwin looked down the fairway. The quartet had quit clowning and finished. "That's a very tempting idea. But come on, we can go now. I need time to think about this."

"Of course, *mi gorrion.*" Rafael remained unusually silent the rest of the game, while Godwin, badly rattled, couldn't make even a double bogey on a single remaining hole.

It was a little after ten on Tuesday, opening-up time. Betsy and Godwin were going through the well-rehearsed motions of preparing to unlock the door. After a few minutes Betsy said to Godwin, in a curious echo of his conversation with Rafael, "You've been awfully quiet. Is something on your mind?"

"No, no," he said, a little too hastily. "I'm just thinking."

"About what?" she persisted.

"Well, Rafael kind of surprised me yesterday on the golf course. He said he wants to open a shop of his own, selling rare coins. And maybe collectible paper money, too."

"Could he do that? I mean, and make a success of it? What experience does he have in retail?" asked Betsy. She remembered her own fumbling and bumbling when she unexpectedly inherited Crewel World from her late sister.

"That's just it, he doesn't know very much about owning his own business."

"Did you tell him that?"

"Sort of. I mean, we talked about it some more last night and I told him he needs to get a job in retail and work there for at least a year. He's very clever and a hard worker. I think he could get promoted to store manager, and then he'll really learn something." Godwin stooped to turn on the radio, tuned to a light jazz station.

"What brought on his desire to open his own shop?"

"I don't know. He has this enormous coin collection, with some of just about everything in it, and he's always buying and selling things over the Internet. He hasn't been doing it for very long, but he really knows a whole lot about coins, so that's not a problem. And I guess his experience with trading and buying and selling means he knows that end of it, too. He just doesn't know very much about the nuts and bolts of owning an actual business. Taxes and rent and hours and employees. I mean, I could tell him a lot — in fact, I *have* told him a lot about working here — but it's not the same as actually getting some hands-on experience."

"That's true." Thank God for Godwin, Betsy thought. His support and expertise had been priceless when she was getting her feet wet. In fact, they still were. "Do you think he'll take your advice and try to find retail work?" Betsy broke open a roll of quarters into the cash box.

"Maybe. Or maybe not. He's been spending time on the Internet lately, looking at different locations of storefronts for rent."

"So he's that close to making a decision?"

"I'm afraid so."

"Why are you so worried about this? Do you think he's making a bad decision?"

"I don't know." He offered a wry smile. "Maybe that's why I'm worried. I just don't know."

But Betsy wondered if there was something he wasn't telling her. Which was very unlike him; Godwin normally wore all his thoughts and emotions on his sleeve. She hoped Rafael wasn't trying to get Godwin to come into the fledgling business with him; it was often a bad idea to mix romance and business.

"Did you get your new plants from Marge at Green Gaia?" he asked, having apparently had enough of talking about Rafael.

Betsy decided to let dogs that had gone to sleep lie. "Yes, I bought lily of the valley and hostas — I know, I said I didn't like them, but they're big and these have showy bicolor leaves. And I bought some bleeding hearts. Connor and I spent most of yesterday planting on the hillside. It'll take a few years to fill in, but then it will be beautiful back there. It already looks nicer." Connor was Betsy's long-time boyfriend. He rented an apartment across the hall from hers.

"Did you ask Marge any more questions about Hailey?"

"A few. Her place was really hopping with customers, so I couldn't get a good-size block of time. She said that Hailey was what used to be called a man-hater. Always badmouthing them. Marge said that one time Hailey was shopping at Green Gaia and overheard her talking about the terrific new man she'd been dating, and when it was Hailey's turn to pay, she told Marge that she should not be looking for a stepfather for her two daughters, that allowing a man in the house was just asking for trouble."

"Would that be Marge asking or the man?"

Betsy laughed, then sobered. "I suppose this could indicate Hailey divorced a seriously bad husband — or maybe an incompatible husband divorced Hailey. Either way, he apparently turned her against his entire sex. I'd look at him as a suspect except he's living out on the West Coast with his third wife and children and hasn't been involved with Hailey or their children for years."

"Aw, too bad he's out, then. Have you found out who profits by Hailey's death?"

"She doesn't seem to have left much of an estate, just the house, a modest one out on the west edge of town. Her son and daughter are going to sell it and split the proceeds."

"Well, there are other kinds of profits, such as it leading to someone gaining peace of mind."

"Yes, of course. I need to talk to more people. I'd like to find others who were good friends of Hailey's. There's this one woman, Ruth Ladwig —"

"Say, we know her, don't we?"

"We know of her. She's an expert on dyes, especially vegetable dyes. I'd never met her face-to-face until she came along on a tour of Hailey's house, the scene of the crime. Have you?"

"No, but Amy Stromberg knows her."

Amy was the weather forecaster on a local news program — and a needlepointer. "Does Amy dye her own yarn?" asked Betsy, surprised.

"No, I'm sure she doesn't. I don't know how they became friends."

"What does Amy say about Ruth?"

"Only that she really knows what she's talking about. And that she's had both her knees replaced — that came up because Amy knows someone who has been having problems with her knee replacement. Amy says Ruth had a good surgeon and followed her therapist's instructions, so she did well. I guess the exercises are painful, especially at first."

While interesting, that wasn't particularly helpful. "Ruth is supposed to contact me. I also want to talk again with Philadelphia Halverson. She was so upset at her mother's house that I didn't have the heart to keep asking her questions."

"Is she going to contact you, too?"

"She didn't say so, but she did say she'd answer any questions I had. Maybe I should call her, take her to lunch or have her come over to my apartment for supper."

"You don't want to revisit the house?"

"I might, but not with her. It was too dreadful for her being in there, and awful to see her trying to be brave when her heart was breaking. I wish she had taken the advice of the police and hired a company to come in and clean up for her. It's sickening to think of having to clean up something like that, especially when it's your own mother."

Godwin nodded. "Yes, but maybe having strangers do it would be awful, too. After all, your mother took care of you, so here's a last chance to take care of her."

It was a little after lunch and business was slow. The door sounded its two notes, and both Godwin and Betsy looked to see who the customer might be.

"Hello, Irene," said Godwin, pasting on a smile that had a nice hint of sincerity in it — Irene might be a nuisance, but she spent a lot of money in Crewel World.

"H'lo, Godwin," said Irene. "Betsy, I want to ask you something."

"Certainly, Irene. How may I help you?"

"Has Mike Malloy been to see you yet?"

"No, why?"

"Because Hailey Brent is dead, and she worked in the needle arts, and so your assistance must be of value to Mike."

"I'm not sure he thinks so."

So exasperated her dark curls began quivering, Irene said, "He's wrong, of course. You *knew* Hailey! She did a dyeing demo in here! You bought her yarn to sell in here! Mike *has* to come to see you so you can tell him about all that!"

"Maybe Mike doesn't think any of that has anything to do with her murder."

"Who knows what has anything to do with her murder? Aren't detectives supposed to collect lots and lots of facts and only then sort through them to see what is important and what isn't?"

"Well, yes, that's true."

"And besides, Mike might be able to tell you something that you can put on your own pile of facts to see if it's important."

Betsy was impressed. Irene actually had a point. But: "How do you know I'm collecting my own pile of facts?"

"It's all over town. I guess Marge Schultz or maybe Philadelphia Halverson told someone, or two someones, and you know how things get around in Excelsior."

Well, that was the truth. Betsy was at first annoyed at this new leaf on the Excelsior grapevine, then thought that perhaps she should be pleased, because now people might come and tell her things. And like Irene said, when you started gathering facts, you never knew what might be important.

"Irene, what was your impression of Hailey?"

"I liked her! She was always interesting. She had an interesting perspective on life. I think she liked me, too. She said I was wise not to allow a man to interfere with my work, that my work was . . ." Irene paused while she searched for the term Hailey had used. "Expressive, I think she called it. And exciting — no, evocative." Irene didn't sound sure she knew what evocative meant, or if it was properly effusive, and was relieved when Betsy nodded.

"I agree with that, your work is wonderful."

"It sets a mood, all right," agreed Godwin.

"Did she say anything about her own work?" asked Betsy.

"A little. She said sometimes it was hard to get people to see that her work had value. I told her I knew what she meant. I have the same problem. Some people still think what I do is folk art."

"Did she mention anyone in particular?"

"The garden-woman next door, Marge Schultz, was one. But another one, as bad or worse, was Joanne McMurphy."

"Who's Joanne McMurphy?"

"I've seen her, but I don't know her. She often looks angry. All I know is what Hailey said, that Joanne has a temper. The way she talked, some of the time I thought she thought Joanne was funny, but other times I think she was just a little scared of her."

"How do they know each other?"

"You know, I never asked her." Irene shook her head, frowning, a little miffed at herself for not thinking of that.

"Have you told Mike this?" Betsy asked.

Another frown. "Yes, but I don't think he even wrote it down. Do you think it's important?"

"I think it might be." Betsy and Godwin exchanged a glance. Here at last was a lead, slim but in a direction away from Marge.

Seven

Betsy found she was right about one thing. The word had spread that she was investigating Hailey's murder, so many of her customers saw to it that next time they came in — some even made a special trip — they told her what they knew, or had heard, or concluded about Hailey.

Over the next few days, Betsy was informed that Hailey was very comfortable with herself, that she was relaxed and competent, but also prickly and opinionated, as well as efficient and hardworking. Three people said they heard she was "sort of a pagan," and four had heard her talking like a militant feminist, which to one of them was the same thing, practically, right? Hailey was good at the needle arts as well as spinning and dyeing. She practiced Tai Chi, said a woman who had seen her down at the beach last summer doing the strange and beautiful slow dance of the practice.

And by the way, said this same woman, she could swim like a dolphin. "I've never seen anyone more at home in the water. You almost want to look for fins, or a tail."

Though Betsy couldn't see how that or even most of what the other people brought to her was of any value in this case, she duly wrote it all down on the long and narrow reporter's tablet she had taken to using while investigating.

On Friday, Philadelphia called. "I've arranged for Ruth to revisit Mother's house," she said, "and that reminded me that I haven't had another conversation with you. How do I arrange an appointment for us to talk? Do you get a day off from work?"

"Yes, I do, though it's often only a day away from the shop — I have to catch up on my usual household tasks, plus things like bookkeeping, placing orders, and so on, things to do with the shop. I'm sure you are as busy as I am with work and your art projects and caring for your family. How about we meet for breakfast?"

Checking their respective calendars brought up the following Tuesday as a day both could manage. They agreed to meet at Antiquity Rose at nine that day.

The waitress at Antiquity Rose gave barely

90

a second glance at Philadelphia's hair. She seemed more intrigued by Betsy's indigo-blue pantsuit. Or perhaps it was the beautiful lapis earrings and brooch she'd bought at the store to match her blue shoes and purse. Was the ensemble over the top? Betsy thought not. Perhaps it was that the blue of her outfit clashed with the blue-green shade of Philadelphia's hair. It had become an interesting world when one had to consider whether the blue of one's clothing might not complement the blue hair of one's breakfast companion.

Betsy was pleased when the waitress brought them into a small side room and seated them in a back corner, where it was quiet.

"How are you holding up?" asked Betsy after they had consulted the menus and placed their orders.

"Better, thanks. I'm glad you suggested we meet here. I haven't been to Antiquity Rose for a long time." Philadelphia, clad in black slacks and sweater with lots of silver jewelry, looked around the pleasant little room. "Too bad they're only open for breakfast and lunch, but not dinner." The place, a converted house, was a tearoom/restaurant and also an antique shop. The front room where they'd come in was full of plates and cups, embroidered aprons and silver spoons, porcelain, books, and jewelry. The art on all the walls, even the furniture they were sitting on, was for sale.

The food was excellent.

Betsy, halfway through her mushroom omelet, said, "I hope you don't mind some personal questions."

"No, of course not."

"Are you married?"

"Yes, and still to my first husband, which is a little unusual in my age group. We have two children, a girl and a boy. I'm a nurse at Hennepin County Medical Center. My husband, Al — Allen, actually — is a program designer at Graphics Design in Minneapolis."

Betsy pulled her notepad from her purse and ate left-handed while she took notes.

"Philadelphia," Betsy began.

"Please, call me Del. It's not that I don't love my name, I do, but it is a mouthful."

"All right. Del, how old were you when your parents divorced?"

"Eleven."

"That must have been a painful age to have your dad move away."

"It was a relief, actually. They were always fighting."

"Who divorced whom?"

"Mother divorced Dad when she found out he was having an affair. JR took it hard, and I thought for a while he was going to go live with him. He threatened to a couple of times, but always backed down. Anyway, Dad had the other woman all lined up, and there was no room in that arrangement for a kid. I'm surprised JR turned out as good as he did, looking back on it."

"What's your father's name?"

"Mark Brent — Mother liked the surname, so she kept it."

"Your mother never remarried?"

Philadelphia smiled wryly. "Heavens, no. Mother liked that old cliché that a woman without a man is like a fish without a bicycle. She was proud to succeed without a man in the house."

"Yet you married."

"Well, I turned out to be of the opinion that this fish could learn to ride a bicycle, and like it. I think my grandparents set the example I followed. Of course, I got lucky: Al is just great, so I'm not handing my mother's opinion on to my kids. Of course, it may be that, working nights like I do, we don't see enough of each other to sustain quarrels."

"What did your mother think of your husband?"

"She put up with him; in fact, I think she secretly liked Al, though she never said so."

Betsy made a note, then asked, "Do you know a Joanne McMurphy?"

"No, why?"

"Apparently she and your mother had some kind of quarrel."

"I don't think I ever heard Mother mention that name."

"There's an entry in the phone book that lists a Joanne and Pierce McMurphy. Husband and wife, I assume."

"I've never heard of either of them, sorry."

"Who were some of your mother's friends?"

"Well, there's Randi Moreham, Randi with an *i*. Randi's marriage is in trouble, and Mother had gone so far as to suggest Randi move in with her until she decided what to do. I've met Randi a couple of times. She's the quiet type, kind of the opposite of Mother. Her husband's name is Walter. I've never met him. Now that Mother is . . . gone, I wonder what Randi is going to do."

Betsy wrote the names down. "Who else?"

"Ruth Ladwig, of course. She knows a lot about dyes, and the two of them could talk for hours about that. You know, what they'd been trying, what colors you could get, mordants — did you know urine is a mordant?" Philadelphia's nose wrinkled. "Too often there's some unpleasant aspect to the crafts, isn't there? Fortunately, most of them aren't as bad as that. Oh, good, here comes the waitperson with the coffeepot."

When Betsy got back to the shop, Godwin said, "Ruth Ladwig called. She wants to know if you and she can find a date the two of you can go back to Hailey's house. She left her number."

Betsy communed with Godwin, her list of available temp helpers, and her own schedule before calling Ruth to set a date.

"I'm not sure why you want to come with me," said Ruth. "I'm going to price the items in the dyeing workshop. How could that be interesting to you?"

"Philadelphia was so upset down there that she became a distraction to me," Betsy replied. "I have a feeling I missed something, some helpful detail. I just want another look. And, I'd like to talk to you about Hailey."

They agreed to meet Thursday, at two, at Hailey's house — Ruth would have a key.

That evening, as usual, Betsy turned on her television to watch the local news. The newscasters were companionable, amusing, and competent. "Okay, Amy," said the good-looking guy, "is spring still sprung?"

Amy Stromberg, a Gwyneth Paltrow look-alike, blond and blue-eyed, appeared in front of that trick screen that displayed mobile weather symbols. A trio of radar beacons was sweeping around the state map, showing no storms present anywhere except in the far northwestern region.

"It sure is!" she said with a bright smile. She was wearing a close-fitting navy blue suit that showed off the figure of someone who Betsy knew cross-country skied in the winter and played tennis all summer. Her prediction for the rest of the week was for seasonably warm weather — upper sixties and low seventies — under clear skies, but rain showers coming in Saturday night and lingering into Sunday.

Good, thought Betsy. Fine weather on Saturday would bring out shoppers, and the rain on Sunday would help root the plantings she and Connor had installed in the back lot.

Betsy was looking forward to next year, when she could pick bouquets of lily of the valley — she loved strongly scented flowers such as those and lilacs and old-fashioned roses. But the back lot was too shady for lilacs or roses.

She turned the TV set off and went into her galley kitchen to sweep and mop the floor. She was about halfway through her chore when her phone rang. "Hello?" she said.

"Betsy? This is Amy Stromberg."

"Hi, I was just watching you do the weather. You were looking very good."

"Thanks. You called me yesterday, left a message, and I'm only now calling you back. What's up?"

"That Mark Parsons needlepoint canvas you ordered came in. I'll hold it for you in the shop."

"Ooooh, thank you! Oh, hey, I've been meaning to call you anyway. I hear you're investigating Hailey Brent's murder, and are looking to talk to people about her."

"Did you know her?"

"No, but I know some people who did."

"Like who?"

"Well, Ruth Ladwig for one."

"Yes, I've already talked with her."

"Joanne McMurphy."

"You know her?"

"I know her husband — well, actually, it's my husband who is Pierce's friend, they both are software developers. I've met Joanne a few times when she and Pierce have played tennis with Jeff and me. I'm not sure what the connection was, but I do know Joanne was a friend of Hailey's. Joanne mentioned her to me."

"What do you think of Joanne?"

"My opinion of her is low enough that I don't want to play doubles with her again. She's a poor sport, challenges every call not in her favor, yells at poor Pierce if he loses a point. She's actually a little scary when she gets angry."

"Scary?" This was the second time someone described her anger that way.

"She opens her eyes really wide, and her eyebrows raise up crooked, and she shows all her teeth — it's like an angry animal."

Wow. Betsy asked, "Has she ever become violent?"

"I never saw her actually strike someone, though last time we played, she threw her tennis racket at Pierce and I think she meant to hit him. He knows how to calm her down, he's very patient with her, more than she has a right to expect. I feel sorry for him, he's such a sweet person, but if I were him, I'd have someone warm and kind on the side — and be damn careful Joanne didn't find out about her."

"Hmmm, interesting. Do you know Randi Moreham?"

"Not to talk to, though I've seen her

around. I think she came into some money. She gave a nice donation to SNAP last year, after a couple of years of much more modest donations." Betsy was aware of the Spay Neuter Assistance Program that Amy volunteered for. It was a Minnesota charity devoted to decreasing the surplus pet population by offering to neuter cats and dogs at little or no cost. They actually had a van that was a mobile clinic, and were looking to buy a second one. Betsy had made a donation herself last fall — she strongly approved of their mission.

"I understand she's on the verge of leaving her husband, and Hailey was offering her a place to stay," said Betsy.

"I'm afraid that's news to me."

"Anyone else you know who was a friend — or an enemy — of Hailey's?"

"I don't think so. We didn't move in the same circles, really." Amy paused, then changed the subject. "How about I come in on Saturday to pick up that Parsons canvas? And could you pull the yarns for me for it?"

"Sure, everything will be waiting for you."

After they hung up, Betsy made another note about the canvas and stuck it on her refrigerator where she'd be sure to see it in the morning.

■ ■ ■ ■

In the shop the next morning, Betsy tried to think of a way to connect with Randi Moreham and Joanne McMurphy. She didn't know either of them, and was pretty sure neither of them had ever been in Crewel World.

Only pretty sure?

She went into her computer's customer database and found that Randi Moreham had in fact come in three times and bought something — the last time over six months earlier.

Godwin came over to look at what she was doing. "I have an idea," he said. "It's something we should do anyway."

"What's that?"

"Do a special mailing — both by e-mail and snail mail — to customers who haven't visited the store in a while. Do a 'We Miss You' theme."

"You're right that we ought to be doing something like that," said Betsy. "How quickly can we put it together?" Then she thought of something else. "And how about we offer to send a dollar out of each twenty spent to SNAP?" That additional sweetener might appeal to Randi.

"Good idea. I can have the mailing ready to send out in a couple of days, if we rush."

"Make it so," said Betsy, smiling.

"Aye, aye, Captain."

Godwin was as good as his word. On Friday morning, after having loaded a file of the finished ad on the shop's computer, he hit the Send button. A little stack of printed ads waited on the checkout desk for the daily postal pickup. Titled "We Miss Your Smiling Face," it offered to broaden the smile with a ten percent discount to anyone bringing the ad to the shop. It also noted that one dollar of every twenty spent would go to SNAP, the charity that neutered the pets of poor people.

And having baited her hook, all Betsy could do was wait.

EIGHT

On Thursday afternoon, June first, Betsy drove over to Hailey Brent's house, where she found Ruth Ladwig waiting for her in the driveway. "The key is to the side entrance," said Ruth, holding up a fish-shaped key holder.

The dead lilacs had been removed from the dining room table. "Philadelphia said she went through the house with an agent," said Ruth. "The estate sale will be next Friday, Saturday, and Sunday, the house will be staged Tuesday and Wednesday, and a for-sale sign will go up Thursday."

Betsy looked around. "Kind of sad, isn't it?"

"Yes, but I think the fact of the murder is weighing her down, and she wants very badly to be freed from this reminder of it."

They went down the steep, age-grayed stairs into the basement. Ruth turned on the lights.

The spinning wheel looked somehow forlorn in its place in the middle of the carpet, perhaps because the sky was overcast. The light coming in through the high little windows was not friendly.

They noted the two bowls with unspun fibers in them. "You're still of the opinion that these are made from soy and bamboo?" asked Betsy.

"Yes," said Ruth. "I have some samples of spun soy and spun bamboo at my station at the museum, and the textures feel the same as those in the bowls. Odd, but the bamboo is softer than the soy to the fingers." She went to put a forefinger on the wheel of the spinning wheel. "I've already got a bid to put on this on behalf of a friend. Now, let's take another look at the dyeing setup."

Betsy looked with trepidation at the spot on the floor where the body had been found, but as before, there was no visible sign of its former presence.

The three long-cooled pots remained on the stove. "Do you smell that?" said Ruth. "Vegetable matter goes moldy pretty fast in water." There was, in fact, a musty, spoiled smell in the air.

"Why is the yarn a darker brown than the dye bath?" asked Betsy, peering into one pot, wrinkling her nose as she confirmed the source of the moldy odor.

"The yarn has taken up the dye," said Ruth. "You see, she hadn't taken the carrot tops out of the other bath; she was probably going to use that to dye the rovings over there in the bowl."

"I *thought* they were carrot tops," said Betsy. "Is there anything that can't be used to make a dye? Rocks, I suppose."

Ruth considered the question. "I don't know. Even crushed rocks can make a dye. Any portion of plant material — roots, leaves, bark — can make a dye. Some are stronger or more beautiful than others, of course. But all the vegetable dyes have a soft quality that's really lovely."

"Yes, and I remember thinking that every color of yarn Hailey brought in went with every other color."

Ruth took down the dried skeins of yarn, then lifted the pot with the brown yarn in it and poured its contents into the sink. She turned on the faucet and began to rinse the yarn in cool water, squeezing it gently from time to time. She draped the yarn on the plastic-coated clothesline where it immediately began to dribble. "I don't know if Philadelphia will do anything with this," she said. "But I'm sure — Irene, isn't it? I'll bet Irene would be glad to have it for her project."

"I'll call her."

"Better check with Philadelphia first. Maybe she wants it for her own knitting projects."

"Good idea, you're right. Do the green one next," said Betsy.

"All right, but it isn't green dye."

Betsy, frowning, watched as Ruth brought the big pot to the counter. When she took the lid off, Betsy could see that the dye bath had turned inexplicably from green to dark blue.

"I thought so," said Ruth. "The air gets into it, by osmosis, I guess. This is indigo." She used the dowel sitting on the counter to reach into the pot and pull out a large amount of thin yarn. It came out green and she held the dribbling stuff over the sink. Right in front of Betsy's surprised eyes, in a few seconds the green disappeared and the roving was blue.

"It's like magic!" said Betsy. "How does it do that?"

"It's the oxygen in the air that causes the change. When you make up the indigo solution you use two chemicals: Spectralite, a brand name for thiourea dioxide, and lye. You have to measure the lye carefully, because too much lye can turn your fibers into mush. But it's the thiourea dioxide that removes the oxygen from the dye bath. This means you stir very carefully, and slip the fibers into it gently, so as to mix a minimum of air into it. But if you let it sit long enough, the air gets in anyhow." Ruth put the dowel into the dye bath and moved it around. "Ah, I thought there was something else in here."

She brought out a knitted square about six inches on a side, but it was yellow-green — then the air did its work, and it turned a pretty red-brown.

"Brown?" said Betsy.

"It must have been orange when it was put in," said Ruth. "Orange and blue make brown."

"Why a knitted square?" asked Betsy.

"I have no idea. Perhaps she was doing it for her own use; certainly if Irene wanted yarn, a finished piece of knitting was of no use." Ruth rinsed the square and draped it dribbling over the clothesline, then rinsed the indigo yarn.

"See anything yet?" asked Ruth.

Betsy looked around the space and sighed. "Not a thing. I guess I'm too ignorant of the whole process to recognize anything wrong or even just a little off. Except the smell, of course."

"I don't see anything wrong or off, either," said Ruth, looking around.

"We should take these with us," said Betsy, gesturing at the yarn and at the knitted square hanging over the sink. "Otherwise Philadelphia or the person doing the staging might throw them away. I've got a deep sink in my basement. I can run a line and hang them over it to dry. I'll let Philadelphia know I've got it. And, with her permission, I know how to get in touch with Irene to see if she wants any of it, and I'm pretty sure she will. I'll have her contact Philadelphia about payment."

"All right, good idea." Ruth shook water off her hands. "Now, where is that cheesecloth? I know I saw it somewhere." She began opening cabinets, and finally found the one that had a tall stack of gauzy white cloths in it. She chose one, spread it over the drain in the sink, and started to empty the pot that had carrot tops into it. Then she paused again. "Or do we want to dye the roving that's in the bowl of mordant?"

"I don't know how to spin it into yarn, do you?"

"No. Kind of a shame, but no." She emptied the pot onto the cheesecloth, gathered it up, and squeezed it out. Then she opened the door to the cabinet under the sink and said, "Darn it, I forgot: There's no liner to the trash can."

She held the sopping cheesecloth over the sink while Betsy went into the big box of plastic bags next to the can and pulled one out.

"Isn't that kind of strange?" asked Betsy.

"What's strange?"

"Well, she must have strained the pot of brown dye, right? And thrown the vegetable matter away. Why empty the trash can when there were still the carrot tops to strain out and throw away? And if for whatever reason she did dump the old liner, why didn't she put a new liner in the can? I do it automatically, pull out the full bag and put a new one in. It's one task, really, not two."

Ruth shrugged. "So do I. But different people do things differently. Maybe the trash can was overflowing and she just quick tied it off and took it out."

Betsy had on occasion put off emptying her trash bin until it threatened to overflow. She nodded. "I can see that," she said.

"We'll have to toss that new liner, though it seems a shame to waste a whole trash bag on just the carrot tops and the rovings." Ruth poured out the mordant in the bowl, squeezed the rovings, and put them in the trash bin. Then she washed her hands thoroughly and dried them on a paper towel.

Finally, she pulled another trash bag from the box of them and shook it open. She put one skein of dry yarn into a bottom corner, twisted it once, put the other dry skein in the other corner and twisted it again, then did the same with the wet items, twisting each until she'd made a sort of compartment for each item, to keep the wet ones from soaking into and possibly spreading their fresh dye. She pulled the drawstring at the open end of the bag to close it and put the lumpy bundle on the counter.

She and Betsy then proceeded to scrub, rinse, and dry the pots, paying special attention to the big one that had held the indigo dye. "It clings," Ruth explained, "and even a tiny bit left over can spoil the next thing you try to dye in it."

"How long have you been interested in dyeing?" asked Betsy as they worked.

"A very long time, years."

"How did you meet Hailey?"

"We both turned up at Murphy's Landing — have you ever been out there?"

"No."

"It's a collection of old buildings, dating back to the late 1800s, early 1900s. People in period costume show what life was like back in those days, and in one of the houses there's a woman who concocts vegetable dyes on a wood-burning stove. She has a loom and a spinning wheel, too. Hailey and I spent most of an afternoon talking with her, and came away friends."

"What did you think of Hailey?"

"As long as what you talked about was dyeing, spinning, and the needle arts, she was amazing. Happy to share what she knew, loved to experiment. But she had a real problem about men and another one about politics. I never tried her on religion. Twice burned, you know?" Ruth smiled as she rinsed the pot she'd been scrubbing.

"I've heard she was willing to bend the rules of ownership when someone had a plant she wanted to try out."

Ruth thought that over. "She never said that to me — not in so many words, at least. But it wouldn't surprise me. She talked a lot about how more things should be shared in common."

"What was she like as a person?"

Ruth thought that over. "Opinionated. Very sure she was right, even when she wasn't. Funny in a sharp-tongued way. Intelligent. Talented." She tapped a forefinger on her lips as she thought some more.

"There was something sly about her. No, not sly, that's the wrong word. She liked, really liked, to listen to gossip, and then carry what she learned to the person being gossiped about." The finger tapped again. "We all gossip, of course. I remember one time I started to tell her something and I said, 'Now don't tell Gladys this, but' and she said, 'Buy my lunch and I won't.' And she meant it. I mean, she laughed, but I ended up paying for her lunch."

"Did she keep her word?" asked Betsy.

"Oh yes." Ruth laughed. "But it cured me of sharing gossip with her unless I didn't care who she told."

They turned the pots over to dry on a couple of layers of cheesecloth. "Now, let's price these things," Ruth said. She got a notebook from her purse and began very methodically looking at every item, including even the dowels, and writing it down with a figure next to it. "If I were only a little more dishonest," she said, mock complaining, "I'd lowball these stainless steel pots and make sure I was here first thing for the estate sale."

As they were about to leave, Betsy said, "Ruth, do you know Randi Moreham or Joanne McMurphy?"

"I've heard their names, but they were

Hailey's friends, not mine. No, wait, I don't think Joanne was a friend, just someone Hailey knew. She knew Joanne's husband, too."

"Did she ever talk about them to you?"

Ruth thought. "Not a whole lot. She was encouraging Randi to go ahead with her plans to divorce her husband. I know that because we were at lunch a few weeks ago and I had to wait while she had a cell phone conversation with Randi. She said something to the effect of 'You know my door is always open to you if you need a place to stay.' I told her that it was almost never a good idea to get involved with a divorcing couple, because if they made up, she would lose Randi as a friend. She said, 'If Randi goes back to her husband, she's already no longer my friend.' "

"How about Joanne McMurphy?"

"Let me tell you a story about Joanne," Ruth said. "A group of friends, two of them from Excelsior, came over to help me out after my knee surgery a year ago, and we were sitting around after drinking coffee, and someone said it was a good thing that Joanne hadn't come along on their mission of mercy. I asked why, and she said that Joanne had always needed to be the boss, but her bad temper was getting worse and worse until it was impossible to deal with her. But that's just gossip, barely worth the breath it takes to repeat it. And I wouldn't repeat it, except that you're looking for any information about Hailey we can offer. So be wary about asking Joanne's opinion of Hailey. I will say her fellow Excelsior-ite laughed but sincerely agreed."

Back at the shop, Betsy found waiting for her an attractive young woman with thick, dark brown hair and candid hazel-green eyes, dressed in subdued bluish gray.

"I've been meaning to come in anyway," she said. "That offer to donate to SNAP put me over the top. I'm Randi Moreham. You're investigating Hailey Brent's murder, right?" She was standing at the checkout desk, in front of a low stack of counted cross-stitch patterns and DMC flosses.

"Well, this is a very pleasant surprise!" said Betsy. "Were your ears burning? I was just talking about you!"

"Nothing bad, I hope."

"No, not at all."

Godwin said, "She was about to leave. I was just starting to ring her purchase up."

Betsy said, "Then I'm glad I came back in time, Ms. Moreham."

"Please, call me Randi."

"All right. Randi. Can you wait another few minutes while I take something down to the basement?"

"Of course."

"Thanks." Betsy took the plastic bag of dyed yarn downstairs and came back up. She said, "You do know that if you have any information about Hailey Brent, you should talk to Sergeant Mike Malloy over at the police station."

"He's already talked to me," said Randi. She was a very slender woman probably in her early or middle thirties. "But I think I also should talk with you. Can I sit down first? These shoes are killing my feet." Her narrow feet were encased in extremely high heels.

"Certainly. May I get you a cup of tea, or coffee?" Crewel World offered free coffee or tea to paying customers as a perk.

"Coffee, black, thanks."

"Come with me." Betsy led her to the back portion of the shop, to a small round table covered with a cloth embroidered with children holding balloons. Two small chairs with cushioned seats were pulled up to it. Betsy usually used it when consulting with a customer trying to select a pattern or to decide what colors or what kinds of floss to use for a pattern.

Betsy gestured at one of the chairs and put her reporter's notebook in front of the other. "Have a seat," she said. "I'll get the coffee."

She moved to a small room at the very back of the shop that held a coffee maker and a teakettle, and brought back to the table two pretty porcelain cups, one with coffee and the other with an herbal tea for herself. "Before we talk about Hailey Brent," she asked Randi as she sat down, "did you find everything you were looking for for your project?"

"Yes, thanks. Godwin was a good help in picking things out."

"Yes, he's wonderful, isn't he?"

"Yes." Randi took a sip of her coffee, then wrapped a slender hand around the cup, as if to warm it. "What did you want to ask me?"

"How well did you know Hailey?"

"I thought I knew her very well. We were friends for about five or six years — I met her at an adult education class in creative writing. I wanted to write children's books, and she was going to write a novel about a woman dyer. We started a two-person writers' group that lasted five months, but neither of us finished our projects. It's harder than it looks, writing. But we stayed in touch."

"Why did you say you only thought you knew her well?"

"Well, she was always sure of herself, and very kind to me. And me, I dither, can't make up my mind about anything, whether it's what to cook for dinner or should we have kids or should I get a divorce. Walter and I started having problems, and I shared my problems with Hailey, and pretty soon I started thinking maybe we should divorce, and Hailey strongly agreed we should. I trusted her opinion. She even offered me a place to stay if I followed through with the divorce. She treated it as if it were obvious that I should divorce Walter, and I got all caught up in the details of it. We discussed why I should get the house and whether the money I inherited from my Aunt Lucy was a sign, and so on, as if filing for the divorce was almost the least part of it.

"Then suddenly she was murdered. I was never so shocked in my life. It was as if someone cut off the air or the sunshine — or maybe more like someone turned on the air or the lights. Because I talked, really talked, with Walter, and I found out he was sick and scared because he didn't want a divorce. And that's when I realized I didn't, either. Neither of us did. So we've started going to couples counseling and I think things are getting better between us.

"That's why I only thought I knew Hailey Brent. She wasn't supporting me in my decision. She made the decision herself, and got me to agree with it."

Betsy wondered if Randi wasn't now reflecting her husband's opinion or even the counselor's, but she just cleared her throat and made another note.

It also occurred to her that unless Randi was lying, she had no motive to murder Hailey. On the other hand, Walter certainly did.

NINE

The timer dinged in Betsy's galley kitchen as a reminder that it was time to make the salad. At the same moment the doorbell buzzed. It was exactly 7 p.m.

"I'll get it," said Connor.

"Thanks, love." Betsy began pulling items out of the refrigerator and putting them beside the cutting board.

Jill and Lars Larson were always so prompt that Betsy sometimes wondered if they didn't stand out on the sidewalk waiting for the second hand on their watches to sweep around to the minute.

Jill came up the stairs to Betsy's apartment ahead of Lars. She was a tall woman, naturally ash blond, with a Gibson Girl face. She was wearing her usual lofty, serene expression, which hid a not-always-subtle sense of humor.

Lars was a very big man, equally fair but in a golden way, with broad shoulders and a little too much chin. He had an amiable air that sometimes fooled people into thinking he wasn't as hard-nosed in his profession as a sergeant on Excelsior's little police department should be.

They were both dressed casually in chinos and lightweight flannel shirts, Jill's light blue and Lars's deep green — it was cool for early June.

Connor was a medium-tall man with a weather-beaten face, kind blue seafaring eyes, and an Irish accent so faint hardly anyone could hear it. He took them into the living room and sat down with them to talk. He wore gray twill trousers and a densely patterned Fair Isle sweater he'd knit himself.

"How does Emma Beth like preschool?" Connor asked. Divorced and with two sons and a daughter, all grown, Connor liked talking about the Larsons' children as if they were the grandchildren he was beginning to fear he'd never have.

"She's doing very well," said Jill. "Of course, she's the brightest child in her class."

"Of course," agreed Connor.

"She asked a riddle the other day. Why can't a bicycle stand up on its own?"

"Beats me," said Connor.

"It's two tired." Jill laughed and said, "She actually understood the pun, isn't that amazing?"

Connor laughed, too. "Amazing."

"Dinner smells delicious," Lars said. "I smell poultry. Are we having chicken?"

"No, some extra-small Cornish hens Betsy found somewhere."

Lars rubbed his palms together. "Oh boy!" he said. "I like those because I can eat them bones and all."

But first there was a spinach salad with red onions, mushrooms, avocado, and pieces of mandarin orange.

"I thought about putting in some little shrimps, too," said Betsy, "but I just never got the chance to go back to the store for them."

"This is great just as it is," said Jill.

The Cornish hens came with wild rice stuffing and tender new asparagus. Dessert was cheesecake with brandied cherries.

"Ahhhh," sighed Lars at last, leaning back in his chair and touching his hands lightly to the sides of his stomach. "That was really nice, Betsy, thank you."

"I'm glad you enjoyed it."

"How's your latest project coming?" Jill asked Betsy.

"I need more practice stitching on perforated paper, so I'm working on Mill Hill's Moonlit Kitties. It's got a wonderful Van

Gogh–like moon."

Jill laughed. "No, I meant the Hailey Brent case. Any progress to report?"

"Not a whole lot."

Connor began to clear the table while Betsy got out the Scrabble game, long a favorite of the two couples.

"I can tell you something, though it's not particularly helpful," said Lars. "It's peripheral to the case you're working on."

"What's that?"

"Someone involved in the case, not a suspect, has a concealed carry permit."

"Who is it?" asked Betsy, eagerly.

"Pierce McMurphy, Joanne's husband."

"That's not peripheral!" said Betsy.

"Depends," said Connor, a stack of dessert plates in his hands. "What kind of gun does he carry? Do you know?"

"A forty-five semiauto — or he did. But it isn't relevant; it was stolen two weeks before the murder."

"Was it a forty-five caliber bullet that killed Hailey?" Betsy wanted to know. She thrust her hand into the little bag of tiles and pulled one out. "T," she said, and handed the bag to Lars.

"Yes," said Lars, nodding. He shoved a big hand into the bag. "Ha!" he said, showing the others the X he'd drawn. "Best you

121

can do is tie me for the chance to go first."
Contrary to normal Scrabble rules, they
played that the letter with the highest score
went first.

"Was it stolen in a burglary?" asked Jill.
"Why didn't you tell me about this?" She
took the bag from him and drew a C.

"I didn't think it was important," said
Lars. "Like I said, he's not a suspect. And
anyway, he didn't have the gun at the time
of the murder."

"Hmm, a burglary," said Betsy.

"Yes, but not a home break-in; the gun
was stolen from the trunk of his car."

"If he had a concealed carry permit," said
Connor as he came to sit down at the table,
"what was the gun doing in the trunk of his
car?" He reached for the bag of tiles.

"He was visiting a client who works in a
building with a big 'Allied Merchants For-
bids Guns on These Premises' sign on the
door. So he locked it in his trunk. When he
came out, his car had been broken into.
They stole his brand new Garmin GPS, a
cowhide attaché case with a three-hundred-
dollar cashier's check in it, and his forty-
five Ruger aluminum-frame semiautomatic."

"What a good memory you have!" said
Jill, laughing.

Betsy watched Connor draw a Z. "But if he was visiting a client, why didn't he take the attaché case in with him?"

"He didn't need it for that client; he was making a delivery of some drawings too big to fit in the case." Lars drew seven tiles from the bag and began to arrange them on the wooden holder.

They settled into the game. With his splendid British vocabulary, Connor always did well at Scrabble, though he sometimes had difficulty with American spelling, and anyway Jill kept him on his mettle. Lars liked to use strategy, blocking Betsy, Jill, and Connor whenever he got the chance. Betsy just was happy to find she had the tiles and the opportunity to form a good word. Such as adding C-O-M to Jill's P-L-A-I-N, and turning the board to Connor.

He was smiling in anticipation and immediately started putting tiles down to link the D in E-N-D-I-N-G with the O of C-O-M-P-L-A-I-N, then going on, spelling D-Y-S-T-O-P-I-A. And the Y was on a triple letter score. He looked around the table, anticipating a challenge, but the other three only nodded. He added up his points and turned the board to Jill, saying, "I was looking for a place to put that Y."

Connor won the game by thirty points,

but Betsy came in second, surprising everyone, including herself.

Jill insisted on helping with the dishes, but once in the kitchen she had something else on her mind.

"Betsy, I don't think you know any licensed private eyes — or do you?" she asked while waiting for the sink to fill with soapy water.

"No, I don't know any. Why?"

"I'm sort of wondering if I shouldn't go for a license myself."

Betsy nearly dropped one of the glasses she was putting into the water. "Jill Cross Larson! What gave you that notion?"

"Watching you — well, more watching the people you help. They come to you desperately scared of being charged with murder, and are relieved and grateful when you prove them innocent. One reason I joined the police force was because I enjoy helping people: keeping the streets safe for honest folk, restoring lost children to their families, investigating traffic accidents. I can't go back to that job, not with two small children to raise, but I could do sort of that same kind of work part-time, the kind of work you do, maybe."

"What does Lars think?"

"He thinks we should get me pregnant

124

again."

Godwin, having loaded the dishwasher, wandered into the study to find Rafael laying out coins on the big antique mahogany desk. " 'The King was in his counting house, counting out his money,' " said Godwin.

"That sounds like a quote," said Rafael absently.

"It's an old nursery rhyme. 'The maid was in the courtyard, hanging up the clothes, when along came a blackbird and *snipped*' " — Godwin snapped his fingers — " 'off her nose!' "

Rafael chuckled. "The things you know!"

"I know, it's a beastly bore. Are you thinking of selling some of these?"

"Yes. I have taken to heart what you said about my working in retail to gain understanding of how it is done, so I have rented a table at the MOON coin show. I will buy and sell coins there. Will you come with me?"

Godwin smiled, surprised and pleased at Rafael. "I'll check my schedule. I should be able to take that day as my day off." He went to his room, a spacious one, with a grand view of the lake, and booted up his computer.

He did a quick check and found he could take the date off. After telling Rafael the good news, he made a note on his calendar. He had gone with Rafael to these coin meets before, but never as a vendor. He was pleased that Rafael was taking seriously his advice to get retail experience. It would be interesting to see how well his partner did when on the other side of the table.

The mailman brought two big, cardboard-stiffened envelopes into Crewel World the next morning. Opening them revealed two entries in the template contest. Ten more had come in the past week, and Betsy got those out of a desk drawer to look them over.

Several contestants had elected to treat the narrow rectangles as a color wheel, running from bright red at one end to cool blue at the other, outlining the rectangles in black. Others had filled the spaces with various stitches or patterns. One person had decided the rectangles' black outline looked like the bars on a sagging cage and stitched a Chinese-style tiger pacing behind them, glaring out at the viewer, tail lashing and teeth on display.

"Ooooooh," said Betsy. "I like this one!"

Godwin looked at the others. "I like the

one she calls Rose Trellis," he said.

"Here's a nice one." It was done in a broken bargello stitch, each jump from rectangle to rectangle acknowledged by a corresponding jump in the pattern. "Wow, that took some concentration," Betsy said. She turned it over and saw the tag had Rafael's name on it. "Hey, I didn't know he gave us an entry!"

"He gave it to me yesterday and I just put it in the drawer with the others. I don't think he wants any special consideration."

"He doesn't need to ask for special consideration; this is really good."

"I agree, but I'm prejudiced. Now, we had said we were going to display the entries, but there's a limited amount of wall space, and if what we've got already is any indication, there are going to be a *lot* of entries."

"I've got the solution all thought out. I bought two bags of toy clothespins at the dollar store and a ball of twine at Menard's. The ceiling's nice and high in here, and we can string the entries up so everyone can see them. Oh, but first we have to retag them with numbers so our judges won't know who did them. Let's not forget to put a corresponding number on the name tags we take off."

Sorting quickly through the rest of the

mail, Betsy found a first-class letter addressed to her in careful printing, with the word PERSONAL printed in red letters in the lower left corner and a Forever stamp in the upper right-hand corner.

Betsy opened it to find a single sheet of lined paper covered on both sides with more printing, this a lot more carelessly done, though obviously by the same hand.

Dear Ms. Devonshire, it began.

I did not want to send you an e-mail message because anyone might see it. My mother, who is Marge Schultz, told me she is being harassed by a police detective named Michael Malloy. He wants to prove she murdered a woman named Hailey Brent. I never even heard of Hailey Brent, and I am sure my mother never murdered anyone. She is a good person, and hardworking, intelligent, and honest.

Mother says you are trying to help her. I hope with all my heart you are successful.

Mother is the hardest worker I have ever known. She worked two jobs putting my father through medical school. My father was a good man, but he got cancer one year after he finished being an intern. He fought it for three years before he finally died. My mother was the rock that got us through.

I am so proud of how she has made Green Gaia a success. She always loved to garden. When we lived with Grand-mama, we had a big backyard garden for mostly vegetables but flowers, too. She worked for a landscape company and then a garden center, which she bought from the owner when he retired.

I have told my mother that she should find a boyfriend and maybe get married. She always says she can't because she is already married to Green Gaia. I think Green Gaia is the most important thing in the world to her, more important even than me or her granddaughter.

She proudly walked me down the aisle herself when I got married. I hoped we would stay in Excelsior so she could be a loving grandmother to my daughter, but my husband got this amazing job offer in Southern California and that's where we live to this day. We only get to Minnesota every third Christmas, because we spend one with his parents in Las Vegas, then one just us, then one with Mother. But we stay in touch by e-mail at least once a month. We plan to come to Excelsior this Christmas. I hope our plans come true.

I can't think what else to tell you about

*how good and wonderful Mother is. I thank
you over and over for coming to her aid.*
Sincerely, Louise French

Betsy, deeply touched, read the letter
again. She, too, hoped this coming Christmas would see the family happily celebrat-
ing in Excelsior.

Later, Betsy was high on a ladder stringing
twine — Godwin was afraid of heights,
especially when seen from a stepladder —
when the door sang out its two-note alarm.

"Oh, hi, Irene!" called Betsy, causing Irene
to jump and look around as she entered the
store.

"Hi, Irene," said Godwin, coming from
the back of the shop.

"H'lo, Goddy, I thought at first you were
Betsy," she said.

"I *am* Betsy," said Betsy, and this time
Irene saw the ladder, ran her eyes up it, and
spotted Betsy near the top of the wall
behind the checkout desk.

Irene smiled broadly. "I *thought* that was
you! What are you doing up there?"

"Stringing up rope so that we can hang
the template contest entries."

"Oh, what a good idea! Mine isn't ready
yet. You said you had something for me?"

Irene looked around but didn't see a mysterious package with her name on it.

Betsy finished tying the rope to the hook and came down the ladder slowly. "I don't know what you'll think of this, but Hailey had been in the process of dyeing some spun yarn for you. I brought it back with me after I visited her house, and it's waiting for you to decide if you still want it."

Irene nodded several times briskly. "Of course I want it! I can think of my piece as a tribute to her — in addition to it being a tribute to progress in the field of fibers. New fibers! New blends! What colors did she finish for me?"

Betsy reached under the checkout desk and came up with a cardboard box. "Here, take a look."

Irene peered in. "Oh my, this is very nice!" She lifted out a skein of brown yarn. "See how it's flecked? That's because of the two kinds of fiber, they take dye differently." She held the skein up a little too close to Betsy's face, and snatched it back again before Betsy could change focus. "Marvelous!" She dropped the skein on the desk and reached for the indigo one. "*Such* a pretty color!"

Godwin came to the desk and picked up the brown skein. "Say, it is a mix of light and dark," he said.

The door sounded its two notes, and he turned to see who was coming in.

Betsy looked around Irene's shoulder but didn't recognize the new customer. She was a handsome woman, about twenty-five, with short blond hair, very light blue eyes, and an athletic build. There was a pugnacious air about her.

Uh-oh, thought Betsy, *a dissatisfied customer.* She braced herself for an outburst.

"Which one of you is Betsy Devonshire?" the woman demanded.

Irene, startled, dropped the skein she was looking at back into the box, and turned to stare.

"I am," said Betsy. "How may I help you?"

"By keeping your nose out of what's none of your business!"

"I beg your pardon?"

The woman walked to the desk. Her fists were clenched and her teeth were showing in a snarl. She didn't have a Crewel World bag with her; this was not someone returning an unsatisfactory item. "You know what I mean! Pretending to be a detective! Snooping around, treating people like criminals! How *dare* you!" The woman slammed a fist on the desk.

Irene made a sound like a whimper and scurried over to hide behind a spinner rack, then peered around it, her dark eyes enormous in her white face. Godwin took a giant step to one side, turned, and picked up a sturdy yardstick that was on the library table. He assumed a determined air.

"Who are you?" asked Betsy.

"You know who I am!"

"No, ma'm, I don't." Betsy was amazed to find there was no quiver in her voice. Her stomach was twisting itself into a knot, and her heart was pounding. The fury on the woman's face was terrifying.

"Don't stand there lying to me!" Again the fist slammed onto the desk.

"I know you," said Irene in a quiet but carrying voice.

"You stay out of this!" shouted the woman, lunging at the spinner rack, which fell toward Irene. She got out of the way barely in time.

Then the door sounded its two notes again, and suddenly Jill was in the shop, looking every inch the cop she used to be. "What's going on here?" she said.

"Ask them!" said the woman, brushing past Jill on her way out the door.

"Wow," said Godwin into the silence following her exit. "Just wow."

"Who was that?" asked Jill.

"She almost knocked me down," whim-

133

pered Irene when Betsy and Godwin looked toward her.

"Are you all right?" asked Betsy.

"You said you know who she was," prompted Godwin.

"That was Joanne McMurphy," said Irene. "She has a terrible temper."

"You can say that again," said Godwin. "Wow."

TEN

It was nearly closing time, the end of a busy Friday. Betsy, glad she had worn her red pantsuit, was up the stepladder again, hanging two new entries in the template contest. Godwin was holding the ladder steady.

"I think the floor must be uneven right about here," he said.

Betsy thought so, too, from the way the ladder had jogged back and forth when she first climbed up its rungs. "This is wonderful; we're going to need more clothespins soon," she said.

"I know, this contest was a great idea!" said Godwin, his voice a little strained as he pushed just hard enough to keep the ladder steady.

The door sounded its two notes and the ladder wobbled as Godwin tried to look over his shoulder to see who was coming in.

"Ack!" Betsy cried, one elbow out, the other hand gripping the top step. She

135

looked under her elbow. It was police detective Mike Malloy. "Hi, Mike, what brings you in here?"

"I'd like to talk with you for just a couple of minutes, when you're free."

"Sure, I'll be right with you."

Betsy clipped the latest contest entry to the line and made her way carefully down. "Thanks, Goddy."

"My pleasure."

"Mike, would you like a cup of coffee or tea?" Betsy asked.

"No, thank you."

Betsy closed the ladder and put it down behind the checkout desk, dusting her hands when she was finished. "This is a good time, since we're about to close. We'll be able to talk without being interrupted. Goddy, could you run the credit card machine? Mike, come with me to where we can sit down out of his way."

She led him into the back half of the shop to the small round table with its cover of patriotic flags and exploding firecrackers — the shop, always running a season ahead of the calendar, was already selling Fourth of July items.

"Now, what can I do for you?"

"I understand Joanne McMurphy came in here yesterday and created a fuss."

"Ah, the Excelsior grapevine is still flourishing."

"What grapevine? I got a call from Irene Potter, an eyewitness. She thinks you and I should form an investigative partnership, or maybe I should have you sworn in as a member of the police force."

Betsy smiled. Irene was sure that with Betsy's help crime could be wiped out in the whole of Hennepin County, if not the entire state of Minnesota.

"Yes, she was here when Joanne came in."

"Irene said she was scary."

Betsy nodded. "I don't think I've ever seen a human being in such a state of rage."

"Did she hit you or threaten to hit you?"

"No. I thought she might hit me, but instead she went after Irene, pushed a spinner rack over at her."

"Deliberately, or accidentally?" Mike had brought out his notebook and was writing in it.

"Oh, deliberately. She was furious at her, I'm not sure why. I was frightened and so was Irene. Godwin was ready to defend us."

"Godwin? Really?" Mike clearly was amused by the idea.

"He's brave, Mike. Not macho, that's not his style, but he's far from a coward. He picked up a yardstick — not one of those flimsy things, but a nice thick one I bought at the State Fair last year. It can certainly be a weapon. He grabbed it and was prepared to use it to defend us. But Jill Larson came in, and you know Jill, she has this presence, and Joanne just ran out."

"What was she angry about?"

"She said I was poking my nose in where it didn't belong. I didn't know who she was so I didn't know what she was talking about. Then Irene said she knew her, and that's when Joanne rushed at her."

"To try to prevent her from telling you who she was?"

"Oh no; I think she hadn't really noticed Irene until then and just resented her trying to be a part of the quarrel. I remember reading a phrase in a book long ago about someone being in an 'ecstasy of rage.' That seems to describe Joanne. I don't think she was thinking, just acting." Betsy thought briefly. "I wonder if she's sane. Have you talked to her?"

"No, but I'm going to."

"I heard that her husband reported a gun stolen two weeks before Hailey's murder, and that it was the same caliber as the murder weapon."

Betsy could see Mike start to bristle. "Where did you hear that?"

"From a reliable source."

Mike, tight-jawed, made a note, doubtless to check with everyone who knew. Betsy hoped he wouldn't figure out Lars was the source. He said, "Okay, it's true Pierce McMurphy used to own a semiauto that could be the right caliber, but he was in an all-day directors' meeting in downtown Saint Paul on the day of the murder. They even had lunch brought in. There's no way he could be our perp."

"Does Joanne know that?"

"Know what? That he was at lunch?"

"Know that he has a perfect alibi."

"I'm sure she does. Why?"

"Because she may have been trying to protect her husband. Has she come on angry to you, too?"

"It's never a good idea to come on angry to a cop. I know she's angry about something, but she hasn't lost it with me."

"Does she have a perfect alibi, too?"

Malloy frowned over his notebook page. "No. But she had no reason to murder Hailey Brent."

"What would Pierce's motive have been?"

"I don't know if he had one, either. Once the alibi was confirmed, I stopped looking at him."

"But the gun —"

"He called the police about the theft the day it happened. A report was filed."

"I assume the gun hasn't turned up."

"You assume correctly. The money order was cashed; the video record showed it was a woman in her teens. The payee line was left blank, so all she had to do was put her own name on it. We identified her — she's got a juvenile record — and she claims she found it in the pocket of a jacket she shoplifted."

"That sounds just crazy enough to be true."

Malloy nodded. "Especially since her record is for shoplifting, not for breaking into cars."

"Why would someone buy a money order and not put a name on the payee line?"

"McMurphy said it was to be given to an individual at one of the companies his business serves, and he didn't know how to spell the person's last name. The payee's company was to be one of his stops the day it was stolen."

"So why would the thief, if it wasn't the teenager, get rid of an easy three hundred dollars?"

"Beats me."

"Has the GPS turned up?"

"No. Maybe the thief needed one."

"Are you going to arrest Joanne?"

"Not unless you want to sign a complaint. Ms. Potter doesn't want to press charges. Which is probably not a bad decision."

"Then I don't, either."

Malloy nodded, unsurprised. If Joanne were arrested, and then bailed out, she would almost certainly want to seek revenge. "But I plan to have a word with her. Maybe scare her some, make her consider being a little more polite in her dealings with people."

"Do you think talking to her will do that?"

"Maybe. You don't know until you try. But she should be made aware that her antisocial behavior is drawing official attention."

On Saturday morning, Amy Stromberg came in to pick up the Mark Parsons needlepoint canvas. Betsy had spent part of Friday morning pulling the yarns for it.

"What an eye! What a mind the artist must have!" Amy said, holding it out at arm's length. At first glance it looked like a set of repeating geometric patterns in red, blue, yellow, and green. Then came the realization that the red portion of the pattern was made up of angular geckos circling one another, that the notches into which the tiny feet fit were seen to be more gecko feet, and, finally, that the whole pattern was made up of geckos.

"Very clever," agreed Betsy.

"This is going to look great in my entrance hall. People can stare at it while they're taking off their coats. How far did you have to go to find it?"

"Just to Needlework Unlimited. But I was lucky; Mark Parsons' canvases are getting hard to find ever since he quit designing."

Betsy meant to take Saturday afternoon off to go to the Hailey Brent estate sale, but things got busy so it was half past three before she could get away. There were cars parked up and down both sides of the street from the house, though probably some of them were Green Gaia customers. Betsy found a place about half a block from the house and walked back.

A sign directed her to the side entrance, but on her way back there her eye caught people wandering through the garden behind the house. She decided to go see what was happening. She found Philadelphia back there, sitting at a card table piled high with a fat stack of newspapers, a cheap cash box, and an assortment of trowels. A spade was leaning against the table.

"Hi, Del, what's all this?" asked Betsy.

"We're selling plants from Mother's garden," Del replied.

Four women and a man were walking up and down the rows. One of the women carried a trowel.

"It's so early in the year, how can anyone tell what's coming up?"

"Trust me, they know. The only problem is, the tulips and daffs are finished, so they have to take potluck on the colors."

"And the newspaper — ?"

"Instead of pots. Three or four sheets will keep the roots intact until you get home."

"How's the sale in the house going?"

"Pretty well, actually. This is the slowest it's been all day. The stuff in the dyeing kitchen went fast, which isn't surprising. Ruth put the word out on a web log for dyers. We've been selling the furniture, too. One reason I'm sitting back here is so I don't have to watch Mother's bed or dining room set go out the front door."

"You could have kept the furniture in the house as part of the sale," Betsy pointed out.

"No, the woman I hired to sell the house is also staging it, and she says the probable buyers will already have furniture. And anyway, Mother's furniture doesn't match the look she's going to try for in the staging."

"I thought the dining room furniture looked great."

Philadelphia shrugged. "I did, too, but she doesn't like it. And she's been staging homes for six years."

Betsy shrugged back. "When in doubt, follow the advice of experts."

"That's right. Speaking of experts, how are you coming with your investigation?"

Betsy grimaced. "Not so well. I'm collecting facts and speculation, but so far, nothing is pointing to a solid suspect."

"Is that usual in your cases?"

Betsy sighed. "This one seems to be unfolding more slowly than usual, probably because I don't know the people involved well at all. And I'm not a police investigator, so I can't go ringing doorbells and insisting that people talk to me. But one reason I came here this afternoon is to ask for your brother's phone number. I'd like to talk to him."

Philadelphia gave it to her, then Betsy asked, "Say, have you got any lily of the valley?"

"Along the fence, near the maple. There's a sickly hydrangea over there, too, that needs to be moved to a place in the sun."

"No, all I can use are shade plants. How much?"

"For the lily of the valley? A quarter apiece."

That was less than she'd paid for the ones at Green Gaia. "Does Marge Schultz know what you're doing back here?"

"I don't know, or care, particularly." Philadelphia didn't sound snotty or rude, just indifferent. "I'm trying everything I can to raise enough to pay what it's costing me to get this house sold."

Betsy selected a trowel and took a thin section of newspaper over to the fence, which was made of broad, dark boards that had not been painted in years, if ever. The boards were damp along the bottom, green with moss. Glad she'd changed into an old pair of jeans, she knelt on the grass and began to dig up lily of the valley, most of which were showing stems lined with tiny white flowers. She inhaled their scent happily, then opened the newsprint and put the plants onto it. Someone was talking on the other side of the fence — Green Gaia property.

The voice — it was a woman's — was saying, "The blue spruce isn't really blue, but a blue-green. By itself you'd think it was a dusty green. One way to make it look bluer is to plant a different variety of evergreen beside it, such as a fir or pine. I'm so glad you came!"

"You know I'll always come when you need me. Is this a safe place to talk?" The man's voice was a slow, warm baritone. He was speaking barely above a murmur.

Uh-oh, thought Betsy, *who is* that?

The woman's voice also dropped. "Over here in the woods? Of course it is. We can see anyone approaching from every direction."

Ah, Betsy knew now where they were standing: in the cluster of young trees that were bagged and potted, waiting for customers.

"Good. Now, what's the problem?"

"I'm frightened. I need you to spend some time with me." Good heavens, the woman was Marge.

"Darling, we agreed that right now we have to be even more careful. I know it's difficult. It's hard for me, too. My wife seems to be extra demanding, almost as if she senses something's wrong."

Oops, thought Betsy.

"But nothing's 'wrong,' that's the problem!" Marge said. "Saying hello when we pass on the street isn't enough! I want to get you alone, just the two of us, and be 'wrong' with you for hours!"

"I feel like that, too, but we agreed,

remember? No meetings."

"Yes, I know, I know. But it's agony being near you."

"Then why did you call? We agreed we weren't to see each other until after the divorce, unless it's urgent — and I don't mean what you think I mean!"

Marge's throaty chuckle made it clear that she knew what he thought she meant.

Betsy, digging among the lily of the valley, was torn between creeping away and wishing there were a chink in the boards so she could see who the man was.

"But we need to talk about your divorce." Marge's tone had become practical.

"There's nothing to be done at present."

"That's not true. Things are not improving; your life is becoming more difficult with her every day. I want to be there for you, but you have to make that important move soon."

A new voice spoke up, young and male.

"Are you going to want some help moving a tree?" he asked.

The man said, "Uh, yes, I want that blue spruce right here. But I parked my car way the hell and gone from here. If you'll bring the tree to the gate, I'll drive up and you can load it for me."

"Sure. I'll just go get the wheelbarrow."

After a pause, the man said, "Now see what you've made me do! Where am I going to plant this thing?"

Marge's voice filled with laughter. "Darling," she said, "I wish I'd thought of this ploy before! You're improving my bottom line in a whole new way! Come on into the store and I'll write this up."

Betsy looked down at the layers of newspaper and realized that while eavesdropping, she'd uprooted over twenty lily of the valley plants. Fortunately there was plenty of room for them in the back lot.

It's probably none of my business, but all the same, I wish I knew who Marge was talking to.

Betsy got back to her shop in time to help close up, then went upstairs to her apartment. She did a little housekeeping, some bookwork, fed the cat her evening pittance of Iams Less Active, then searched out the phone number of JR Brent, Philadelphia's brother. Brent was at home, and at first he sounded puzzled by her request for an interview.

"Who are you?" he kept asking, then at last a light dawned. "Oh, you're the woman who owns that store that sells embroidery hoops! I've heard about you. And no, I'm not interested in talking to you. I think the police are doing a fine job."

And that was that.

ELEVEN

On Saturday evening, Jill was in the kitchen fixing dinner — steamed broccoli, fish sticks, and mac and cheese. Bjorn, the family's huge black Newfoundland dog, lay asleep on a strip of carpet in a corner. Bjorn adored the two children of the household, but he occasionally sought a break by hanging out with an adult. Fortunately, the kitchen was large and he didn't interfere with Jill moving around.

The back door, which let into the kitchen, opened, and a very tall and broad uniformed policeman with sergeant stripes on his sleeve came in. Lars was home. He was a watch supervisor in the little Excelsior department and was on weekend duty that day. Jill came to greet him with a kiss. As she went back to work, he opened a little cabinet high on the wall in the entryway and locked his gun in it.

"Daddy!"

"Daddy!"

Two towheaded little children, the girl almost six and the boy just four, came rocketing into the kitchen to attach themselves to his legs. Bjorn lumbered to his feet to join the trio, bushy tail wagging, pink tongue lolling.

Lars picked the children up to kiss them while they hugged him hard.

"Kiss Bjorn!" demanded Erik.

Lars obediently stooped and the dog's big wet tongue slurped him on the mouth and nose. The children shrieked with laughter.

"Good dog, Bjorn!" said Emma, reaching to stroke the dog's black head.

"Bjorn loves Daddy!" declared Erik.

"*I* love Daddy!" said Emma.

"No, *I* love Daddy!" said Erik.

"We *all* love Daddy," said Jill. "Now go wash your hands, dinner will be ready very soon."

The children broke their embrace and, cheering, ran from the kitchen.

Lars got to his feet, pretend-staggering under the sudden release of his burden. "And we've been talking about having another one," he said.

"It's you who wants another one," said Jill, turning off the flame under the steaming broccoli. She pushed her hand into an oven mitt and brought a cookie sheet out of the oven. The smell of breaded fish intensified. "What I long for is the day when the kids' appetites evolve so that meals like this are a fading memory. Bring on the shrimp scampi. Please."

Lars, passing through the kitchen, paused to snort. "Yeah, please. If you go for that PI license, we'll be down to TV dinners. The hours those guys work are crazy." He headed for the bedroom to change out of his uniform.

Jill made a face as she arranged the fish sticks on a plate. It wasn't as if she really felt she was wasting her valuable talents raising the children. What she was doing as a stay-at-home mom was important and challenging. She loved Emma and Erik so much that she couldn't bear the thought of turning them over to a day care facility, no matter how good it might be, and thereby missing the milestones of their development.

On the other hand, watching her good friend Betsy struggle to find time to investigate, to follow meager leads that led nowhere, made her yearn to assist. Betsy, though not as inexperienced as she had been at the start of this curious second career as a sleuth, didn't have Jill's formal training. Having passed the notoriously difficult sergeant's exam on her first try, Jill was reasonably certain she could pass a test to get a private eye license. And then she could be of signal use to Betsy — not to mention able to follow through on some cases of her own.

She already had a concealed carry permit, and a nice Rossi snub-nosed .38, something Betsy refused to consider getting. That wasn't a good decision, in Jill's never humble opinion. Going up against a murderer unarmed was not intelligent.

Jill was glad Betsy was bright enough to inform the police when she was sure of a culprit's identity, but one of these days she was going to do or say something in front of someone she only suspected — and that might put her in real danger. Betsy was brave, but sometimes it was difficult to tell the difference between being brave and being foolhardy.

Supper went about as expected, noisy and a little messy; and neither of the children took more than the required single bite of broccoli.

Afterward, there was the usual fuss of getting them bathed and into pajamas, their nighttime stories read (tonight Lars read to Emma, Jill to Erik), their final glasses of water brought. Silence fell at last when they went to sleep.

Lars and Jill met in the living room, their expressions alike: love and indulgence mixed with aggravation and relief.

"If we have another one, they'll outnumber us, you know," said Jill.

"I think I can talk Emma into joining our side," said Lars.

"Seriously," said Jill, "what do you think?"

"I want another girl," said Lars. "I think they're easier."

"I said, seriously."

"I am serious. Remember when we got married we said we wanted a house full of children?"

"I think the house is full. Although —"

"Although what?"

"Erik will start preschool this fall and Emma will be in first grade. That means the house will be empty part of the day —"

"Which will give you time to focus on Elsa."

"No, it would give me time for a part-time job. And who is Elsa?"

"Our second daughter. I'm not stuck on Elsa, it just begins with an *E,* like the other two. I like Ellen, too. And Eleanor."

"You've really been thinking about this."

"Yes, I have," Lars said. "Haven't you?"

"Yes. But I keep coming down on the side

that says no. I want to look into getting a PI license."

"Look, once upon a time PI work was mostly following a husband or a wife suspected of playing around, or finding a teen runaway. Nowadays, criminal defense lawyers hire them to do real investigations, to interview suspects and uncover admissible evidence, and that kind of thing can be dangerous. Betsy's gotten involved with some hairy stuff and she's an amateur."

"I would love to work with Betsy and do it with legal recognition. She doesn't always follow the rules of evidence."

"Yes, but what might you get yourself into? I think one of us with a potentially dangerous job is enough for this family."

"Oh, Lars, I could get hit by a truck, or the house could blow up, or who knows? Just being alive can be dangerous to your health."

"I know, I know. I don't think you know how worried I can be. I don't want to shorten the odds, that's all. If you really want to get back into action, I'd prefer that you come back on the cops."

"You mean come back to a desk job."

Lars hesitated. "All right, yes. But you'd be officially part of what was going on, have some input, and be of real service. Please, darling, think about that, will you?"

Jill didn't reply, and the air in the living room took on a slightly frosty chill that lasted the rest of the evening.

It was the quiet hour after dinner. Godwin was working on a needlepoint canvas, and Rafael was going over some coins from his collection.

After forty minutes or so, Godwin sighed and parked his needle in a corner of the canvas. It was a beautiful face of a chicken in bright reds and yellows, completely surrounded by a swirl of its small feathers, in shades of cream and off-white, each oval shape coming to a black point, an image at once surreal and realistic. No Name Chicken it was called, from CanvasWorks Traditions. It was going to look terrific in the remodeled kitchen, but stitching all those feathers was becoming a bore. He decided to take a break and go talk to Rafael.

Rafael kept his medieval English coins in a three-ring binder whose "pages" were clear plastic. Each page consisted of five rows of four pockets each. Godwin had seen the collection, though he had not paid much attention to it. He knew Rafael had collected one coin from each English monarch from William the Conqueror to Elizabeth I, twenty-three monarchs in all — there were no coins minted during the brief reign of Edward V — and devoted a row to each coin. In the first pocket he had put a square of paper with the name of the king or queen in whose reign the coin was minted, the year of birth, and year of death. In the second pocket he put the actual coin. In the third he put the little envelope the coin had come in, which had such details as the city in which it was minted and where the coin was found. In the fourth he put another slip of paper with a very brief bio of the monarch.

The coins themselves were silver, darkened by age. Most were pennies; for centuries, pennies were the only English coin. They varied in size, each a little larger or smaller than a nickel. None was perfectly round; each had been struck by hand. As Godwin entered the den where Rafael worked on his collection, he saw him pull one of the coins from its pocket. He slid it out, balancing it on a forefinger, and looked closely at it under the light from a strong desk lamp.

"I thought you weren't supposed to touch coins without wearing one of those thin cotton gloves," said Godwin.

"That rule doesn't apply to these," said

Rafael. "These are not gold or the highest quality uncirculated, where a scratch or bit of wear can knock down the value."

Godwin came to the beautiful antique desk Rafael was sitting at. "Which coin is that?"

"Edward II. He was one of us, you know."

"What, you mean you're related to him?"

"No, I mean he was gay."

"Really?" Godwin bent for a closer look. The front — the "obverse," Godwin knew — portrayed the clean-shaven face of a man whose hair, in an out-and-up curl, covered his ears. There was a simple crown on his head. "How do you know he was gay?"

"Unfortunately, he was notorious for his dalliances. He wasn't a very good king, though his father was — and so was his son."

"Son?"

"Oh, he married and had children — although there is a story that at his wedding feast his boyfriend paraded around the court wearing the queen's royal jewels. His queen, a French princess named Isabella, eventually had enough of Edward and his 'favorites' and took a lover, a Frenchman named Mortimer. The two of them knocked Edward off his throne and ruled in the name of his minor son."

"Wow. How long ago did all this happen?"

"He died in a dungeon, probably murdered, in 1327." Rafael held the coin up. "I wonder what the original owner of this coin thought about his king."

"I wonder what his son thought of him."

"Well, his son was fifteen when his father died, and I'm sure his mother had filled his ears with ugly stories. On the other hand, the older Edward was handsome and probably a lot of fun. He liked the kind of work performed by commoners — he could shoe a horse and thatch a roof. Isabella and Mortimer ruled in his son's name, but when he turned eighteen, and they didn't seem about to let him take over, he pulled a raid on his mother's quarters. He killed Mortimer and sent Isabella off to a distant castle with a warning not to meddle in the affairs of the kingdom again. And she never did. She was clever and very beautiful, but Edward III was not to be played. He proved to be a strong, brave king, good-tempered and very popular. He was king for fifty years, an enormously long time for that period."

Godwin chuckled. "You talk about these people like the Monday Bunch gossips about the citizens of Excelsior."

Rafael shrugged. "That's all history is,

really. Gossip." He smiled. "That's why I like it."

"And that's why you like the coins. They are a real piece of history you can hold in your hand."

"You are very perceptive. And it's true, these coins are an affordable way for ordinary people to hold in their hands an actual artifact of a very long-ago time. They can imagine who the first owner was, what he was like, what he could have bought with the coin, how he came to lose it."

"You're not an ordinary person who needs to collect at bargain prices," Godwin noted. A lot of Rafael's other coins were high-quality rarities that cost a lot of money.

"I always appreciate a bargain. And I am more ordinary than you think." Rafael held out the coin. "In the case of these coins, not all of them were expensive. It was the hunt that brought me to acquire them."

Godwin took the coin. It was paper-thin, almost weightless. The narrow face on it looked back at him enigmatically. "Where was this one hiding all these centuries?"

"It was part of a hoard. Back in the fourteenth century, someone took his life's savings and put it in a pottery jar and buried it in a field — then went away and died. In modern times a farmer was plowing the field and broke into the jar, which had been lifted by frosts to a level where the plow could reach it." Rafael had done an Internet search but found the coin through a local dealer — he preferred doing that, so he could see the actual coin before buying it.

Godwin turned the coin over. On the reverse was a long cross interrupting uncial lettering he could not read. "Latin, right?"

"Yes, like all coins of that time." Rafael took the coin back. "Why don't you try collecting?" It was a question he'd asked before.

And Godwin gave the answer he'd given before. "I'd rather buy needlepoint canvases. They're more interactive."

Rafael put the coin back in its little envelope and put the envelope back into its pocket. "Speaking of interactive," he said, "I've been going through my collection, deciding what I'm willing to part with at the coin show. I'm going to bring along my medievals, though I don't think I'll sell any. They're not expensive — well, except the gold ones, and they're too hard to find to make me want to sell the ones I have." He turned and pulled another three-ring binder from the bookshelf behind the desk. A label on its face read simply SPAIN.

Godwin didn't want to hear — again — a

disquisition on the complex history of Spain, so he changed the subject. "Want to eat out tomorrow night?" he asked. "As you know, the shop is closed Sundays. Besides, Betsy is really busy with her sleuthing."

"All right. Biella's okay?" The restaurant was a favorite of theirs.

"Fine."

"Betsy is spinning her wheels this time, isn't she?"

"No, of course not. The case is working its way through a dry part right now. But it's moving, and she'll get it, she always does."

"Aren't you afraid for her? Meddling in crime is no occupation for an amateur. Perhaps you should ask her if she has a will. Maybe she intends to leave the shop to you if one day she should be killed."

"What an awful thing to say!"

"If she is behaving foolishly, you should act to defend yourself. You have worked there for years, and for low wages, too. She owes you compensation if you should suddenly lose your position because she dies."

Godwin stepped back from the desk, about to say something in anger. Then, just in time, he caught himself. "You're joking, of course." But he said it in a tone laden with warning.

Rafael looked up at him, surprised. "Yes, of course. Sorry you did not find it amusing. I like your boss, she is a very nice lady, and very clever. But sometimes I think she should not interfere in the business of the police, who are quite competent."

"She's not interfering, she's helping!"

"If she wants to help, why doesn't she get the license? The private detective license?"

"Because then it would be a full-time job, and she already has a full-time job. I think for her to be sleuthing all the time would break her heart. There are too many horrible things in the world for her to get mixed up in them day in and day out."

"So she prefers to remain a, a *dabbler,* is that correct?"

Godwin frowned at Rafael. "Why are you picking on her? She does damn good work. And she's not 'dabbling.' "

Rafael sighed. He reached out and stroked his book of coins. "You're right. She doesn't dabble. I'm the dabbler. That's why I want to open a business of my own. I want to contribute something to this community, to this state, perhaps even to this country." He sighed again. "It would mean breaking my grandmother's heart. She thought a gentleman did not soil his hands with trade."

Godwin laughed. "Your grandmother is

dead. But I think I know what this is about. I think you're jealous."

"Jealous of Betsy?"

"Yes, but not because she owns her own business. You're jealous of her relationship with me. You think we share things you have no part of."

"Well, don't you?"

"No. I tell you everything I tell her, truly I do."

"Then why am I still jealous?"

"I don't know. I think this is a stupid and dangerous conversation, so let's stop it right now. Would you like a bowl of ice cream? I'm going to get one for myself."

"No, thank you. I want to look on the Internet for small shops to rent."

Godwin, heart sinking, went to the kitchen and filled a bowl — a big bowl — with cookie dough ice cream. He didn't know which was worse: Rafael's notion that he could run his own successful small business, or his sudden perception that Betsy and Godwin had a special relationship. The trouble, Godwin thought, was that it was true.

Twelve

Sunday, after church and a hearty breakfast, which was becoming a tradition with Connor and Betsy, the two of them went out in a light drizzle to plant lily of the valley on the steep hill behind the shop.

They worked in a companionable silence for a few minutes, then Connor said, "*Machree,* I wonder if you shouldn't give up this latest case. You're not making any progress, and I can see that the frustration is making you very unhappy."

"Giving it up won't cure my unhappiness."

"Are you sure? It might be like putting down an impossible burden. I don't like to see you frustrated like this."

"I don't like it much, either. But quitting would leave me unhappy, too. Besides, I haven't decided it's impossible yet. Hand me another lily."

Connor, bless his wise heart, didn't argue,

or even bring it up again.

On Tuesday morning, Jill came in with a stitching project she wanted stretched and framed — finished, in other words.

"Wow, this came out really well!" exclaimed Betsy.

It was a counted cross-stitch pattern, a big one that took eighty different colors of floss to complete. Teddies and Friends was the name of it, from Artecy Cross Stitch, and it depicted two shelves piled with two teddy bears, a plush puppy, a toy duck, and two clowns, all in soft, realistic colors.

"For Erik's room, I take it," said Betsy.

"Well, yes . . ."

"Oh, have you decided to have another baby?"

"Not quite. Lars really thinks we shouldn't wait."

"But you're still thinking of that PI license."

"Yes, though Lars keeps coming up with reasons I shouldn't do that."

"One reason is that you probably wouldn't have time for another big project like this one."

Jill chuckled and obediently turned her attention to the piece of stitchery. "What do you think, double mat?"

"Yes, I agree, but how about a modest frame, something narrow and dark?" Betsy suggested.

Jill put her hand, palm down, on the canvas and tilted her head a little sideways. "Hmmm, yes, I like it." She got out her credit card and made a deposit on the estimated cost of the project and left.

A few hours later Betsy was cutting fabric into salable pieces when the phone rang.

"Crewel World, Betsy speaking, how may I help you?"

A man's voice said, "Betsy Devonshire?"

"Yes?"

"I'm Pierce McMurphy, and my wife and I would like to come in and talk to you."

Betsy was nonplussed for a moment. "All right," she said at last. "When would you be able to come in?"

"How about right now? We're parked less than a block away — it gives us less of a chance to chicken out."

"That's fine. We're not busy right now. Come on in."

"Thank you."

"Who was that?" asked Godwin after Betsy had hung up. Clearly the look on her face had made him curious.

"Uh-oh," he said when she told him.

Less than two minutes later the door rang

its two notes and a medium-tall man with lots of gray in his dark hair came in behind a rigid-faced Joanne McMurphy.

Godwin was making a production of re-arranging the knitting yarns in a basket near a wall, standing so he could keep an eye on the pair as they approached the checkout desk where Betsy was waiting.

"First of all," said Joanne, speaking quickly and mechanically, "I want to apologize for losing my temper. I have some anger issues, and I want to tell you that I'm going to be doing something about that in the very near future." Her tone made Betsy wonder how much of this apology was Joanne's idea and how much was Pierce's.

"And I want to thank you for not pressing charges against Joanne for her serious lapse of judgment," said Pierce in his warm, deep voice. He had strongly marked and attractive features, and an athlete's build. His eyes were sad, but his fists were clenched, and Betsy wondered if he'd ever had to express his gratitude before. She felt profoundly uncomfortable and couldn't think what to say.

But then his wife turned to look at him, and he returned a smile so warm and tender that she fairly bloomed back at him.

Godwin, unable to see this exchange,

spoke up. "Have you talked to Irene?" he asked.

"No, not yet," said Pierce. "But we will."

"I can't think what came over me," said Joanne without turning around. Her voice was smooth and gentle. Pierce rewarded her with a broader smile.

Betsy shot a quashing glance at Godwin, who had drawn a breath, doubtless to make a caustic remark.

"Is there anything we can do to show we're really sorry?" asked Pierce.

"Nothing I can think of," Betsy said.

But Godwin spoke up. "You can answer a question."

"All right," said Joanne, turning toward him. "What is it?"

"Godwin," warned Betsy. She turned to Joanne then. "There's nothing we want to ask you."

"Did you murder Hailey Brent?" asked Godwin.

"No, I didn't," said Joanne, her voice calm but her face ashen. "I had no reason to murder her. I hardly knew her."

"Godwin, that was incredibly rude!" said Betsy. "I apologize on behalf of my store manager."

"I don't think I accept your apology," said Joanne stiffly. "Come on, Pierce, let's go."

"For heaven's sake, Goddy!" said Betsy when the door closed behind the couple.

"Well, someone had to ask, and you didn't seem about to. What do you think about them coming here like that?"

"I'm not sure." Betsy turned and frowned at the closed door. She had never met Pierce McMurphy before, at least not that she could remember. But there was something familiar about him. She closed her eyes, remembering the details of his dark hair and eyes, his muscular build, his warm, deep voice — there it was.

Pierce McMurphy was the man behind the Green Gaia fence in a love quarrel with Marge Schultz.

"But the person Marge should have wanted to kill was her lover's wife — Joanne, right?" said Godwin. It was later that day, and he and Betsy and Jill were sitting at the library table in the shop, eating sandwiches from Sol's Deli. Jill's son Erik was playing with Sophie the cat in the back. This wouldn't distract him for very long; Sophie was far too lazy to be an agreeable game player with an active boy like Erik.

"No," Betsy said. "Marge talked to Pierce about his divorce. She didn't say anything about Joanne's death."

Jill said, "So Pierce was the one with a motive to kill Joanne."

"Yes, but Joanne is alive and well," Betsy pointed out. "Hailey is the person who is dead — and Pierce not only had no motive, he has a solid alibi."

Godwin said, "So the question is, who had a motive to kill Hailey? Joanne, maybe? She certainly has the temperament for it." He gave a dramatic shudder.

"But no motive," said Jill.

"In her case, she doesn't need a motive. Not much of one, anyway. Maybe Hailey looked at her funny while passing her on the street."

Betsy ate a potato chip and said thoughtfully, "Maybe we need to look at what sets Joanne off. In my case, it was investigating Hailey's murder. I don't know if she felt personally threatened, or if she was protecting someone else — Pierce, for example."

"But Pierce has an unbreakable alibi," said Godwin.

"Maybe Joanne didn't know about the alibi, or thinks it's not unbreakable," said Jill, after a sip of tea.

"Hmmmm," said Betsy.

"You're good," Godwin said to Jill. "You should go back on the police force. You'd pass the detective test in a minute."

Betsy said, "Jill is thinking about becoming a private investigator."

"Lars is against it," said Jill. "He says it's too dangerous."

Godwin looked surprised. "But his job is even more dangerous," he said.

"All the more reason why he's not in favor of it for me. We shouldn't both have dangerous jobs."

"So you've given up the idea?" asked Betsy.

"No, not completely. Not yet." She smiled. "It's just so interesting, trying to figure things out, drawing conclusions from an assortment of facts. It's like reading a novel that has every other line missing."

"And every tenth page missing, too," said Betsy with a rueful laugh.

On Wednesday, Betsy decided it was time for another talk with Marge Schultz. She left Godwin in charge of the shop and drove over. Though a weekday, there were plenty of customers walking up and down the long wooden tables lined with potted plants. The warm and sunny weather certainly wasn't hurting business. Many shoppers were carrying plastic baskets, and some were wheeling shelved carts filled with their selections, the carts' tiny wheels juddering over the

172

uneven ground. The season had marched ahead, and the plants were blooming: petunias, lilies, marigolds, Indian paintbrush, and some that Betsy couldn't identify.

Betsy found Marge consulting with two women in the marigold section.

"We just love marigolds," one woman was saying. "They're so hardy, and they bloom right up until frost. And the deer and rabbits won't eat them like they do our other plants."

"I think they're like shards of sunlight," said the other, poetically. "The pure yellow ones are like noon, and the different shades of orange ones are like sunsets. Let's buy lots of them for edging."

"Marge?"

The woman turned, and her eyes widened. "Oh, hello, Betsy! I didn't see you standing there. What can I do for you?"

"I need to talk with you."

"Right now? I'm kind of busy."

"It won't take long, just a couple of questions."

"Is it about — um?"

"Yes."

"All right. Hannah, Mimi, you just bring those into the shop when you're ready and someone will cash you out."

"Thank you," they chorused.

"Follow me," Marge said to Betsy, and she led her to the small, cluttered office in the back of her shop. "Here, sit down. Now, what's this all about?"

Betsy took a breath and plunged in. "How long have you and Pierce McMurphy been lovers?"

Marge's mouth fell open. She said, "What on earth?" in a strange, high voice, caught herself, cleared her throat, and tried again. "Whatever gave you *that* idea?"

"I overheard the two of you talking."

Marge stared at her. "When was this?"

"When he told you that you shouldn't see each other until after his divorce. You sold him a blue spruce."

The stare continued. "But you weren't — I didn't — How could you — ?"

"I was in Hailey Brent's backyard, by the fence."

"*Spying* on me? How *dare* you!"

"I wasn't spying on you. I was at the estate sale at the Brent house, digging up lily of the valley to plant behind my shop. I recognized your voice, but not Pierce's — at least not until he and Joanne came to talk to me yesterday."

"Oh my God, you didn't tell them —"

"No, of course not. I've had a glimpse of Joanne's temper."

Marge sat back in relief. "This is awful, this is so awful. Now you must think —"

"I don't think anything, except that I happened to be by Hailey's fence, and if I could overhear you speaking, then she could have, too. Really, you two ought not to have revealing conversations where other people can overhear what you're saying. Is that what happened? Did Hailey find out about you two and threaten to tell Joanne?"

"We never talked back by the evergreens before, so I don't know how she could have overheard us. She never told me she knew about Pierce and me. You think I murdered Hailey, don't you?"

"I don't know what to think."

"But I didn't! I came to you to help me prove that!"

"I know. The problem is, this looks very bad. Killing Hailey might seem an intelligent thing to do to keep Joanne from finding out about you and her husband."

"But I tell you she didn't know. All right, she'd been hinting around that she knew something bad about me, but I didn't know what it could possibly be. Pierce and I have been so very careful it didn't occur to me that she was referring to our relationship. She didn't want me to file a complaint with the police about her stealing flowers, and I thought she was trying to prevent that by pretending she knew something bad about me. If I thought she knew about Pierce and was willing to share that knowledge, I would have told her, told the police — I would have told everyone! I would have taken out an ad in the paper: Marge Schultz and Pierce McMurphy are lovers. That would have stopped her gossipy mouth."

"But what about Joanne?"

"If something happened to me, the police would know who to arrest."

"So you had no idea what Hailey was hinting about."

"Well, after a while I thought maybe she really *did* know something, because she was so gleeful about it. But I was sure it wasn't about Pierce and me. I know my employees wondered why I didn't make a police report, especially after Hailey took about a quart of my red marigold blooms."

"So why didn't you?"

"Because I didn't want even more trouble than there was between us. You know how marigolds bloom: a week after she took them, the plants were covered with flowers again. She didn't strip the plants of all the flowers, and she didn't damage the plants; she was careful about that. Like I told you before, she was more of a nuisance than

176

anything."

Marge leaned forward. "Please believe me. I didn't know Hailey knew about Pierce and me."

But Betsy was remembering Philadelphia saying Hailey knew something about Marge she called "illicit." That was a term often used about an adulterous love affair. On the other hand, if Hailey knew, surely her hints would have clued Marge in to what she knew. Right?

And there the case seemed to come to a halt.

THIRTEEN

The Monday Bunch was in session. An informal club of stitchers, its members gathered early Monday afternoons in Crewel World to stitch and gossip. Present at this session were serene Patricia, earthy Bershada, naive Emily, stalwart Jill, bluff Alice, friendly Doris — and rakish Phil, the lone male member.

Phil wasn't a hanger-on, he was a committed counted cross-stitcher. Normally, he worked on train-themed pieces, but he'd been taken by Winter Retreat, a twelve-by-sixteen-inch Gold Collection outdoors pattern, and was working hard on it. It featured four boldly marked Canada geese standing in a field of tall tan grass beside a body of dark water. There were glints of gold in the grass and a gray, overcast sky into which more geese were vanishing. It was a finicky piece, he was finding, with lots of changes of subtle colors in the grass, sky, and water.

Working on the piece was stretching his talent and his patience to their limits. Which, after all, was not a bad thing.

Betsy had an errand to run and so she wasn't there when the meeting convened.

"Anyone know how Julie's doing?" asked Doris in her husky voice. She was working on a small needlepoint canvas of two swans, a gift for a friend who liked birds.

"She's home from the hospital," said Jill, who was crocheting a tiny cap to be donated to a neonatal care unit. "But she's not able to drive yet."

Phil said, "She's already got a plastic thumb and a pacemaker; with that new hip she's turning into a geriatric Barbie doll. Damn." He consulted his pattern, grimaced in confirmation, and began to unpick a couple of stitches.

Bershada looked up from the birth announcement she was cross-stitching and said, "You better pray you don't need a joint replaced one of these days."

"Why? I might enjoy being a bionic Ken!" He lifted his chin and looked sideways to give them all the benefit of his profile. While he might once have been a rather handsome young man, he was, now in his seventies, looking a bit shopworn. But his wife, Doris, smiled tenderly at him.

Patricia paused in her work on a very intricate candlewick pattern of snowflakes to ask quietly, "How is Betsy doing?"

After a pause, Jill said, "She's not happy with the way the Hailey Brent case is moving."

"Because it's not moving very well, is it?" said Emily diffidently. She was knitting the second of a pair of sky blue mittens for her second-oldest daughter, who was on a growth spurt and might not even be able to wear these bigger ones come November.

"No, it isn't," said Jill.

"Poor thing," said Emily.

Alice put down the afghan square she was crocheting. "Godwin," she called in her deep voice, "does Betsy seem depressed to you?"

"Not especially, why?" Godwin came out from the back, where he'd been sorting a shipment of cross-stitch patterns to be put into bins. "Have you noticed something?" He looked concerned.

"I think we all have," said Alice, looking around the table. The others seemed as if they'd like to disagree, but none did.

There was a little silence, then Doris spoke up. "I think we're all worried about Betsy's investigation into Hailey Brent's death."

Phil nodded in agreement. "This thing is taking a long time, longer than any other case she's tried her hand at."

"Is she making any progress at all?" asked Bershada.

"She's made a lot of progress," said Godwin stoutly. "It's just taking a while to pull things together. And important parts are still missing."

"Like what?" asked Bershada.

"Yes, maybe we can help," said Phil.

"Well, I know for one she would like to be able to interview Walter Moreham."

"Who's he?" asked Emily.

Godwin gestured while he considered how to explain, a book of cross-stitch patterns in one hand. "Randi Moreham's husband. Hailey was trying to persuade Randi to get a divorce, and when Hailey was killed Randi realized she really didn't want one. And Walter had said from the start he didn't want one, either, so now they're working on staying together. But you see, that gave Walter a motive for removing Hailey's influence."

"So why doesn't Betsy just go talk to him?" asked Emily.

"Because she has no legal standing. He's a stranger to her, and she's not a police investigator, so she can't just go knocking on his door."

"Does he know she wants to talk to him?" asked Patricia.

"I don't know. Probably not."

"Well, now, maybe he does," said Jill. "Betsy has talked to Randi, and I can't imagine that Randi didn't tell her husband about it."

"So why hasn't he come forward?"

Jill raised an eyebrow with a little twist of her head, encouraging them to consider the question.

Patricia said, "Betsy's trying to prove that Marge Schultz didn't do it, so that means she's looking for other suspects. And Walter is not interested in being one."

The door sounded and Betsy came in, using her back to push the door open because she had a big box in her arms. Godwin hurried to hold the door for her.

"Thanks, Goddy," she said. "These must be the baskets we ordered." Betsy used baskets to display yarn and counted cross-stitch patterns in the shop. She also sold baskets. She carried the big box to the checkout desk and put it down with a sigh. "No wonder the post office wanted me to come pick this up," she said. "This box would've taken up half the back of their little van. Hello, everyone," she added, looking at her friends around the table.

"You must have more muscles than you look like, carrying that box by yourself," said Emily, whose grammar was not her strong point.

"No, baskets aren't heavy, just bulky," said Betsy. "Sorry to have missed the start of your meeting. What were you talking about?"

"You, of course," said Phil.

Betsy sighed. Any member not present was often talked about. "Nothing too unflattering, I hope."

Phil said, "Well, we hear there's someone you'd like to talk to: Walter Moreham."

Betsy had been rummaging in a drawer for a box cutter. She stopped and looked at him. "Yes, that's so."

"Well, I think I can arrange that. Walt plays poker every other Wednesday evening with a group I'm also a member of."

"Well, there you go, girl!" cheered Bershada. "Good for you, Phil! Are you meeting this Wednesday?"

"As a matter of fact, we are." He looked at Betsy. "Shall I speak to him?"

"All right, yes. Thank you. But don't be disappointed if he says no."

With wifely pride, Doris said, "I think Phil can get him to say yes."

■ ■ ■ ■

Phil wasn't so sure. He didn't know Walt all that well. The man was one of the quiet ones, a conservative player who, while cheerful, rarely laughed out loud, and who rarely either lost or won big. Yet he was a faithful player, hardly ever missing a session.

Phil tried to think how best to approach Walt. Would a direct appeal work? Or should he play it cool, let someone else bring up the topic of Hailey Brent's murder? Surely someone would. The fact of it going unsolved for over a month was a complaint heard everywhere. Then he could brag a little about Betsy and work it around to her still needing to talk to some people.

This week they were meeting at Paul Miley's house. Paul had beer and soft drinks set out, along with chips, dip, and crackers and cheese. They gathered in the "man room," down in the basement, which was furnished with a pool table, a poker table, a big elderly refrigerator, and a little wet bar. Neon signs advertising beer lit up the cream-colored walls and strewed patches of color across the Berber carpet.

The six men each bought forty dollars in

chips from their host. The highest value was five dollars, a chip rarely used.

They popped open beers and began with a complaint about the weather. It had been a slow-opening spring, but now it was too warm and dry.

Kurt, the youngest, who lived with his severely handicapped brother in a condo apartment, said, "If they don't run the sprinklers every other evening the grass turns brown."

"My dad washes his car twice a week, trying to make it rain," said Paul, a big, genial man with a close-cropped gray beard.

"Maybe we should start a movement," suggested Parker, a very obese man in his fifties. "Everyone washes their car twice a week."

"Can I run it through a gas station car wash?" asked Mick, a short man with big ears and a crooked smile. "Or does that superstition only work if you wash it by hand?"

Paul appeared to consider that. "I think washing by hand makes it stronger — but only if you do it yourself. Hiring a neighbor kid to do it doesn't count."

Walter, a tall, handsome man not yet forty, with steady light blue eyes, said, "We have two cars. Do we have to wash both of them, or can we alternate?"

It was clear to Phil that they weren't going to talk about the murder. He said, "Let's get this show on the road. Come to the table, and let's cut the cards to see who deals first."

They began playing at around seven thirty and stopped for a break at nine thirty, rising from the table to walk around the big room. They made jokes about the neon signs. "If the county attorney peeks in a window and sees all that advertising, he'll make you buy a liquor license," laughed Kurt. They ate chips and dip — the cheese and crackers were for during the game, as they did not mess up the cards like greasy potato chips did.

Phil walked over to Walter, who was standing near the refrigerator. "Get me a brewski, too, will you?" he asked.

"Sure," said Walter.

They lifted the tabs on the cans, and Phil took a swig from his. Then he said, "Can I ask you something?"

"What about?" Walter cocked his head a little, hearing the discomfort in Phil's voice.

Phil, wincing at Walter's perception, abandoned any attempt at subtlety. "I have a friend who would really, really like to talk to you."

"Male or female?"

"Female."

Walter smiled and proved himself not so perceptive after all. "No, thanks, I'm happily married."

Phil forced a laugh. "No, no, it's not like that. My friend's name is Betsy Devonshire and she owns a needlework shop. But she investigates crime on the side, and she's damn good at it. She's working on a case, and she needs to talk to you about it."

Walter's mouth opened, then shut again. "I don't think so."

"It's important. The work she does on these things is important."

"This must be about Hailey Brent's murder," Walter said.

"Yes."

"I've already talked to a police investigator about that."

"Of course you have. Your wife knew Hailey Brent."

"You seem to know a hell of a lot about this."

"That's not important."

"Yes, it is. What, has this Betsy person got some kind of pipeline to the police department?"

"No, this is information she's obtained on her own."

"And shared with you — and who else?"

Phil shrugged and lied. "How would I know? She asked me to ask you if you'd talk to her."

"What about?"

"I don't know that, either. She's just gathering information, and she thinks you might be able to help. She's solved a couple of murders in her time, and she would like to help the police solve this one. You can ask Mike Malloy about her, if you want. He'll tell you she's good. Hell, ask your wife."

"Come on, you two," called Paul from the poker table. "You're holding up the game."

"Think about it," urged Phil. "Let me know before we go home."

Walter had three sevens, a good hand in a game with no wild cards. He saw the bet of fifty cents and raised it a quarter.

He didn't know Phil very well. He saw him as a wiseass who was fond of bluffing at poker and who played more for fun than to win pots. Not his favorite kind of person — though Phil was very witty, and occasionally even laugh-out-loud funny. This request — that he talk with Betsy Devonshire — came as a total surprise; he hadn't known Phil was acquainted with the woman. He had suspected Ms. Devonshire wanted to talk to him — Randi thought it might be so — but he was against it.

Phil saw his quarter raised, and raised it another quarter. He was smiling in a superior way, but he often did that when he was bluffing. The other two remaining players folded. Walter studied Phil's face, shrugged internally, and called the bet.

He won the hand — Phil had a pair of nines.

"Good call," said Phil, his smile turned rueful.

Then it was Phil's turn to deal and he called seven card stud, deuces, and one-eyed jacks wild.

Typical, thought Walter, whose favorite game was five card draw, nothing wild. He studied Phil as he dealt cards facedown, then faceup, calling each faceup card as he put it in front of a player and remarking on it.

"King of hearts, nice but no help; ten of spades, that's a pair, watch out; jack of clubs, that's three clubs," and so forth.

Still he must not let personal dislike of a man's style at poker affect his judgment regarding his request.

Randi, bless her heart, had found Ms. Devonshire a kind and sympathetic listener

— but she had found Hailey Brent to be the same, and she was certainly wrong there.

Walter couldn't figure this Devonshire woman out. She wasn't a cop, she wasn't a private investigator for hire, so what was she doing messing around with a murder she had no real interest in? Was she just some kind of super snoopy person? That couldn't be it; Phil wouldn't have invited him to talk to Sergeant Malloy about her unless Malloy knew and approved of her poking around. Walter had heard of her, of course; just about everyone in town had. Funny how they all seemed to accept her investigating as if she were just another branch of the police department.

"Your bet," said Phil, calling him back to the game. Walter had three clubs showing and another one in the hole. There was another facedown card to come. A look at the cards on the table showed fewer than average clubs faceup. That fact was not enough to make him raise, but he called the bet.

"Down and dirty," announced Phil, distributing the final card facedown.

Walter took a look and carefully prevented his expression from showing his pleasure. He raised fifty cents in the next round of betting. Two players dropped out, his bet was called — and he lost when Paul had four tens, a deuce, and a one-eyed jack making two of them. *I should have considered all those wild cards,* thought Walter. Phil's request that he talk to Betsy Devonshire had distracted him.

Knowing he was distracted didn't help. His mind returned to the request again and again during the evening.

It hadn't been apparent to Randi that her story made it seem he had a motive to murder Hailey. He could not help thinking this Devonshire woman hadn't missed that point.

But if he refused to talk to her, that would probably make her sure he had something to do with it.

So like it or not, he'd better agree to meet her. He told Phil so as they were leaving. Phil's triumphant grin left him uneasy. He hoped he could convince the Devonshire woman he was innocent of murder.

FOURTEEN

It was a sunny Friday in June, and the start of a multistate coin show. It was being held in two big rooms at a conference center at the crossroads — Godwin would have said the armpit — of Highways 694 and 100. The single-story wooden building had a rural theme, down to its barn-red paint and white trim. The Minnesota Organization of Numismatists — MOON — had rented half the big building; a large wedding reception was under way in the other half.

There were about a hundred dealers present in the bourse, or sellers' room, with tables up against all four walls and two sets of double rows down the center, making three aisles. One of the eight-foot tables, halfway down the first row, had been rented by Rafael. Godwin helped him put out his albums of coins and the one glass case he'd bought for the occasion, about thirty by twenty inches by three inches deep. All the other tables had several cases apiece, the better to display the dealers' wares.

"We're going to have to get more glass cases," said Rafael, looking enviously at the tables on either side of them. He was using a soft cloth to polish the glass of his case.

Godwin knew the cases were expensive, and hoped Rafael didn't invest too much in his new enterprise before he knew he would make a success of it.

When the show opened to the public half an hour later, there was a brief rush of customers. Rafael, with his good looks and amiable manner, soon had a little cluster of people around his table. But most of the coins he had for sale were oddities — he had all four Canadian bimetallic five-dollar coins, for example, made of silver and niobium, and representing the four Algonquin seasonal moons; and a trio of 1965 British crown coins, each with its evocative portrait of Winston Churchill. There weren't many collectors of those, so most of the customers soon melted away. He did sell two uncirculated Morgan dollars at a good price, and was happy with that.

Godwin was impressed. Rafael had a merchant's heart and a natural charm, both necessary assets for a successful businessman.

Along came a dark, Hispanic-looking man, about twenty, with a patchy three-day growth of beard. He was dressed in too-long jeans over shabby cowboy boots, a faded flannel shirt that he had not tucked in, and a worn black leather vest. He carried a wrinkled manila envelope bulging at the bottom. He had been stopping at tables along the row, and stopped again at Rafael's table to look over Rafael's assortment of American coins. Several were in clear plastic PCGS holders, called "slabs" by collectors.

"I have some coins I'm trying to sell," he said, in Spanish-accented English. "My uncle's" — he hesitated, then said in Spanish — *"suegro."*

"Father-in-law," translated Rafael.

The young man brightened at this understanding. "Ah, yes, thank you, my uncle's father-in-law. He had many coins in . . ." He gestured. "Books? But not books."

"Albums, I think you mean."

"Yes, albums. The father-in-law, he died, and my uncle, he sold the, er, albums, but there were some coins . . ." Again he gestured. *"Sueltas?"*

"Loose," translated Rafael.

"*Si*, loose. My uncle is a busy man, he work every day, so I said I would try to sell these coins. My uncle and I, we are not collectors, so we not know where to bring them. Then I see in the paper about this show, open to the public, so I am here. Some are in . . ." He gestured. "Like those things." He pointed to the slabs. "Is that good?"

"It's very good," said Rafael. "It means they've been professionally graded by a top company."

The young man frowned. *"Que?"*

Rafael said something in rapid Spanish. Godwin recognized the words *monedas* and *valuadas:* "coins" and "appraised."

The man, greatly relieved, replied at length, concluding, *"Pues, mira estas."* He opened the envelope and slid eight or ten coins out onto the top of the glass case. Two were in old-style white PCGS holders, and Rafael picked them up first.

"Hmmm," he said, and Godwin leaned in for a look. One coin he recognized right away as a beautiful silver Morgan dollar, the "king of collectible coins." The obverse of the coin was the face of a woman with a lot of hair dressed to the back of her head, slightly too much chin, and a serene expression. The date on the coin was 1876. On the back was an eagle with open wings, holding in its claws a bundle of arrows crossed with an olive branch. PCGS had given it a grade of MS-65, Select Uncirculated, a very high grade.

Godwin glanced up and saw the young man watching Rafael very intently. *"Es buena?"* he asked.

"Si," said Rafael. *"Muy buena."*

"Pues, cuanto me darías por ella?" How much would you give me for it? Godwin recognized the question from his happy hours of shopping in Mexico.

Then started the bargaining. Godwin could not follow the words, but he understood the language. He could tell Rafael was going easy on the young man, as they did not bargain hard or for long. They agreed on an amount that made both of them happy — seventeen hundred dollars — and Rafael handed over the money in cash.

The other coin in a PCGS slab was a silver dollar dated 1874 with a seated Liberty on the face and a spread eagle on the back. The words Trade Dollar were around the bottom of the reverse, and above it was spelled "420 grains, .900 fine."

Again with the intent look, the young man asked, *"Es buena?"* Is it good?

"Si, es buena." Rafael frowned over it, however. The grade for this coin was EF, Extremely Fine.

"Que sucede?" What's the matter?

"No me gustan los Trade Dollars." I don't like Trade Dollars.

"Porqué?" Why?

"Muchos son falsos." Many are fake.

"But it is in that holder, right?" The man's English was suddenly a bit better. "That is a guarantee."

"Si. Yes, it is." But still Rafael frowned.

"It's okay, you don't have to buy it. I will sell it to someone else." He reached for the holder.

"No, no. Está bien, me arriesgaré." Okay, I'll risk it.

"Entonces, cuanto me darías por ella?"

Again the bargaining began. This time the young man wasn't as happy with Rafael's offer, but at last, with a shrug, he took seven hundred dollars.

The other coins the young man offered were loose, ungraded, and somewhat worn. But there was a standing Liberty quarter dated 1917 with the obverse worn but the eagle on the reverse looking clean and sharp. Rafael offered twenty dollars for it and the young man seemed happy to accept. Another coin was a very badly worn Spanish dollar — one of the famous "pieces of eight," which was legal tender around the world from the seventeenth century to the nineteenth. Spanish-born Rafael, not unnaturally, loved finding them, and had a large collection of them. He made the young man smile with his generous offer of fifteen dollars.

The two parted with words of gratitude, shaking hands, exchanging names.

Business fell off completely after that, and around one o'clock Godwin opened the little cooler he'd packed that morning with sandwiches, pop, and corn chips, and the two sat back to have lunch.

Another dealer came by to talk about how poor business was and to see how Rafael and Godwin had been doing.

"Nothing too much, Jim," said Rafael. "I am too heavily invested in oddities and medievals for this show. But I did strike it lucky with two PCGS-rated coins." He reached into a box under the table and brought out the coins. "Take a look."

Jim looked at the Trade Dollar and said, "It's a good thing this has been graded by PCGS. There are so many Chinese fakes of this coin that I've sworn off buying them."

"Chinese fakes?" said Godwin.

"But the Chinese fakes are castings, this is struck," said Rafael.

"You haven't been keeping up. They've gotten damn clever and turned it into an industry," the man said, his voice warming with indignation. "They bought old stamping machines from the US years ago for their own coinage, and some of them got diverted into making fakes. You're right about their early attempts, they were just trash, cast instead of struck, but they're getting better all the time."

He looked at the PCGS holder, turning it over in his hands, examining the lettering on it. "This is a good-looking dollar. Let me see the other one, would you?"

Rafael produced it, and the man examined the coin. "Uh-oh," he said.

"What's the problem?"

"The Morgan dollar was first minted in 1878, and this coin is dated 1876."

Rafael snatched it out of the man's hands. "I do not believe it! You are reading the date wrong."

"No, I'm not, the date is perfectly clear, and you better believe something's screwy, because it's true."

"But this is a PCGS-graded coin!"

"I will bet you the best coin in my private collection that slab is fake, too. It's an old one, hasn't got their new holographic emblem on it. Jesus, I've been hearing they're doing that, but I haven't seen one till now." He turned and shouted down the room, "Hey, Milo, come take a look at this!" He said to Rafael, "Is the guy you bought it from still here?"

Rafael looked around, standing on tiptoes, looking hard. "Of course not. Damn."

"What's his name?"

"Pedro Alvarez, he said, though if he's selling fakes, that's almost certainly not his real name."

"What's going on?" asked a tall, cadaverously thin man with a slender graying mustache trickling off the end of his chin.

"Our friend here was suckered into buying two fakes."

"Two!?" exclaimed Rafael.

"If one's a fake, what do you wanna bet the other one's not a fake as well?"

"God *damn* it!" Rafael stooped and brought out the other two coins he'd bought. "What about these?"

Jim looked them over. "I'd say they're authentic. Not high-grade enough to be fake. Did he nick you good on the price of the copies?"

Rafael named the amount and the man said, "If they were real, I'd've said you made a heck of a deal."

"Yeah, I was feeling pretty good about what I paid for them. And so was Pedro — he seemed satisfied with the price — and no wonder! *Pedro me vió la cara* — Pedro made a fool out of me!"

There was a policeman at the entrance to the show, and Rafael filed a report, though without faith he would ever encounter Pedro Alvarez again.

He was still fuming about the loss hours later. "How was I to know?" he grumbled over a late supper that evening at home.

"How did Jim know?" asked Godwin. "What's he reading that you aren't? Is there a publication that talks about frauds and fakes?"

"Not one I'm aware of. I'm a member of the American Numismatic Association, and I usually read most of each issue of their magazine. I go to Northwest Coin Club's monthly meetings but not faithfully. And I've only been to two of ANA's annual meetings. Too lazy. That, I see now, was a big mistake."

"You're a lone wolf in a lot of ways," said Godwin, stacking the plates and carrying them into the kitchen. "That hasn't been a problem up to now, I guess."

"I wonder," said Rafael. "It makes me question a lot of my recent purchases. I'd been thinking I'd become an expert in this coin collecting business — and maybe I am in my own small sphere of medieval coins.

But that's a small sphere, and I see now I only have a shallow understanding of other arenas. I'm a long way from being educated enough to open my own shop, I guess." He sounded so depressed that Godwin left the dishes in the sink to come and speak words of comfort to him. But his heart was singing and he was careful not to disagree.

FIFTEEN

Betsy had never spoken with someone as reluctant to sit down with her as Walter Moreham. Though he didn't say a word about his reluctance, his body language was eloquent. He sat very stiffly in his chair, avoiding eye contact, his hands folded in his lap. He spoke in short, sometimes incomplete sentences, and the cup of coffee she brought him sat untasted on the table in front of him.

They were sitting at the little table in the back half of the shop. It was Saturday. Walter had been at work all morning, had eaten a quick lunch — he had refused to join Betsy for lunch — and had come in with a face like a stone to sit down with her. What made this all a bit strange was that he had called her to offer to talk. All right, it was Phil who persuaded him to do it, but it wasn't by threats of violence, was it? Nonetheless, clearly he was really spooked.

So Betsy started gently, off topic. "What is it you do, Mr. Moreham?"

"I work at an ad agency."

"Do you write the ads?"

"I illustrate them."

"You're a photographer?"

"A graphic artist."

"Really? Have I seen any of your ads?"

"Probably."

"Do you do newspaper or magazine ads?"

"Both. Label designs, too."

"Label?"

He shrugged. "Cereal boxes, hot dog wrappers, things like that."

"Interesting. Did you always want to be a commercial artist?"

"No."

Betsy waited, but he said nothing more. She sighed and got down to business. "Had you ever met Hailey Brent?"

"No."

"Why not?"

"She was Randi's friend, not mine." Betsy tried her waiting game, and this time he continued. "I have a friend or two Randi hasn't met."

"Were you aware that Hailey was encouraging Randi to leave you?"

"No." But there had been a slight hesitation before the reply.

"You suspected it."

Walter looked at Betsy with sad eyes, then took a big drink of his coffee. His mouth firmed and he looked down into his lap. He sighed. Betsy waited. He sighed again, the way a person sighs when making a decision.

"My job is very stressful," he began, speaking slowly and still not looking at her, "with lots of short deadlines and demanding clients with screwy agendas. It's been like that for me since I started working as a commercial artist. What I wanted when I married was a quiet home, with a wife who was on my side. I had that for almost six years."

"That sounds really sweet."

"It was bliss." He smiled, remembering. "I'd come home from a hellish day and my dinner would be waiting, the house would be clean, and Randi would be cheerful. I wouldn't complain about my work and she would tell funny stories about her part-time job at the auto parts store."

He fell silent, and though Betsy tried her waiting game again, he appeared oblivious.

"So then what happened?" she asked, as sympathetically as she could.

He looked up at her, his eyes unhappy. "It started with little things, but pretty soon all I heard was how I wasn't helping enough around the house, and why was I against having a child, and why didn't I talk about my job. Everything I did irritated her. My home stopped being my safe house." His head dropped again and he said so softly it was hard to hear him, "I didn't understand what was happening. I was sick and scared."

Betsy's heart filled with compassion and she let it show in her voice. "That must have been a dreadful time for you." She paused, then asked, "Did you try couple's counseling?"

"Not then. I thought maybe it *was* my fault. I thought we could work it out. She was seeing a doctor. I thought he'd prescribe something. An antidepressant, maybe. But he didn't."

This was wonderful; he was really opening up to her. She was careful to keep her tone sympathetic, although it wasn't hard; she was really feeling for the poor fellow. "Who was Randi talking to about your troubles, did you know?"

"No. I didn't know she was talking to anyone at all. I know I wasn't. I was just hoping it was some idea she got from a book or television, that she'd get over it. I wasn't paying that close attention. I should have been, but I wasn't. I was tangled up in a big project at work; the client was crazy, demanding lots of changes, short deadlines. A new product was being introduced, we couldn't get anything right, we thought we might lose the client altogether, it was just nuts. And Randi got more and more unreasonable. She started saying maybe I should move out. It was a nightmare. I just about quit sleeping altogether. Then I come home from work and Randi is almost hysterical, her very dearest friend Hailey Brent is dead, shot dead. I was like, Hailey who? But I could see it was a shock to her — hell, even to me. I mean, *murdered.* That just doesn't happen to people we know. She wants to talk about it, she can't stop talking about it — and then I begin to understand. Hailey thinks — thought — all men are pigs, that we exist to exploit women. It was Hailey's idea that Randi should divorce me.

"Now, I love Randi more than any other woman in the world. She's sweet, intelligent, hardworking, kind, and beautiful. I'm the luckiest man alive to have her for a wife. But she always thinks everyone else's opinion is better than her own. Once I listened to her talk about Hailey, it occurred to me that this divorce business wasn't entirely her own idea.

"So I stopped agreeing with her that I was a sexist pig. Stopped sympathizing with her.

I reminded her that I worked very hard, lots of extra hours, and didn't have time to do half the housework, too. I asked her if she wanted me to get an easier job, for less pay, so that I could do more housework. Maybe she could make up for the loss in pay by putting the money her aunt left her into our joint accounts."

"Now, Walter, that wasn't very nice," said Betsy. But she kept her tone sympathetic.

"I know. And I didn't really mean it; it was more like shock therapy. But it started her thinking, and in a week she agreed we needed couples counseling, and it took only three sessions of that to make her decide maybe she didn't want a divorce after all."

He sighed and took another drink of coffee. "When I found out Hailey Brent was to blame for our troubles, I hated her. I was glad she was dead. But you know something? Now, I think our marriage has come out of this stronger than before, so what the heck, maybe she did us a favor."

"Only by getting murdered," said Betsy.

"Well . . . yeah, I guess that's so."

"Did you murder her, Walter?"

"No! I told you, I didn't know her. I barely knew she existed until after she was dead, and it was only then I found out she was the one trying to get Randi to leave me."

But Walter's alibi was that he was locked in a conference room at a far end of his company's headquarters in downtown Minneapolis. A big DO NOT DISTURB sign was taped to the door, and he was not answering his phone. He was frantically redesigning three illustrations for an ad campaign.

"So you were blocked in, right? Couldn't leave?"

"I wasn't a prisoner; there weren't guards at the door." Walter wasn't looking at her again.

"There was a back way out, wasn't there?"

After a pause: "Yes. The corridor went both ways: One way led back to the offices; the other went to a stairwell to the street."

"So you could have gone out for an hour or two without anyone being the wiser?"

"No! I couldn't have done that and gotten the redesign done!"

"Did you get the redesign finished?"

"Yes. Barely, but yes. And it was good; they bought it. And that's my alibi. I couldn't possibly have left that room for any reason but to visit the men's room and still got that project done on time."

Betsy sighed. She had only Walter's word for that.

"I assume Mike Malloy asked you if you own a gun," she asked.

"Yes, he did. I don't. I had a twenty-two rifle when I was twelve, did some tin can plinking with it, but I gave it to a cousin when I turned seventeen and haven't even held a gun since then. I was never very good with one anyway. My eyes don't work well together at a distance."

"No military service?"

"No. Couldn't've gone if I wanted to with my bad eye."

Betsy thanked Walter for talking to her and let him go back to work. Then she wrote up some notes on their conversation. His alibi was shaky. And what about his claim not to know until after Hailey Brent's death that she had been the source of his marital problems? That might be false. Didn't Randi ever quote Hailey to him? Or wasn't he listening?

On the other hand, he did come to her, and he didn't seem evasive once he started talking.

Still, she couldn't cross him off her meager list of suspects.

Sixteen

On Tuesday, Betsy left the shop in Godwin's capable hands. The day started out gloomy, and by the time Betsy and Connor finished their breakfast it was raining. It was not a heavy downpour that might finish and clear off, but the kind of steady rain that could settle in for the day.

The temperature was in the high seventies, so Betsy dressed lightly in denim shorts, a chambray shirt, and sandals.

The rain had chased away a lot of customers from Green Gaia Gardens, Betsy noticed, as she hustled from her car to the garden center's office. That was good; maybe she could talk to Marge without taking her away from business.

But Marge wasn't there, either. Betsy looked around and didn't see even an employee inside. She went back out and found a tall young woman picking up a spilled four-pack of Indian paintbrush, expertly tucking the roots into a clay pot and replacing the soil.

"May I help you?"

"I hoped to talk to Marge," Betsy said.

"Her mother fell and they think she broke her hip. They're at the hospital," she said, using the rain to sluice the dirt off her hands then pushing her wet blond hair back behind her ears. She wore a short, waterproof yellow jacket and tennis shoes oozing water.

"Oh gosh, that's awful! I hope she'll be all right," said Betsy.

"Yes, so do we all. Her mother is a lovely woman. I'm Katy, store manager; is there some way I can help you?"

"Well, I'm not sure." Betsy definitely did not want to ask the woman if she knew Marge was having an affair with McMurphy. "Did you know Hailey Brent?"

Katy frowned at her. "I'm sorry, we've pretty much decided not to gossip about poor Ms. Brent. May I show you some flowers or vegetable plants?" Betsy started to say no — the rain was soaking into the shoulders of her shirt — when Katy said, "Wait a minute, you're Betsy Devonshire, aren't you?"

"Yes, that's right."

"Ohhhh." There was a world of comprehension in that drawn-out syllable. Betsy could see Katy was shifting gears by the rearrangement of her eyebrows.

"Are you really going to help Marge?"

"I hope so. I'm trying to find out just what happened to Hailey. What she was like, who her friends — and enemies — were."

"Well, I've worked here for six years, but I wasn't either a friend or an enemy. I knew her on sight, but she wasn't over here a whole lot. She bought her plants through the Internet or by mail, mostly. Sometimes she'd come over just for a look, to see a plant she'd been reading about in person — photographs in catalogs aren't reliable. Just once in a while she'd buy something. What she'd do —" Katy looked around for eaves-droppers and leaned forward to continue in a murmur. "She'd steal."

"She'd steal plants?"

"No. This is going to sound weird, but she'd steal blooms off of flowers."

"Oh yes, Marge told me about that. She stole flowers to use in her dye-making. I bought some of her yarns to sell in my shop. Beautiful colors."

"I remember one time she cut a lot of blooms off our new variety of marigold. Marge was really upset about that, but one good thing about marigolds, they come back fast. I think maybe Ms. Brent didn't know they were a spendy variety of marigolds, just that they were an unusual color."

"I think I remember hearing something about them. They're pure red, right?"

Katy smiled proudly. "Green Gaia developed them — well, Marge did, really. I don't know how she does it. I didn't even notice one of the marigolds we were growing was a spontaneous new variety until I saw a whole row of them, but she's always got an eye out for something different. She propagated it, and now she's patenting it. The variety will be a real moneymaker, we hope."

"You can patent a plant?"

"Sure. Then you license other greenhouses to grow them or sell the seeds. Marge's first big expansion of Green Gaia was paid for by another patent of a new variety of aster."

"She's selling a lot of the red marigolds this summer, then?"

"Oh, not that big a number. We're keeping almost all of them for seed, so we're just selling a limited quantity to the public. That's why Marge was so angry about Ms. Brent taking the blooms. There's a lot of money involved. We can expand this operation again if it hits like Marge thinks it will. But we have to be able to fill the orders for seeds."

But marigolds, red or otherwise, weren't for sale, or even blooming, when Hailey was shot. "When did this theft of blooms happen?"

"Last year. We were charging ten dollars a plant. Even though we had a very limited quantity, I was surprised when we sold out."

"Novelty sells," said Betsy, the voice of commercial experience.

"You bet."

"So Hailey stole the red marigold blooms last year. Did she steal anything this year?"

"I don't think so. There weren't many potted plants blooming back when she was killed."

"Did she ever steal whole plants?"

"Just blooms, as far as I know. Like I said, she'd buy whole plants once in a while."

As the rain continued pattering down, Betsy began to feel chilled. She wished she'd brought the little umbrella she kept in the glove box in her car. Or worn her raincoat. "Did she buy any red marigold plants?"

"No. Actually three people bought all of those we put out. One came back in the fall and said she was the envy of her neighbors. They really are a pretty shade of red. They get covered with flowers, and it takes a hard frost to kill them. I like the deep orange ones better myself, but the reds do make a nice show in borders."

"When will Marge know about the patent, whether or not it's granted?"

"By the end of summer, probably."

"How certain is it she'll get it?"

"She's already writing up the announcement to send out."

"Do you have any red marigolds for sale right now?"

"No, not for sale. But the seed beds are out back. Want to see them?"

"Okay, thanks." Betsy was already soaked through; a few more minutes couldn't get her any wetter.

The back half of the grounds was marked off by a sturdy Cyclone fence with a padlocked gate. Most of the land back there was a sea of warm red, the multipetaled flowers blooming profusely on closely packed plants each about seven inches tall. Except for the color, the plants looked like ordinary marigolds, compact and with feathery leaves. "Very pretty shade of red," remarked Betsy.

"We're letting them all go to seed, of course," said Katy. "One interesting feature of these new marigolds: They seed themselves better than the regular kind. If you grow a row of them, then next year you'll get one or two volunteers."

"Interesting." Betsy couldn't think of any intelligent question to ask, so she thanked Katy and started back for her car.

It was parked on the street, almost directly in front of Hailey's house. Betsy knew that Philadelphia had reduced the asking price three times and still had no takers. So much for her desire to be unburdened of the house. Betsy stood behind her car for a few moments. She didn't have any reason to go up there.

On the other hand, she was about out of ideas. Jill, she remembered, once said that police detectives, stymied in an investigation, started going over things they had already covered, trying to see if there was something they had missed.

What had she missed at Hailey's house? She didn't have the combination to the little Realtor's box attached to the door, which held the house key, so she couldn't go inside. Could she see something from outside? She went up on the porch and, shading the sides of her eyes against the window, tried to look inside. All she could see were pale and dark shapes barely identifiable as a couch and two chairs.

Leaving wet footprints behind, she came off the porch and went around the side of the house. She started to go up to the side door when her eye was caught by a tiny splash of color from the backyard. She walked back to the overgrown remnants of Hailey's flower garden. And there, almost hidden by weeds, was a bravely blooming red marigold.

"I'm sorry, I couldn't tell you if my mother had red marigolds in her garden or not," said Philadelphia on being asked. "I couldn't even tell you for sure if she had red flowers. I don't remember any during the estate sale, but I can't tell a marigold from a petunia unless you give me three guesses." Philadelphia was sounding hassled.

Betsy apologized. "I'm sorry if I interrupted you at work."

"Yeah, well, I'm off nights right now and trying to get my clock reset and it's not going too well. Plus, my last three knit pieces haven't sold so I'm trying to find a new outlet for the Red Hat Ladies — though what I think is, the market's saturated and I need to find a new theme altogether. My mind's all clogged up. It's like my muse died."

"I'm really sorry to hear that."

"Yeah, well . . . How's your sleuthing going?"

"It's stalled. I think I have most of the pieces, they just don't add up to an accusation."

Philadelphia said, "I guess Mike Malloy's in the same boat, right? He hasn't arrested anyone."

"That's true."

"And that's the one bright spot so far as Marge is concerned," Betsy said to Godwin before she went upstairs to change out of her wet clothes. "He may still think she did it, but he hasn't got any proof."

"So what's next?"

Betsy sighed and thrust her fingers into her hair. "I don't know."

"How about we invite Jill over to brainstorm? You know she's just itching to get involved."

"Yes, and I know Lars is just itching to forbid it."

"He wouldn't dare!"

"That doesn't mean he doesn't want to."

"Why is he being like that?"

"He's afraid she'll get into some dangerous situation."

"That can't happen if we just sit and talk."

"He doesn't want me to encourage her to even think about sleuthing."

"So what are you going to do?"

"Think of something else, I guess."

Betsy peeked in again after lunch to find Jill and Godwin sitting companionably side by side at the library table. No other customers were present to distract them.

"Come in, come in!" said Godwin cheerfully.

Jill was working on a small painted needlepoint canvas from Jelly Bean Stock. It was about a foot square, depicting a magnificent tom turkey standing behind a wicker cornucopia overflowing with white and orange pumpkins, grapes, apples, gourds, and a thin sheaf of wheat that draped over the elaborate border. She was nearly finished with it, working the scroll in the border in silver braid.

Godwin was knitting another in his endless series of white cotton socks, his fingers moving as if they had a life of their own.

"Rafael is turning into a gourmet chef," he said, continuing a conversation. "I'm going to have to do more exercise or by Christmas I'll weigh two hundred pounds. Sit down for a minute, Betsy."

"All right. H'lo, Jill," said Betsy. "How are the children?"

"Just fine. Emma Beth wants me to buy her some floss of her very own — 'and a box to keep it in, like yours, Mommy.' " Jill imitated her daughter's tone.

"Aw, that's sweet! And I think I have just the thing for her."

"Terrific. Meanwhile, Goddy and I were talking about your investigation of Hailey Brent's murder, but we discovered we're missing one thing."

Betsy sighed. She might've known that's what this was really about. "What's that?"

"You. If you haven't got a ton of things you need to do, could you talk about it for a little while?"

Betsy gave Godwin a look that should have knocked him off his chair, but he returned it with only his most limpid gaze. She said to Jill, "Does Lars know you're over here?"

"I didn't know until an hour ago that I'd be headed this way myself. And no, I didn't call him to tell him I was going to Crewel World. Why?"

"Oh, Jill, Lars doesn't want you getting mixed up in another one of my cases. I feel like we're going behind his back doing this."

"Talk isn't going to do anyone any harm. Besides, you and I — and Goddy — have talked about your cases before."

"Yes, but — Well . . . that's true."

"And Godwin thinks you're in a sticking

place with this case. Talking about it may help, right?"

"That's true, too."

"So talk to us."

Betsy sighed and settled back. "Where do we start?" she asked.

"How's business?" asked Jill, surprising Betsy with that entirely off-topic query.

"Slow. Slower than it's ever been. But it's slow everywhere." Betsy's gesture might have included every small shop in the state. "We're hanging on; things will get better."

"Do you think being worried about the shop is affecting your investigation?" So Jill wasn't as off topic as Betsy thought.

"I don't think so. I've been worried about business before, and it hasn't hampered my sleuthing." Though right now both things were as bad or worse than they had ever been.

Godwin said, "Why don't you just review the case from the beginning? Maybe we can see something you're missing. Or maybe *you'll* see something — I've done that, talked about a problem with someone and suddenly the solution is right there in front of me, without the other person saying a word."

Betsy didn't want to admit she'd been discussing the case with Connor without enlightenment happening, so she just nodded and set off on a too-familiar trail.

"Back on the seventeenth of May, Hailey Brent was found in the basement of her home, dead of a bullet wound to her head."

"Was she shot in the front, back, or side of her head?" asked Jill.

"I don't know."

"Is that important?" asked Godwin.

"It could be," said Jill. "Was she facing her murderer, or did he sneak up on her from behind? Maybe she knew him and wasn't afraid of him, or maybe he was chasing her and trapped her in the basement."

"She wasn't being chased, she was in the middle of dyeing some yarn," said Betsy. "There were pots of dye on the stove — she had what looked like a kitchen down there: stove, refrigerator, sink, cabinets. But she only did dyeing down there."

"Tell me about it," said Godwin, irreverently.

Jill made a hushing gesture at Godwin. "Go on," she said to Betsy. "Did you see anything that struck you as unusual?"

"No — well, nothing important. Just little things. Like there was a knitted square in a pot of indigo dye that otherwise had a skein of yarn. The square had already been dyed some other color, probably red or orange, so it came out brown."

"What was strange about that?"

"Well, there wasn't anything else in the dye kitchen that shade, and no other fiber, either dyed or waiting to be dyed, was knitted. It's probably nothing, but it was a little unusual. Did you know indigo in the pot is green? When you lift the dyed material out into the air, it turns blue."

"I'd read that somewhere," said Godwin. "What's even more interesting to me is that indigo dye has been known for thousands of years, but the formula for making it is complicated and not obvious, so how some really long-ago people without university chem labs figured it out is a real mystery."

Jill said, "But that's not the one we're out to solve, is it?"

"I guess not." He said it cheerfully, then gestured at Betsy. "Go on, go on, what else struck you as strange?"

Betsy thought. "This is probably even less important, but the wastebasket was empty, it didn't even have a liner — and there was a box of liners right beside it."

Jill said, "And that was strange because — ?"

"Well, the flowers or whatever Hailey was using in one pot had been strained out and thrown away, but a second pot still had carrot tops in it. Not strained out. It was as if she strained out one pot of dye, threw the material away, big plastic can liner and all, while leaving the second pot with its material sitting right on the stove. It just seemed — inefficient. And from the orderly way everything else in that kitchen was set up, I don't think Hailey was inefficient."

"What do you think it means?" asked Godwin.

"I have no idea," said Betsy. She flung her hands into the air. "I have no idea."

Seventeen

"All right, then, never mind, let's keep going," said Jill. "What happened next?"

"Philadelphia Halverson, Hailey's daughter, and Ruth Ladwig, Hailey's friend, went through the house with me. Philadelphia — isn't that a great name? But she wants to be called Del. Anyway, Del grew up in the house. So did Hailey, actually. Hailey moved back in as an adult after she divorced her husband, and she took care of both her parents and her children. The house is to be sold, and the proceeds divided between Del and her brother, JR."

"Is the brother —" began Godwin.

"No, he's out of it, not desperate for money, so no motive, solid alibi." Betsy put a hand flat on the table, then turned it over. "On the other hand, he refused to talk to me."

"What about Philadelphia? Does she have an alibi?"

"Not really. She's a nurse; she was working the night shift at HCMC. She says she was home alone, asleep. And she agrees with Hailey's sentiment, that artists — and she's an artist, she sells knitted figures in art galleries — are allowed special liberties with regard to the law."

"Hmmm," said Godwin.

"On the other hand, she has no motive I can discover."

"What about Hailey's ex-husband?" asked Jill.

"He lives on the West Coast, married to his third wife, with two young children. It wasn't a happy divorce, but he seems to have moved on. He hasn't been back here for years, and he didn't come to Hailey's funeral. It seems Hailey didn't like him or any other man; she acted like she didn't like Del's husband, and she tried to convince her friend Randi Moreham that her husband was a rat and she should divorce him. Which gave Randi's husband, Walter, who didn't want a divorce, a motive to murder Hailey."

"Does he have an alibi?"

"Yes, but it's not a very good one. He was at work, he says, but locked away alone in a conference room working on an urgent project — he's a commercial artist for an advertising company. No one was allowed to interrupt him. The room had a door into a back corridor he could go out of without being seen. His only proof that he didn't leave is a finished project. Plus he says he didn't know Hailey was the source of his wife's discontent until after she was killed."

"Is he a rat?" asked Godwin.

"I've only talked with him once, but I don't think so. And now that Hailey's out of the picture, apparently Randi doesn't want a divorce, either. They're in counseling, working things out."

"It would be a shame," said Jill, "if it turns out he is a rat after all, just not the kind Randi was thinking he was."

After a thoughtful silence, Godwin asked, "All right, who else besides Walter are you looking at?"

"Well, there's Joanne McMurphy. I can't find what the connection was between Joanne and Hailey, though at least they knew each other."

Godwin turned to Jill. "She came in here the other day to yell at Betsy for sticking her nose in where it wasn't wanted. I was here, and so was Irene Potter. She frightened poor Irene half to death. Very scary person, very."

Betsy said, "If I could find evidence of a quarrel between those two, I'd put her first on my list of suspects. Goddy was not exaggerating about her being scary."

"Anyone else?"

Betsy started to tell them about the love affair between Pierce McMurphy and Marge Schultz, but thought better of it. Jill was entirely trustworthy, but Godwin . . . well, he was Godwin, and with all the goodwill in the world, he still might let something slip. And Joanne was a dangerous person to anger.

"You know what's missing?" said Betsy. "I don't really know any of these people, not them or their friends and relations. I don't have a deep sense of what they're like, or any way to find out."

"We know what Joanne is like," said Godwin with a dramatic shudder.

"We know what she's like when she's lost her temper, which I've heard she does frequently. But what's she like when she's calm? And does she have a job? What do you suppose she does?"

"Works for the IRS," suggested Godwin promptly. "Or a collection agency."

Ignoring him, Jill said to Betsy, "You've talked with Philadelphia — Del — about her mother, haven't you?"

"Yes, but she spoke of a woman with an artistic soul who secretly liked Del's husband, not a woman who was a thief and a man-hater." Betsy consulted her notes. "Actually, I think I got a, a *different,* maybe more accurate, feel for Hailey from Ruth Ladwig."

"What did she say?"

"That Hailey always thought she was right about everything. That she had strong opinions about politics and religion. That she was intelligent and talented and had a sharp sense of humor. That she loved to listen to gossip and then go tell the person being gossiped about what was said. Ruth forgot that one time and had to bribe Hailey with the cost of her lunch not to repeat something Ruth told her."

Godwin laughed, but Betsy looked up from her notes. "Does that jar any ideas loose?"

Jill shook her head. Godwin, still laughing, said, "Obviously, the murderer is Ruth. Bribing Hailey with lunch wasn't enough; she had to shoot Hailey to keep her quiet."

Jill said, "Goddy, if you're not going to be serious, you should leave the table!" But she was laughing now, too.

After dinner that evening, Betsy and Connor sat down in her living room to work on projects. He was knitting a glove — he had given several pairs as Christmas presents last year, and friends who hadn't gotten a pair gave envious glances to those who had; so he figured he'd better get busy. The current pair was being done in pink with purple "fingernails."

Betsy was working on a piece of counted cross-stitch made from one of Valerie Pfeiffer's paintings: Fuchsia Chick-Chat. The chart was designed and produced by Heritage Crafts and featured a pair of young, fuzzy-headed chickadees, one open-beaked in song, the other glaring as if wishing his brother (sister?) would Just. Shut. Up. The illustration was an enlarged photograph of the finished chart, the stitching very visible. Betsy found this to be part of its charm, and instead of working it on 27-count fabric, as the pattern called for, she was working it on 11-count Aida. At the moment, she was stitching the bright pink and red fuchsia bloom hanging from the twig the birds were sitting on.

"How about a movie on Sunday?" asked Connor.

"Anything good playing at the Dock?" The Dock was Excelsior's movie theater, small but comfortable, with good popcorn.

Connor named two possibilities, one an animated comedy from Pixar, and one an action film with lots of explosions.

Though Betsy preferred comedies, she knew Connor had an affinity for pulse-pounding action. "All right, either one," she said, knowing which one he'd choose. Rather than try to follow the action plot, she could put her fingers in her ears and plan an ad campaign for the shop.

A pleasant silence fell, as the two continued doing their needlework projects.

An idea began nudging Betsy, but she was focusing on backstitching the flower petals and ignored it.

The idea came back, insisting she pay attention, and she put her cross-stitch away. As she had done before, she got out her knitting — she was working on a plaited basket weave–stitched scarf in bright russet. Once the pattern had been established in her mind — it was a two-row pattern — it wasn't difficult. And it was good-looking. Betsy was thinking it would make a nice Christmas present for Rafael. But knitting a simple repeating pattern was also a way to clear her mind for some serious thinking.

The idea was to make a list of what she needed that would push the puzzle of Hailey Brent's murder forward. She wasn't prepared to do any deducing; she wanted more information. For example, she needed to find out what the connection was between Joanne McMurphy and Hailey. Who was it who said she thought Hailey was a little afraid of Joanne? Irene. *Hmmm, how reliable is Irene?* she wondered. But Amy also mentioned Joanne as a friend of Hailey's. *Must be something to it if both of them knew about it.* But what could Joanne and Hailey possibly have in common?

Was Joanne a man-hater? More like a people-hater. Had she always been like this? Probably not, or Pierce would never have married her. Betsy needed to find out what changed her. Was part of it Hailey's malign influence? Had Hailey and Joanne found common ground in a shared belief in the uselessness of men? Would Pierce know? Though Joanne had yet to cause anyone actual physical harm that Betsy knew of, she had come close enough often enough to make her a valid suspect. And, after a period of thought long enough to finish two rows of knitting, Betsy recalled Mike Malloy saying Joanne had no alibi — something to ask Joanne herself about.

The problem was, of course, that Betsy didn't want to talk to Joanne unless the woman was tied securely to a chair.

And then there was that red marigold blooming in Hailey's overgrown garden.

What did it mean? According to both Marge and her employee Katy, Hailey didn't buy plants from Green Gaia, and she only stole blooms. Anyway, last year's commercially sold red marigolds were purchased by just three gardeners, none of them Hailey; and this year's weren't yet for sale when Hailey was murdered. Red marigolds sometimes seeded themselves, but where did Hailey get them, if the only ones available were sold by Green Gaia?

What if the solution to Hailey's murder had something to do with red marigolds?

Which made her think of Marge. Betsy knit a row and was halfway down another when she remembered something Godwin had said in jest.

But what if he was right? What if someone murdered Hailey to stop her mouth forever?

And what if that someone was Marge?

EIGHTEEN

Over a bedtime snack of frozen yogurt, Connor said, "I can tell this case is still weighing on you, *machree*. Or is it something else? Something wrong down in the shop?"

"No, it's the case, or more like one aspect of it. I need somehow to talk to Pierce Mc-Murphy, or, better, his wife, Joanne. I've been trying to think how to approach them."

"I think a phone call would be the best way to start."

"I can't just call them up!"

"Why not? Joanne can't get at you through the phone."

"What would I say?"

"How about, 'Joanne, we need to talk. May I buy you lunch?' That's harmless enough. Meet in some public place, of course."

"Of course." Betsy meant it sarcastically, but before she could voice it, she changed her mind. Why not try it? She turned to Connor with a smile. "You are such a brilliant darling, going straight to the center of a problem!"

He laughed, pleased. "Anything else I can help you with?"

She frowned and sighed. "I want to tell you something that must not go outside this room. It's a piece of very dangerous information."

He sobered at once. "All right. What is it?"

"Marge Schultz and Pierce McMurphy have been having an affair."

He stared at her. "Are you sure? How did you find out?"

"I actually overheard them talking. I was uprooting lily of the valley in Hailey's backyard — you remember, I brought home another batch of them for the hill in back — and heard their conversation right through the fence. He was saying he loved her, but they needed to avoid each other for now. She told him he needed to get working on a divorce. I didn't know who the man was until Pierce and Joanne came in to apologize for Joanne's outburst, and that's when I recognized his voice. If somehow Joanne found out — No, wait a minute, that won't work. Joanne would kill Marge, not

Hailey." Betsy bit the inside of her cheek, thinking.

"So obviously Hailey didn't find out about it and tell Joanne," said Connor.

"But I think she did find out about it," argued Betsy. "Marge said Hailey had been teasing her about some secret she'd discovered. And Hailey told her daughter, Philadelphia, that she'd found out something 'illicit' about Marge. And when Hailey did that dyeing demo in my shop, she wondered out loud if Marge hadn't stolen the flowers she brought to use in her dye bath. Unless Marge has a slew of secrets, I think Hailey was hinting about the affair."

Connor held up a hand. "Hold on, stealing isn't the same as adultery."

"Well, I guess you can think of it as stealing another woman's husband. But Marge is adamant that she and Pierce have been very careful and she's sure Hailey didn't know. But what other kind of hold could Hailey have over Marge? Marge says Hailey wouldn't do more than hint. But what else could it be? Marge says she doesn't know what Hailey's secret was. See what I mean?" she said, throwing up her hands. "Every time I learn something, all it does is lead me to something else I need to find out!"

"All right, all right, settle down," said

Connor in his calm voice. "If something doesn't make sense, it's because we're not looking at it right. I think it's possible Hailey didn't know about Pierce and Marge. So she didn't tell Joanne. Maybe Hailey was just bluffing."

Betsy smiled. "You know Godwin and his love of old-time customs and beliefs. He told me that it was widely believed back in the 1800s that if you sent a telegram to a random bunch of people reading, 'Fly, all is discovered,' that most of them would immediately pack up and slip out of town."

Connor laughed. "I doubt that's true anymore."

"All the same, I really need to talk to Joanne. Or Pierce. Or both."

"So call them tomorrow."

The next morning — a slow one in the shop, unfortunately — Betsy was looking through the current issue of *Needlework Retailer* to see what new products might interest her customers. She was also building her nerve to make the phone call. She had looked up the McMurphy phone number, and wavered between hoping they were both out, or both at home, doing something pleasant around the house and therefore in a good mood.

Godwin had the day off and was out on the links with Rafael, so she couldn't ask his advice. Jill and Lars had taken the children up to their cabin in Cass County, so she couldn't talk to Jill, either. It had been Connor's idea to call the McMurphy home, so she couldn't bounce her indecision off him and expect him to suggest she just skip it.

Oh well.

She picked up the phone and, before she could change her mind again, dialed the number.

It was answered on the second ring by Pierce, who said in his pleasant, slow baritone, "Hello?"

"This is Betsy Devonshire —"

"It is you! I saw the name on caller ID, but I didn't believe it."

"Mr. McMurphy, I'm sure you will think me audacious for calling, but I really need to talk with you about Hailey Brent."

"I have already spoken with Sergeant Malloy about Ms. Brent."

"I'm sure you have. But sometimes talking with a different person will bring a new perspective. If you really feel you won't bring anything new to the case, perhaps if I spoke with Joanne —"

"You're insane if you think Joanne will

239

talk to you."

There was a brief, faint sound of a struggle, then a new voice, a harsh woman's voice, said, "Who is this?"

Betsy replied in her gentlest voice, "This is Betsy Devonshire."

"I thought I warned you to keep your nosy nose out of what doesn't concern you!"

Betsy had to yank the phone away from her ear. She paused for a couple of seconds, then said in a conciliatory voice, "I'm sorry you think it doesn't concern me, Ms. Mc-Murphy, because it does. I've been asked by someone to look into Hailey's death, and I have been doing so, so I am involved."

"Who asked you?"

"I don't think I ought to tell you that, at least not right now."

"Oh yeah?" The rude, childish taunt made Betsy smile. Joanne was suddenly merely cross, not scary.

"Yes."

"Wait a minute, I think I would like to talk to you! You think you know so much? I bet you don't know anything!"

Betsy hesitated. What to say to this volatile person? "That's possible. But I appreciate your agreeing to talk with me. When do you want to do it?"

"How about right this minute?" Now

Joanne's tone was belligerent.

Betsy managed not to sigh. "I can't right now. I'm at work. But I can meet you for lunch somewhere. My treat."

"You think I can't afford to buy my own lunch?"

Betsy bit down hard on her exasperation. "I don't know what to think, that's why I want to talk with you."

Joanne snorted, but said amiably enough, "That's probably the first honest thing you've said to me."

Betsy laughed. "You could be right. Where shall we meet?"

"Maynard's. Outside on the deck. One o'clock." She was not asking, she was telling.

"Fine. Will you bring Pierce?"

"Ha!" She hung up.

I guess not, thought Betsy. *Wow, talking to her is like taking that carnival ride that goes up and down while it spins around while it's going in circles.*

Betsy had barely blinked the feeling away when the door opened and a handsome, plump blonde in her fifties came in, limping on her cane. Her name, Betsy remembered, was Susan Okkonen — a Finnish name. She was dressed all in brown and gold with a gold mouse-shaped pin on her blouse.

"Hello, Betsy," she said shyly, and came to the desk to rest her big leopard-print purse on it.

"Hi, Susan. How may I help you today?"

"I have an entry for your template contest, if that's okay." She opened her purse and brought out a big manila envelope from which she took the pattern, which was on black evenweave fabric.

Betsy was a little surprised. Susan was a cross-stitcher, all right, as well as a knitter and crocheter, but she liked to do extra-fine work, sometimes as small as thirty-two count over one. Betsy reached out and took the piece.

Wow.

"This is really nice," said Betsy, after she'd admired it for a few seconds. Using floss that shaded from pink to deep red, Susan had worked each rectangle of the template in a different pattern of delicate, lacy stitches.

"I call it Leaded Glass Windows," said Susan.

"It's beautiful," said Betsy. "I'm really glad you decided to enter." She looked up to see Susan's hazel eyes shining at the praise, and took advantage of the moment to persuade her to take over a small knitting class whose students were struggling with their learning skills. Susan was a superb teacher if the class was small, and she seemed to do best if the pupils were hard to teach.

By noon the day had turned hot. Though Maynard's was within walking distance from Crewel World, Betsy elected to drive; no reason to arrive breathless and perspiring when she needed her wits about her.

Maynard's was a good restaurant in an orange-brick two-story building right on the lakeshore. Inside, it was dark and cool, with big, multipaned, floor-to-ceiling windows on three sides. Out back was a broad, long deck overlooking the bay, set with nautical red chairs around high round tables, and green mesh benches marking the booths.

Betsy arrived exactly on time and was shown to a booth. The shoreline here had a nice marina, wooden ramps lined with slips. Customers could arrive in boats, tie up, and step ashore for lunch. A young couple on a Sea-Doo was doing just that as Betsy watched.

It was a really pretty day. Sailboats and sailboards dotted the bay and the lake beyond. A welcoming little breeze was coming off the lake; the loose silk sleeves of Betsy's pale green dress fluttered in it. After fifteen minutes, when Joanne had not appeared, Betsy decided she wasn't coming. She ordered a glass of white wine and began to study the menu.

Suddenly Joanne was there, dropping with a sigh onto the bench across the table from Betsy and offering a slightly insane smile. "I'm late," she announced. Her face was shiny with perspiration. "I decided to walk," she continued. "I didn't realize how hot it is outside today."

"Would you like a cold drink?" asked Betsy.

"Of course," she said, as if thinking Betsy was stupid to even ask.

Betsy twisted on the bench to signal a server.

"Lemonade with extra ice," said Joanne to the server, a nice-looking young man with extremely short dark hair.

They both turned to their menus. When the lemonade came, Joanne dropped her menu, picked up the glass, and rubbed it across her forehead. "Ahhh," she said of its cooling effect. Then she drank deeply.

Betsy ordered first. "I think I'll have Frannie's chicken salad, please," she said to the waiting server.

"Buffalo chicken wrap," said Joanne brusquely, "and another lemonade."

When the server was gone, Betsy said,

"Do you mind if I take notes while we talk?"

"Turning pro?" Joanne sneered, then touched her fingers to her lips apologetically.

Betsy replied mildly, "No, I just can't always rely on my memory."

"I won't be saying so much that you can't remember all of it," said Joanne, less sharply this time. She drank the last of her lemonade.

"All right." Betsy stopped reaching for her purse and took another sip of wine.

"Do you always start drinking at lunchtime?"

Betsy tilted her head. "Are you deliberately trying to start a fight?"

"Why would I do that?"

"Because you've changed your mind about talking to me."

Joanne's eyes twinkled. "You're pretty astute."

"So you don't want to talk to me. Then why did you come?"

Joanne hesitated. "Because I keep changing my mind. I said I'd come, then I wasn't going to come, then I decided I should come so I started hurrying, then I slowed down, then I hurried again. You confuse me!"

"I don't mean to. I'm just trying to figure

out who killed Hailey Brent, and I'm hoping you can help me. How well did you know her?"

"Oh, pretty well. We met at Tai Chi class, mostly. And at the beach. She was a good swimmer."

"One of these days I'd like to take up Tai Chi. It's so beautiful, all those slow movements, like an underwater dance."

"Underwater dance, I like it!" Joanne's smile grew broader and broader until it turned into raucous laughter, which then quickly faded. "Even just thinking about it calms me down," she said.

Wondering if thinking about it had helped Joanne stop laughing, Betsy said, "How long have you been doing Tai Chi?"

"About three years. I'm still a beginner."

"Really? How long does it take to stop being a beginner?"

"It depends on the person. Hailey had been doing it for about ten years. She said she was still learning, but I think she got good at it right away. She had the patience and temperament for it. She helped me with some of the trickier movements — it takes good balance. You move slowly" — Joanne turned her head to one side and moved her arms in a slow motion, one palm up and one down — "so you can't slip-slide fast-forward your way through the hard ones."

"Is there a teacher right here in Excelsior?"

"No, but there's one in Wayzata and another one in Saint Louis Park. Hailey would have made a good teacher, but she said she didn't have the time."

"She was a good teacher," Betsy agreed. "She put on a good dyeing demo in my shop."

Joanne's pale blue eyes widened. "D-dying — ?"

"*Dyeing* with an *e*. Vegetable dyes."

"I knew that!" Joanne shouted angrily, startling patrons at other tables around them. She shut her eyes tight for a few seconds while her lips moved. "Sorry," she muttered as her eyes opened again.

What was the matter with this woman? "It's all right," said Betsy. "It's a mistake other people have made, too. She died in a place where she dyed — a horrible meeting of homophones."

Joanne stared at her while she parsed this. "Oh," she said at last, "she was killed in that basement where she mixed her dyes." She added disapprovingly, "That's a grotesque joke."

"It's not a joke. It just sounds like one when we try to talk about what happened.

Do you remember where you were when it happened?"

"No. Yes. I'm not sure." Joanne drew her shoulders up high, and her eyes darted from side to side. "You make me nervous!" Her face was growing red.

"Think of Tai Chi!" said Betsy, desperately. "Tai Chi, Tai Chi!"

Joanne nodded and closed her eyes. Slowly, her shoulders lowered and her face unclenched. "Yes," she said, nodding. "Thank you."

"You're welcome. Who told you Hailey was dead?"

"Pierce. I think he heard it on the radio on his way home from work. I hardly ever listen to the news, so I didn't know. I was home all day ironing. I like to iron; it's almost as good as Tai Chi, but not as beautiful." She made a motion as if ironing the tablecloth, then smiled, amused at herself. "I liked Hailey. She was so calm. She never talked strongly to me, always nice and smooth. She didn't get me excited."

"I understand. Was she a good friend?"

"Well . . . not really. We couldn't be real with each other, because I get angry so easily. I don't have many friends." She made a self-deprecating face.

"That's very sad."

"Oh, it's not my fault, or not exactly. Ever since my accident, I've had this problem with my emotions."

"What accident was that?"

"Car. It was, let's see, almost four years ago. Pierce and I had been married seven and a half years, yes, so four years ago. He was driving and I was asleep. I might've been drunk. He might've been drunk, too. I don't remember any of it, even riding in the car before it happened. We'd been at a party, I remember that, and it was late and it was raining. He was driving too fast, and lost control and went off the road, and the car flipped over a couple of times. Fractured my skull in two places when the roof collapsed. Like I say, I don't remember it. Or anything else, for about a week after. I woke up in the hospital with my head shaved and a terrific headache and skin draped across a hole in my skull where they took out a hunk of bone."

"Oh my goodness!" said Betsy.

"Yes, but at least I was alive. And I knew I was going to live. Pierce had a mashed knee and a broken elbow, so he wasn't going to die, either. But we were both changed. His knee still bothers him quite a bit, especially when he plays tennis, and my personality was . . . different. I don't feel any different, except that I get mad really easy, especially when I'm stressed, and I can't get hold of myself for a minute or two. I know that's not the way I used to be, and it's scary. But I take precautions. I won't allow a gun in my house. I don't have a knife in my purse or a baseball bat in my car. I scream and yell and throw things, but I don't stab or shoot." Her voice deepened, and she leaned forward to look deep into Betsy's eyes. "And I don't kill people."

NINETEEN

The sun was shining brightly again on Thursday, the next day and Betsy's next day off. The temperature was forecast to rise only to the upper seventies, and the humidity was low — a lovely day.

She fed the cat — Sophie made a nuisance of herself in the morning until she was fed, so she had her little scoop of Iams while Betsy was still in her pajamas — then Betsy had a leisurely breakfast with Connor. She got dressed, washed the dishes, and called Marge Schultz. Marge was at her garden center and would be there all day.

Betsy was feeling energetic, so she decided to walk to Green Gaia. All the way over there, she pondered how she was going to conduct the conversation. Did Marge know what Betsy now knew about Joanne?

Because now Betsy was pretty sure why Pierce McMurphy hadn't divorced his terrifying wife.

What had seemed a very short drive was turning into a rather long walk — partly because Betsy walked at a leisurely pace past the shop windows on Water Street. Shaggy Leipold's had its usual mix of new, used, and antique gifts, books and toys spilling out its door onto barrels and benches on the sidewalk. Lillian's, which was only open a few days a week, displayed some lightweight, flowing dresses in soft pastel prints. Across the street, Cynthia Rae had some of her strikingly original skirts, tops, and dresses in her windows. If Betsy hadn't been on an errand, she would have stopped in.

Past the car dealership, she was into a residential neighborhood and her steps became more brisk. Though the houses along here were modest, they were all in excellent repair and their lawns, many set behind picket fences, were ornamented with summer flowers in shades of yellow, orange, and blue. Somewhere not far off a jay screamed, "Thief, thief, thief!" Leaves on the big trees lining the sidewalk ruffled in a light breeze. A white clapboard house had a big, old-fashioned rosebush near its front porch, the kind whose heavy scent rolled like a benediction across the grass. Betsy's footsteps slowed again and she inhaled deeply.

Around a corner and she was on the street that went past Hailey Brent's house, which was still for sale. The realty company's sign was a different one; Philadelphia must have gone to a new real estate agent.

Then came the gentle slope up to Green Gaia. There was only one customer wandering among the plank tables, and there were fewer than usual plants for sale, most of them looking overgrown and depressed. Spring and summer buying was winding down, and customers searching for the asters and chrysanthemums of autumn hadn't turned out yet.

The windows on the greenhouse were filmed with dust. Betsy's eyes wandered up its multipaned windows to note the white-painted wrought iron trim. The shape of the building was Victorian England meets modern-day Japan, and it was very attractive.

Looking sturdy and healthy outside the greenhouse's nearer door was a big hydrangea bush. Last time Betsy had been to Green Gaia, the plant was producing enormous green flowers, each composed of hundreds of smaller flowers. Now they had turned pink. Except some were shading into blue. Betsy paused to admire this phenomenon. She had heard the story of this particular plant, how it began as a potted plant years ago that an employee had dropped by the greenhouse door near closing time on a long weekend, and how the following Tuesday it was seen flourishing amid the shards. So Marge had simply dug a hole and moved the plant into it, where it continued to flourish. It was now almost as high as Betsy's head and had to be cut back on one side so it didn't block the door. Its blooms had always been pink. Betsy had heard that pink was Marge's favorite color; that she considered it her lucky plant and she let no one but herself tend to it. Betsy had read that hydrangeas could be made to change color, but it seemed strange that Marge would allow her lucky plant to change from her favorite color.

But the blue blooms were a very pretty shade and made a striking combination with the ones that remained pink. So maybe it was a way to advertise the fact that Green Gaia knew how to effect a beautiful, seemingly magical change of color in hydrangeas.

As Betsy's gaze turned away, it was caught by a display down toward the end of a row of tables. On the last table stood a long row of potted hydrangeas, some pink and some blue, some with both pink and blue flowers on them.

Betsy nodded to herself at having solved the riddle and went into the shop to look for Marge.

She found her in her little office, sighing over a legal-looking document.

"Problems, Marge?" Betsy asked from the doorway.

"What? Oh, hi, Betsy. No, I'm checking to make sure I've dotted all the i's, and crossed all the t's on that patent application for the red marigolds."

"How's it coming?"

"All right so far. But it's been a while since I filed, and since I haven't heard, I'm getting nervous. If I have to refile, I want to be ready, so I'm refining my application."

"I hope you don't have to start over. Do you have an attorney's help?"

"I did with the first one, for the asters, but I felt confident I could do it alone this time, and save myself some money. You know how it is with small businesses in today's economy."

"I sure do. But meanwhile you may have a winner with those hydrangeas. They're spectacular."

"Thank you. I sure hope so. I'm going to run an ad about them on my web site and in the paper. Two of my employees are tweeting and talking about them on Facebook."

"Where did you get them? I didn't notice them last time I was here."

"A flower shop in Saint Paul was closing. The flowers were in sad shape, but it only took some water and a little fertilizer to bring them back. But you didn't come here to talk to me about potted hydrangeas — unless you want to buy one?"

"No. I seem to have a fatal effect on plants that don't take care of themselves."

"Well, then, sit down and let's talk." Marge opened the center drawer of her desk and slipped the document into it.

Betsy sat on the wooden armchair indicated and squirmed a little in her seat. This was likely to be an uncomfortable conversation. She began, "How did you meet Pierce McMurphy?"

Marge closed her eyes briefly and her mouth thinned. Then she said, "I hired his company to design my new greenhouse. He brought me several designs, and I picked the one you see out there today."

"It's really pretty. I was just admiring it."

"Yes, it's beautiful, isn't it? He got me a good price and supervised the construction of it, and we became friends. He's a charming man, and he admired my business sense. We both tried to fight our feelings, but his home life was terrible and I was . . . well, I was lonesome for someone who could make me feel warm and wanted."

"How well do you know Joanne McMurphy?"

Marge snorted softly. "You're asking me, the person most likely to avoid her company?"

"Hasn't Pierce ever talked to you about her?"

"Only to complain." She spoke lightly, making a jest of it.

"She was in a car accident four years ago, did you know that?"

Marge hesitated, then acknowledged, "Well, yes, I'd heard that."

"Did you know that before her accident, she didn't have an anger control issue?"

Again Marge hesitated. "Yes."

"Did you know that Pierce was driving drunk the night of the accident?"

"No, no, no!" Marge said, gesturing with one hand as if to erase Betsy's words. "That's a lie Joanne tells! She doesn't remember the accident, so she makes up things!"

"Does she hate her husband that much?"

Marge looked exasperated. "She — she

doesn't hate him, not exactly. She gets mad at him and lashes out. She gets mad at everyone. Even herself — maybe especially herself. She knows what she's become. Sometimes she even wishes she'd been killed in the accident."

Betsy's heart constricted. "How awful to wish that!"

"How awful to live with someone as angry and miserable as she is."

"So why does Pierce stay with her? He's in love with you, you're in love with him, Joanne makes his life desperately unhappy. Why doesn't he divorce her?"

Marge sighed and leaned back in her chair. "He feels responsible for her." She looked around the little, cluttered office and sighed again. But Betsy bit her tongue and waited her out.

"Okay, there are two reasons." Marge held out an index finger and tugged on it. "One. He feels guilty. He wasn't drunk, but he had been drinking that night. It was raining and the rain was turning to sleet, and the roads were slippery. But what happened was, a panel truck being driven by an exhausted driver lost control on a curve and hit them. Their car slammed across a ditch and rolled over three times. There was a lawsuit and the company that owned the truck *and* the

driver's insurance company were required
to give the McMurphy's big payouts. Over
a million, I guess, maybe more. A good
thing, too; Pierce had good medical insurance, but there were still tens of thousands
owed to doctors and the hospital. But, in
the end, there was quite a lot left over when
the accounts were settled and Joanne came
home.

"Pierce was assigned to manage the settlement because it's obvious Joanne isn't able
to make fiscally responsible decisions."
Marge stopped, and when Betsy didn't say
anything, she touched the hair at the nape
of her neck, then scratched the tip of her
nose. She glanced sideways at Betsy, who
continued to hold her tongue.

"Well, that settlement enabled them to live
comfortably," she conceded, adding hastily,
"or as comfortably as a couple can live
when one of them is as unstable as Joanne
is."

"It seems to me that she's dangerous,"
said Betsy. "I'm surprised he hasn't had her
committed."

"We — he's thought about it. But a place
that could give her proper care, a really
good place, would cost a great deal of
money, probably all that's left of the settlement. And — and, well, Pierce would lose

control of her funds. Plus, despite all her outbursts, she hasn't actually hurt anyone; it's just shouting and throwing things. And she's very attached to him. When she's not in a temper, he says she's actually kind of sweet. He can calm her down, most of the time, and she takes directions from him. It's complicated, but he's decided that, at present, she's better off staying at home with him."

There was another pause. This time Betsy broke it. "What's number two?"

"Two? Oh yes. Two." Marge held out her first two fingers and tugged them. "Red marigolds. I believe the patent on the seeds of the red marigold will bring in a great deal of money. With that, and with what Pierce is earning from his work, the two of us could maintain the standard of living he's used to — and without the constant worry of watching out for Joanne. But if I can't provide a good income, he's better off staying with her." She sighed. "Sometimes I think he'd prefer things to stay as they are."

"What does Pierce think of finding a place for her?" Betsy asked.

"If we could find a good place, one nearby so he could visit her frequently, he thinks this would be an excellent solution."

And what would Joanne think about it in

those sweet moments of clarity? Betsy elected not to ask that question.

"Betsy," said Marge, her expression troubled, "I'm worried because this has gone on so long. The police don't like murders going unsolved, and I'm afraid Sergeant Malloy is feeling pressure to arrest someone, anyone, so he can mark the case closed. Please, I hope learning about Pierce and me hasn't made you decide to back off trying to help me."

"No, of course it hasn't. I'm trying hard to find out what really happened. I hope you can be patient with me."

"Is Mike looking at anyone else, do you know?"

"He is looking everywhere, I'm sure."

As she started walking back home, Betsy reflected on the story Marge had told her. Betsy had thought Pierce stayed with Joanne because he felt guilty about causing the car wreck that damaged Joanne's brain. But Marge said the accident wasn't Pierce's fault; he stayed because of a significant settlement that, added to his income, provided a comfortable lifestyle — so long as he let Joanne live at home with him.

And as long as they remained married, he

could not join the woman he really loved: Marge.

Now Marge was reaching toward a fiscal solution to Pierce's problem. If she could make a success of her new variety of marigolds, Pierce was — according to Marge — willing to put Joanne in a secure facility, use the settlement to keep her there in comfort, divorce her, and marry Marge.

The moneygrubbing bastard.

But Betsy, remembering the enraged Joanne in her shop and her unsettling behavior over lunch, was not inclined to condemn Pierce altogether. Doubtless he had once loved her, and perhaps the occasional glimpses of her former self made him reluctant to set her aside now. And the monetary settlement had at least in part the effect of keeping her at home with her husband. But Joanne's behavior represented a threat to the community, and possibly even to Pierce himself. Amy Stromberg had described an incident where a furious Joanne threw a tennis racket at Pierce. That was likely not an isolated event. Her behavior toward Pierce had to be one of the elements leading to a decision of what to do about her.

Was she happier staying with Pierce, even if provoked by the ordinary stresses of living in freedom? Or would she do better confined in a more controlled environment? It was not a conundrum Betsy felt competent to solve.

But how did any of this pertain to Betsy's problem: Who murdered Hailey? Did it pertain at all? If so, how? Thinking about that kept Betsy so occupied on her way home that she didn't notice the sparrows quarreling charmingly in the gutter or a special on old cross-stitch pattern books in Leipold's window.

TWENTY

It was coming close to the deadline for the template contest. Incoming entries were arriving less frequently now. On Monday, someone brought one in but was too shy to hand it directly to Betsy and instead left it on the checkout desk, facedown, covered with a note. It was a simple but effective pattern, each panel done in shades of russet brown, of straight stitches up and down in the first, then across and back, then diagonal, and then alternating blanks. Each caught the light differently, giving an interesting texture to the template as Betsy tilted it up and down in her hands. She smiled over it for a while before entering the information on an entry blank — the customer had apparently mislaid hers — from the note she'd left with the entry.

Betsy did not envy the trio of judges of this contest. The ceiling of the shop was aflutter with entries, many of them very high caliber.

Godwin came through from the back room, a little stack of cross-stitch patterns in one hand. He was whistling a chipper air Betsy knew but could not identify.

"You sound cheerful," she remarked.

"Do I? I guess I do feel pretty good today."

"Played a good round of golf last time out?"

"Yes, pretty good. Got three pars and a birdie."

"Very good! What's that you're whistling?"

" 'Hooray for Captain Spaulding,' Groucho Marx's theme song for his radio show *You Bet Your Life.*"

"Wasn't that also in one of the Marx Brothers' movies?"

"*Animal Crackers.*" Godwin assumed a slight crouch and said in a Bronx accent, " 'One morning I shot an elephant in my pajamas. How he got into my pajamas I don't know.' "

Betsy laughed. "Paint on a black mustache and you'd be a perfect Groucho. Are you doing something with those patterns?"

"I'm starting to think about our Halloween window." Like most businesses that dealt directly with the public, Crewel World was always looking ahead to the next season.

The shop had a big window up front, and Godwin and Betsy took pride in the artistic trimmings they used to advertise the patterns, floss, and needlework accessories the shop offered. They had already put up their back-to-school window, though it was not quite yet the Fourth of July.

Godwin put the patterns one by one on the library table. They were of witches, ghosts, and jack-o'-lanterns. "I'm thinking we could use a creepy font and letter 'Ghosties and Ghoulies and Long-Legeddy Beasties' across the top," he said.

"Hmmmm," said Betsy. "Yes, all right, that might do very well. But we need a nice long-legged black cat — Mill Hill has a pattern of two going up a moonlit path, but I don't know if they're leggy enough so folks will get the reference." She thought a little more. "Or, we could say 'Things That Go Bump in the Night,' so we could use haunted houses as well as the others — and that Happy Halloween design by — who is it? Sue Hillis, I think — of assorted monsters, ghosts, and witches."

It was Godwin's turn to go "Hmmmm."

"Let's think about it," suggested Betsy.

"Okay, let's," he agreed.

Three customers came in before lunch, and one bought two needlepoint canvases and the wool it would take to stitch them, making for a very happy addition to the cash box.

Betsy sent Godwin next door to Sol's for sandwiches and chips to celebrate. While he was gone, the door announced someone coming in and Betsy turned to see Pierce McMurphy. He was wearing an expensive navy blue pinstripe suit, gray tie, and highly polished shoes.

"Mr. McMurphy," Betsy greeted him politely, waiting to see what this was about.

"Joanne's at her doctor's office, which is not far from here, so I thought I'd take this opportunity to speak with you," he said in his slow baritone. "She said your interview with her went well."

"I think it did. She's a little . . . disconcerting."

"Volatile is probably a better word." He smiled and came to the checkout desk. His attractiveness struck her like a blow. She thought about Connor and managed not to bat her eyelashes at him. "She wasn't always a difficult person," he said quietly. "She was — and sometimes still is — a very sweet, kind, funny woman."

"I understand," Betsy replied. "It must be very hard for you, coping with her the way she is now, with her sudden changing emotions."

He nodded. "Sometimes it is. That's when I try to remember that part of the wedding vow, 'in sickness and in health.' "

Betsy wanted to ask him about Marge Schultz. But she didn't. Still, she wondered, hadn't Marge told him that Betsy knew they were lovers?

"What brings you in to see me today?" she asked.

"I want to know if you suspect my wife of murdering Hailey Brent." Betsy could see sincere anxiety on his face and could hear it in his voice.

Betsy hesitated. "That's a difficult question."

The anxiety burst into anger. "How can it be difficult? Either you do or you don't!"

"I'll try to explain. Your wife has a serious impulse control problem. Relatively minor things set her off into scary rages. If Hailey did something to seriously anger her, how might she react? If Hailey had been stabbed or bludgeoned with a weapon right at hand, Joanne would be high on my list of suspects. But shooting Hailey took some forethought. Joanne doesn't carry a gun, so she would have had to go get one — and could she hold on to her anger long enough to go through with the purchase? I doubt it; her emotions, while powerful, are also ephemeral. So while I think Joanne is capable of murder, I don't think she is capable of Hailey's murder — unless she somehow got immediate access to a gun. Where did the gun that killed Hailey come from? Did Hailey own a gun herself, and keep it in her basement kitchen? Was there an argument between Hailey and Joanne in that basement?"

Betsy took a breath before continuing. "You owned a gun, Mr. McMurphy —"

"It was stolen well before Hailey was shot!"

"Was it?"

Pierce took a step back — Betsy had grown heated in her argument, and asked that last question with considerable emphasis.

Seeing his shocked face, she apologized. "I'm sorry. This has been a difficult case for me. I can't get all my questions answered, and the answers I do have don't make up a story I can understand. It gets frustrating, and I'm aggravated by my failure. I shouldn't have come at you like that."

"It's all right," he said, but unconvincingly. Then he gave a short sigh and said, "No, really, I understand what it's like to be frustrated. You're probably sorry you ever started looking into this. Marge had no right to ask you."

"She had the same right as others have had to ask me to investigate. It's not my job, no, but it's something I've done before. Are you angry with Marge for asking me?"

He stared at her. "Why should I be angry?"

"I don't know. I'm just asking. You know her very well, of course."

"I do?"

Betsy let that evasion hang in the air like the lie it was trying to be.

"Oh, Lord," he breathed. "Who told you?"

"No one. I overheard the two of you talking the day you came to buy a blue spruce evergreen."

"That's impossible," he said flatly.

"I was on the other side of the fence, digging up lily of the valley to transplant to my own property."

The wait was longer this time, but at last he asked, "Who have you told?"

"Someone I trust not to repeat it."

"My God, if Joanne finds out . . ."

"You're sure she doesn't already know?"

"Positive. She'd go after Marge."

"Not you?"

"That might depend on what she's told,

270

maybe on who tells her. Actually, she might go after the person who shared the information with her."

Betsy felt a deep chill. "Is that possible?"

"Is what possible — ? No! Hailey didn't know. *Nobody* knew!"

"Hailey Brent was holding something over Marge's head. Do you know what it was?"

The door sounded and Godwin was back, a big white paper bag in his hand. "I remembered your pickle!" he announced happily. Then he felt the atmosphere in the shop and stopped short. "What's going on? Hey, aren't you Pierce McMurphy?"

"That's right," said Pierce, and he turned toward Godwin with a smile.

Betsy could see Godwin respond to that charm and sent him a wish that he should think of Rafael. "I'm Godwin DuLac," he said, and didn't bat his eyelashes, either.

"Ms. Devonshire and I were just talking." Pierce turned back to Betsy, that charming smile still on his face. "Thank you for being so patient with Joanne the other day," he said. "She thinks well of you. Now I have to be getting along. Good-bye, and thank you."

He went out.

"Whoa!" said Godwin, looking after him. "Smooth and sweet!"

"Goddy . . ." said Betsy warningly.

"Totally immune," said Godwin, pressing his other hand to his chest. "Trust me, totally immune. What did he want, really?"

"To find out what Joanne told me, and to express a hope that I don't have her on my list of suspects. But unfortunately I had to disappoint him. Now, let's eat."

TWENTY-ONE

Connor fixed breakfast the morning of July 3: fried potatoes mixed with two beaten eggs, onion, and sweet pepper. "Let's go swimming this evening," he said as he shoveled the food into his mouth.

Noting the calories in the breakfast — Connor had made toast and put a jar of marmalade on the table with it — Betsy readily agreed.

"Are we all set for the picnic tomorrow?" she asked.

"I'll boil the potatoes today and make potato salad tonight. What else are we to bring?"

"A munchies tray. I've got the baby carrots, celery, two kinds of olives, and a head of cauliflower in my fridge. But I still need to buy a tub of dip."

"Let me make the dip," said Connor. "I saw a recipe on the Internet yesterday that sounded interesting. It's got jalapeños in it, but I'll cut the amount in half. What's the head count so far?"

"A baker's dozen." A group picnic had been organized by Bershada of the Monday Bunch, to meet at the Excelsior Commons park at noon. Bershada's new boyfriend, Trey, was bringing a grill, so there would be hamburgers and brats, courtesy of Bershada. Jill was coming, with Lars and the children. They were bringing a cauldron of calico beans, which, Betsy knew, would begin simmering this evening. Phil and Doris would bring soft drinks, lemonade, and potato chips. Alice was bringing two chocolate cakes with her famous marzipan icing. Patricia and her husband Peter were bringing beer, three bottles of wine, and tablecloths, paper plates, plastic flatware, and lots of napkins. Everyone was bringing something to sit on, and they were going to eat, play games, and talk until it was time for the fireworks.

For a small town, Excelsior had a terrific day of entertainment on tap, including several bands playing a wide variety of music, and a marvelous fireworks display, shot off from twin barges anchored out in the bay. People came from all over the area to see the show.

"Are we going to the parade in the morning?" he asked.

"Oh, we have to! Emma Beth is riding her new bicycle in it — she's decorating it herself — and Jill is pulling Erik in his decorated wagon. We are instructed to stand on the curb and clap especially loudly for them as they go by."

"What time does it start?"

"Eleven sharp. Comes down Water Street, ends at the Commons."

"And then we buy them Popsicles when it's over."

"No, there are going to be free Popsicles this year over by the bandstand. Then we have lunch, and games, and supper, then fireworks."

"Sounds good." Connor drank the last of his coffee. "What's on your agenda for today?"

"Just the usual. Why, do you have something in mind?"

"I was wondering if you've talked with Mike Malloy lately. Is he still focusing on Marge Schultz as his primary suspect? Does he know something you don't? Do you know something he doesn't, to wit, the McMurphy-Schultz affair?"

"Well, I certainly haven't told him. But we kind of tiptoe around each other when it comes to exchanging information. Of

275

course, he's always more interested in hearing what I've found out than in telling me what he knows."

"Is he a gossip?"

"Not at all."

"So why haven't you told him? Are you protecting Marge from him?"

Betsy picked up the last piece of toast — cold now — and tore it in half. "You're making me uncomfortable, asking that."

"Why?"

"Because now I wonder if I have a duty as a citizen to share that information with Mike."

"I can't think that you do. After all, it isn't information about a crime. Adultery isn't illegal."

Betsy, still troubled, stood and began to clear the table. "You're right. But I need to think about it."

She did a quick wash of the breakfast dishes, except the frying pan, which she put aside to soak in detergent and hot water — Connor had a talent for frying things that left chunks welded to the bottom of the pan.

Then she went downstairs to unlock the door to the shop.

Business was up slightly that morning, mostly because tourists in town for the

Fourth were out looking for souvenirs and bargains. But one local came in with an entry for the template contest.

"Annie!" Betsy exclaimed, smiling. "Good to see you!"

Back when Annie Summerhill was a homeless woman, she had been very helpful to Betsy's investigation of a case, and Betsy, seeking to return the favor, rented an apartment for her in a safe neighborhood in Minneapolis. Annie soon managed to get a job with a company that cleaned offices at night. She was such a hard and reliable worker that in a few months she was in charge of a crew with a raise in pay. She told Betsy, "If I keep this up, pretty soon I'll be on his books, which means I can join the union and get benefits."

"What do you mean you'll be on his books?" Betsy had asked.

"I'm being paid under the table right now," Annie replied, surprised that Betsy was unfamiliar with the term. "I like it, 'cause I ain't got no withholding. Every cent he pays me goes right into my pocket." And she had winked and tapped the side of her nose.

Later Annie had gotten a second job, light factory work, assembling medical devices. She worked both for a while, then quit the cleaning company for a job as a security guard — the kind where she sat at a desk most of the time, checking office workers in and out at night. Both were "on the books," and one offered benefits.

Despite working all those hours, Annie found time to do a little needlework — some of it while sitting at that desk — and she visited Crewel World about every other week. Betsy continued to pay Annie's rent and to help out in the occasional fiscal emergency. The last had been a trip to the dentist.

Now Annie stood smiling proudly at the checkout desk, template entry in hand. "I bet you thought I wasn't going to get it done, but I did, and here it is!"

Annie had used the theme of a color wheel, stitching in plain x's using overdyed floss that shifted in shades of each color, giving a shimmering effect. "Very nice," said Betsy. "These stitches are nice and even; you're getting better all the time."

"Thanks." Annie walked around the shop, eyes lifted, admiring the other entries hanging from the ceiling. "I like the tiger," she said, pointing to it.

"Me, too," said Betsy. She was putting a dab of masking tape on Annie's work. It had a number inked on it. Betsy wrote a matching number on Annie's entry form. The entry forms were kept in a file folder in the checkout desk, and would not be shown to the judges. There were twenty-seven entries so far, a goodly number.

She was putting the file folder away when she became aware of Annie still standing in front of the desk, a troubled look on her face.

"Is something wrong?" Betsy asked.

Annie said doubtfully, "Oh no, I don't think so. Maybe. Yes." That last was a confession.

"What is it?"

"My son's in town. And he needs a place to stay." Annie's son was a rarely employed alcoholic who when last heard from was living in his car in another state.

"Annie, you're in a one-bedroom apartment. Where would he sleep?"

"On the couch. Just temporary, he says." Annie's face was a fist, full of doubt, grief, anger, and fear.

Betsy asked, "Do you believe him?"

Annie began to cry. "No. But he's my son!"

"How on earth did he find you?"

"I don't know, not for sure. His call came out of the blue. Donna Campbell's a friend of mine, and she's on Facebook, and she probably posted about me, bragging how I'm doing so well. She talks about everyone she knows. I've known her forever; she used to babysit Cole after his father left us so I could work. I guess Cole checked me out on a library computer. I didn't even know he knew how."

"Do you want him to stay with you?"

"What else can I do?"

"Annie, what do you think would happen if you let Cole stay with you?"

"Oh, he'd probably be all right, he'd sleep for three days." Her face darkened as she considered further. "Then he'd steal my TV and sell it to buy liquor, then invite some new friend to come over, and they'd get in a fight and trash my place that you got for me — which I'm getting fixed up so nice — and we'd both get thrown out." She sucked back a sob. "And you'd be mad at me."

"Darn right I'd be mad at you. Right now I'm mad at your friend Donna for telling him where you live."

A faint smile tugged at Annie's mouth. "I guess I'm mad at her, too."

"So what are you going to do?"

Annie looked away and mumbled, "He's coming over tomorrow."

"You told him he could?"

"I told him don't come over. But he thinks

I don't mean it."

"Do you mean it?"

Still looking away, she said humbly, "I want to mean it."

"What else did you tell him?

"I can't loan him any money." Annie's posture straightened and she stuck her trembling chin out. "I got to mean that. I got bills to pay!"

"Do you really want him to stay away?"

Annie hesitated, then said firmly though her eyes were filled with pain, "Yes. If I let him stay with me, he'll have us both back on the street."

"All right. Tomorrow you won't be home. You come out here — no, we'll come and get you, the buses won't be running. We'll pick you up early, you can stay all day. Some of the Monday Bunch are having a picnic and you can join us. Okay?"

Annie's face slowly lit up. "Thank you!"

Betsy came out from behind the desk to take Annie in a strong embrace. "I know that was a terribly hard decision for you to make, a heartbreaking decision." She stepped back. "Now, be sure to tell the apartment manager that no one is allowed into your apartment when you aren't there, so Cole doesn't talk his way in while you're over here eating brats and watching fireworks tomorrow."

"Okay. I'm glad I came out today."

"Me, too. We, the women who make bad choices for husbands, have to stick together." Annie had spoken of the ne'er-do-well husband who abandoned her, and Betsy empathized. Her own ex-husband, while once a college professor, had lost his position after a series of affairs with his students had come to light.

Annie laughed, though her cheeks were still wet with tears. "Yes, we do. Oh, Betsy, you're such a good friend to me!"

"I love you, too, Annie."

Betsy sent Annie on her way, then called Connor to tell him to put an extra potato in the pot.

Twenty-Two

As in other years, Lars led Excelsior's Fourth of July parade in his Stanley Steamer, blowing its whistle frequently, releasing steam in great clouds. The family's Newfoundland, Bjorn, sat proudly erect in the seat beside him. The steamer was followed by a high school band playing John Philip Sousa marches.

They were followed by two dozen children riding, pulling, or pushing bicycles, tricycles, coaster wagons, doll buggies, and strollers. Very young children were pulled in the wagons by older siblings or parents. Crepe paper, ribbons, balloons, and flags ornamented the vehicles and even some of the children. Some children loved being in the parade, some didn't seem to understand what they were doing walking up the street in front of all those people, some wept in confusion and fright.

Emma was very much of the first school.

She rode her bike — the training wheels recently removed — with aplomb, and when she saw Connor and Betsy standing with Annie on the curb, she smiled broadly, pointed and waved like a politician spying a major donor in the crowd. She wore a dozen sparkly plastic bracelets on each arm; a garland of red, white, and blue plastic flowers over her silver helmet; blue shorts; and a white T-shirt with an American flag on it. She had decorated her bike herself, very thoroughly, except for the bare spots where some crepe paper rosettes had fallen off.

Erik, riding in a coaster wagon pulled by his mother, was crying — he wanted to pull it himself. Nevertheless he waved to the people. Jill chose to ignore his tears until near the end, when she lifted him from his decorated wagon and carried him on one arm. Then he stopped crying and waved shyly. He wore denim overalls and a straw hat.

Everyone met at the bandstand, where free red, white, and blue Popsicles were being handed out.

"Where's Phil?" asked Lars, the last to arrive because he had to find a parking spot and then shut down the Stanley, which took about twenty minutes.

"He and Trey are guarding our spot on

top of the hill," said Doris. Members of the party had started arriving early in the morning to search out a good spot on the Commons, and when one was decided on, they marked it with folding chairs, ice chests, picnic baskets, and a magnificent big charcoal grill.

"When are the fireworks?" asked Erik, who had loved them at Disney World, the bigger and louder the better.

"Not until dark, hours and hours from now," said Jill.

"How long is hours and hours?" he asked.

"Long enough for you to eat hot dogs and potato salad twice!" said Lars. "*And* take a nap!"

"I'm not sleepy!" objected the child.

"No, of course you're not," said Jill. "But maybe later you will be."

"I'm hungry," announced Emma, having fed half her Popsicle to Bjorn.

"And on that note," said Bershada, "let's eat."

Annie, on hearing the picnic was a potluck, had insisted on contributing something, so on her way to Excelsior in Connor's car, they had stopped at Cub Foods. She went in to the deli section and picked up a big carton of mixed chopped fruit.

Betsy had mock-scolded her. "You

brought fruit? Not even fruit with a gooey sweet dressing? Well, all right, if you don't mind being the only person who brought something healthy!"

Annie had laughed, proud to be different.

And her choice was popular. Even Erik took a spoon and fished around in the clear plastic container for a red grape, which he ate with relish.

Trey, Bershada's boyfriend, had started the charcoal burning while everyone else was at or marching in the parade, so there was a minimal wait for the protein part of lunch.

They ate and talked, then stretched out on blankets or sat in canvas chairs to talk some more and watch the children play. Other picnickers brought their children by, and one of them had a soccer ball. Soon some sort of game whose rules were a bit fuzzy was started and played to exhaustion.

"Who won?" Lars asked Emma when she came back to his blanket, Erik close behind her.

"I did!" she declared. "And so did Paul, and Russo. Airey scored *one*!" she concluded scornfully. Airey was Erik's nickname, bestowed by herself, but now universal.

"I maked a point!" boasted Erik. His pale

blond hair was darkened around his forehead by perspiration.

Jill gave the two of them bottles of water and had them sit down on a blanket in the shade to rest. Inside five minutes they were both sound asleep, Bjorn between them.

Things grew quiet. Down in the bandstand, a group of five musicians was playing classic rock, but not loudly. Over on the baseball diamond, a pickup softball game was under way, but the diamond was halfway across the park from the hilltop, so the cheers were muffled. Somebody not too far away was playing a hot flamenco guitar.

The group began to break into smaller groups for conversation. Annie and Alice seemed to have struck up a friendship based on comfort-food recipes; Connor, Phil, and Trey — who had discovered similar tastes in off-color jokes and elaborate puns — huddled out of earshot; Lars and Jill talked politics and shared cop stories with Betsy; Bershada and Patricia were doing needlework and talking children and grandchildren; Peter, a hardworking attorney, was asleep on his own blanket not far from Erik and Emma.

"I think you should consider getting a concealed carry license," Jill was saying to Betsy. "I've got one. Lars and I could go with you when you buy a gun and give you shooting lessons."

"I don't want a gun. It might make me more willing to take chances, make me feel all brave and macho."

"Mine doesn't," said Jill.

"Yes, but you got used to carrying a gun when you were a street cop. And now that you're not on and off duty, how do you decide when to stick it in your purse? Only at night? Only when going through a bad neighborhood? Never to church?"

"I don't carry it in my purse. What would I do if a purse snatcher grabbed it and ran off? I carry it on me. And I always carry it. Because you never know."

"You mean you have a gun on you right now?"

"This very minute."

"I don't see it."

"Of course you don't. I don't intend for it to be seen." Jill was not fat, but she was curvy. Still, Betsy could not detect a curve that wasn't Jill — and Jill wasn't wearing an outsize man shirt or sloppy-loose jeans, but a white knit short-sleeved shirt with broad blue horizontal stripes, and blue capri pants.

Jill, noting Betsy's up-and-down survey, laughed. "Don't worry, it won't fall out the bottom of my pants leg. And it's not tucked away in a place I can't get at very fast and easy."

"What do you think about carrying a gun? I mean, is it like life insurance?"

Jill laughed again. "Life insurance only kicks in when you assume room temperature. My little thirty-eight is life *assurance.* Remember, when seconds count, the police are just minutes away." She made a face to show it was an angry kind of joke.

"All right, I understand, I suppose. But I'm still not going to buy one."

Jill shot a significant glance at Lars and shrugged. "That's your decision."

"Lars," Betsy asked, "what do you think about a wife who goes about armed?"

"Same as she thinks about me, I guess."

Betsy stared at him. "You, too?"

He nodded, smiling, and patted his side toward the back. "Me, too."

The steamboat *Minnehaha* — which was not a paddle wheeler, but a restored antique whose engine was powered by steam — let loose its breathy whistle. The boat was running brief tours, just out and around the Big Island and back. It was on its return trip, and a young couple passing by stopped to watch it make its way to the dock. They were making cynical remarks about the state of the world, sad to hear in a couple so freshly facing tomorrow. As they started back on their way, the young man said, "I hear the euro was seen at Disney World last week wearing a Make-A-Wish T-shirt," and his girl laughed harshly.

"Poor things," said Betsy when they were gone.

"Yeah," sighed Lars, drawing the word out. "Were we ever so lacking in illusions?"

"I'm sure we thought so," said Jill.

"Hello, Betsy!" said a new voice, and they all three looked up to see Marge Schultz, resplendent in pink shorts and pink sleeveless shirt, smiling at them. She continued, "I ate so much I decided I'd better walk some of it off. Isn't it a nice day?"

"It's a splendid day," said another new voice — Connor's. He came to stoop by Betsy's chair.

"Marge, this is Connor Sullivan. Connor, this is Marge Schultz."

"How do you do, Ms. Schultz?" said Connor, rising and extending his hand.

"Nice to meet you, Connor," said Marge, her eyes moving speculatively between him and Betsy as she took his hand. "Please, call me Marge."

"Did you see the parade, Marge?" asked Connor.

"Yes. The children were sweet. It's so nice

the town does that parade just for them. But I do find Sergeant Larson's steam car kind of scary. All that smoke! I was afraid it was going to blow up and kill half the band following behind it."

"Naw!" said Lars. "That's not smoke, it's just steam, coming out the whistle. Why, if I didn't let off steam like that, no one would hear me coming!"

Betsy said, "It's true, Marge, there's no engine sound when it's moving. And it's very safe. Lars takes the children for rides in it all the time, and he wouldn't do that if it wasn't safe."

"All the same, I'll keep my distance, thank you," said Marge. "I see you're here with a big group. Who are they, Betsy, employees?"

"No, mostly they're a stitching group that meets Monday afternoons. Who are you here with?"

"Three employees and their significant others. We do this every year."

"That's nice." Betsy's annual party for employees came in December.

Jill said, "Betsy told me you have some beautiful hydrangea plants for sale."

Marge nodded. "They're young ones, in pots, but suitable for transplanting in your yard, if that's what you're wanting."

"Betsy said some of them are pink and

some blue. Is there a difference between them besides color?"

"No, actually they're the same variety, Endless Summer. It's naturally pink" — she smiled, tilted her head a little sideways, and touched the collar of her shirt — "of course; but you can turn the blooms blue with a product called Color Me Blue. If you have a blue hydrangea, I can sell you some Color Me Pink."

"What is it, a dye?" asked Betsy.

"No, they're two different chemicals, harmless to the plant, but they change the pH of the soil around it, and hydrangeas are sensitive to pH. Alkaline makes pink, acid makes blue."

"Amazing," said Jill. "Okay, I'm going to have to come in tomorrow or the next day and buy a couple of plants. I just love those huge bloom clusters. They look great in people's yards, and they look fantastic in dried winter bouquets, too."

"Yes, they do," said Marge. "I look forward to seeing you." She nodded at the others and went on her way.

"She seems a nice lady," remarked Connor.

"Yes, but there's something sad about her," said Jill with compassion. "And who wouldn't be, with a police detective suspecting you of murder." She turned to her husband. "Mike surely doesn't really think she murdered Hailey Brent?"

"Why don't you ask him?" replied Lars, nodding toward a figure climbing the hill in their direction.

Jill and Betsy looked to see Mike Malloy, wearing a red, yellow, and green Hawaiian shirt and tangerine shorts, lifting one arm in a wave.

"We were just talking about you," said Lars, grinning wickedly at his wife.

And she boldly said, "I was saying I don't see how you can possibly think Marge Schultz murdered Hailey Brent."

"She remains on my list of suspects," said Mike, calmly.

Jill said, "I hope Betsy can prove she didn't do it."

Connor gave Betsy a significant eyebrow lift, and Betsy said, "Oh, all right." She turned to Mike and said in a voice so low he had to lean toward her to hear it. "I have good reason to believe Marge Schultz and Pierce McMurphy were having an affair."

"Wow!" said Jill.

"Where did you hear that?" asked Mike, suddenly looking very much like a police investigator, despite the shirt and shorts.

"I overheard them talking."

"They had the conversation in a place where they could be overheard?" Mike sounded disbelieving.

"No, they thought they were alone. I was in Hailey Brent's backyard, near the fence between Hailey's place and Green Gaia. Pierce was there ostensibly to buy a blue spruce, but Marge wanted to talk to him, to encourage him to get moving on his plans to divorce Joanne."

"Oh, Lord," said Jill.

"Now wait," said Betsy. "It seems to me that the person to kill in that unhappy triangle would be Joanne. Marge insists that no one — *no one* — knew of the affair."

"You found out — and you did it while standing in Hailey's backyard," Mike pointed out.

"Mike," said Betsy, "you've interviewed Joanne McMurphy, right?"

"Yes. A very strange-tempered lady."

"Do you know how she came to be that way?"

Mike nodded once. "I talked to her husband, too. I remember that car accident — my Uncle Vince was a highway patrolman and talked about it for years afterward. He rode up on it and was surprised to find two live people inside. He helped get them out of that car, which was like a wadded-up piece of aluminum foil. They're a pair of walking miracles, despite her mental problems."

"Do you think she could have murdered Hailey?"

"If the gun used was sitting in that basement where she could grab it easily, yes."

Betsy nodded. "Yes, that's what I think, too. She told me she's careful not to have a weapon at hand. Did Hailey by some peculiar chance have a gun permit?"

"No. But you don't need one just to keep it in the house."

Jill said, "Hailey Brent loved gossip. If she knew about Pierce and Marge's affair, why wasn't she spreading it around instead of keeping it a secret? Especially if Marge or Pierce knew she knew?"

"That's right," said Betsy. "So maybe Marge is right, Hailey didn't know." But Betsy remembered the dyeing demo and Hailey's strange, cruel hint that Marge stole the flowers she brought to be made into a dye bath. No, Hailey knew *something.* But what?

Mike went on his way, newly burdened with the information, and Betsy fell into a troubled reflection.

But before she could talk some more about it, Philadelphia came by with her husband Allen and their two lively children, Chloe and Mitchell, nine and twelve. She introduced them to Betsy, who in turn introduced Jill and Lars. Allen was quiet, almost shy, smiling behind his dark beard, keeping his hands in the pockets of his shorts. Philadelphia's blue-green hair was done up in spikes. Their children, dressed alike in jeans and tie-dyed T-shirts, were patently impatient to move along — until Mitchell saw the big black dog. "Wow!" he exclaimed. "What kind of dog is that?"

"A Newfoundland," said Lars. "He helps babysit our children. He's especially good at keeping them from drowning."

"Really?" Mitchell didn't know whether or not his leg was being pulled.

"Really," said Jill. "They love to go out into the water and pull drowning people to shore. You don't have to train them, they do it naturally."

Mitchell and Chloe stared at the dog, dozing on a blanket with Erik and Emma, as if expecting him to dash into the lake any second. When he didn't, Mitchell said, "Mom, I'm hot, can we have some ice cream?"

"All right," said Philadelphia. "Come along." And off they went.

A few minutes later, Patricia's husband

Peter woke up full of energy. His enthusiasm soon had the other adults up and moving, which woke the children up. They organized a three-legged relay race which included some adults and children from other groups and resulted in some strenuous efforts and embarrassing, no-injury tumbles. Jill and Connor proved so great together a hasty rule was passed that they could no longer pair up. Annie proved enthusiastic but clumsy, and Alice refused all attempts to be recruited as a contestant. Lars won a heat with his son as a partner by lifting Erik off the ground by his arm, and another rule was passed: no carrying.

The competition was declared over when no one wanted to run anymore.

Everyone retired to a sitting place and lemonade was passed around.

"Whew!" said Lars after half a glass. "That was fun."

"I winned with Daddy!" boasted Erik.

"Yes, you did, Airey," agreed Jill.

"I almost won," said Emma, not as boastfully. She had finished a surprising second with Phil as a partner.

"You were great!" said Phil, raising his glass to her. "Next year you'll be a couple inches taller and you and me, we'll finish first every time!"

"You bet!" said Emma, much gratified, raising her glass in return.

Half ashamed of their returning appetites, members of the group began wandering by the ice chests, taking a slice of cake, a fistful of potato chips, a soft drink, "just a dab" of potato salad. The talk became general. Jill mentioned the hydrangeas she planned to buy, and Alice offered some planting advice. "Dig a bigger hole than you think you need, fertilize it right away, and give it plenty of water the first week."

"Thanks, Alice. Marge said the flowers on the variety of hydrangeas she has are naturally pink, but I'm thinking I'd like a pink one and a blue one, for Emma and Erik, so I guess I'll buy the chemical mix to change the color of one of them."

"You don't need chemicals," Annie said. "Just bury a set of aluminum measuring cups under one and it'll change to blue. That's what a neighbor of ours did, back when I was a kid."

Jill stared at her. "Measuring cups?"

"*Aluminum* measuring cups," said Annie. "It's the aluminum that makes the color change. I bet when you look at the bottle or can of whatever is supposed to turn the pink flowers blue, you'll see that it contains aluminum."

"Annie's right," said Alice. "My cousin Tillie did it with her hydrangeas. Only she did it with alum — which is aluminum and something else."

"Aluminum sulfate," said Bershada. She added darkly, "Used also as a mordant in dyeing."

Betsy looked thoughtfully at Bershada. Wasn't alum one of the mordants in Hailey's arsenal?

TWENTY-THREE

The fireworks display didn't start until a little after ten and lasted for an hour. Connor, world traveler, politely remarked that it was nearly as good as any he'd ever seen. Other towns around the lake had displays, too, so there was a continuous shower of sparks no matter where you looked. The children cheered and clapped at everything, though Erik got a little cranky toward the end, it being well past his bedtime.

Betsy had to work the next day and so gratefully accepted Connor's offer to drive Annie home.

Connor's car was a Chrysler, bought used three years ago, scrupulously maintained. He was a good driver, but his right foot had a high lead content.

He had to be very patient getting out of town, as the lake blocked several directions, and traffic was heavy. Fortunately, he was as patient as he was lead-footed. Annie sat quietly in the passenger seat.

At last she said, "You and Betsy still getting along good, I can tell."

Amused, Connor said, "How can you tell?"

"You don't interrupt when the other is speaking, and you like to cuddle in the dark."

It was true that when darkness fell, Connor and Betsy sat close together — Betsy had given her chair to Annie, so Connor sat with her on a blanket. And Connor, after a bit of reflecting, agreed that he and Betsy tended to hear each other out.

"You're very perceptive," he said.

"You don't think it's a bad thing that she likes to act like a detective?"

"I wouldn't dream of imposing my opinion on her."

"So you don't like it much."

"I worry that she's not always careful."

"Me, too. I don't know what I'd do without her. She turned my life around."

"Oh, I think you would have turned it around all by yourself sooner or later."

"Maybe I would," Annie agreed loftily. Then she said, "And then, just like now, my no-good son would come around looking for me to support him."

"Betsy told me something about that. I

know it must be hard to turn your back on your own son."

"Especially since he's my only child." Annie fell silent for a while. "But needs must when the devil drives. Did I say that right? Godwin taught it to me. He says it means you have to do what there is to do when there's no other choice."

"You said it correctly. I'm sorry it's come to that, Annie."

"Look, there's an opening," she said, and sure enough, traffic suddenly thinned and they went roaring up Highway 15.

The road curved back and forth along here, following the contours of the lake. Connor slalomed along it expertly, about twenty miles an hour over the limit.

"Wow, you drive really good!" cheered Annie.

"Thank you." He was pleased she wasn't fearful.

In a few minutes they drove up a long, curving ramp onto I-394 East and were on their way to Minneapolis.

"Now you can really go fast," said Annie.

"No, there's a highway patrolman three cars behind us," said Connor, who had long ago learned to keep a sharp lookout for cars with low-rise complications on their roofs.

Annie laughed. "I like you," she said.

"You're smart."

Connor took the Dunwoody exit into the western edge of downtown and followed Annie's directions to an old-fashioned, four-story, dark red brick building with a modest glassed-in porch marking the entrance. It was a decent neighborhood; not far away was the Minneapolis Art Institute.

"Home," said Annie with a contented little sigh.

Connor stopped beside some parked cars to let her out, but then spotted a figure by the porch. A thin man, wearing a loose-fitting white T-shirt and sagging jeans, was leaning against the door to the place, and something about his pose told Connor he was drunk or stoned.

"Uh-oh," said Annie, also looking at the man.

"What's wrong? Do you know who that is?"

With a sharp, scared edge to her voice, Annie said, "I wonder if it's Cole, my son. If it is, there might be trouble."

"What kind of trouble?"

"I don't know. Yelling, maybe. Maybe crying, to make me give in and let him come inside with me."

"You don't want him to come inside with you?" Betsy had told him about Annie's problematic son but hadn't gone into too many details.

"No. No, absolutely not." But Annie was trembling, whether from fear or irresolution, Connor couldn't tell.

But the problem was Annie's, not Betsy's — or his. He needed the solution to come from her. "What do you want me to do? Shall we just drive away?"

Annie took a deep breath and her voice firmed. "Drive where? And what, not come back, ever? I live here, this is my home! I want him to go away!" Her head bowed. "But I'm scared."

"How about I have a word with him?" Connor pulled ahead, into a space a few cars down.

"No, he's my problem, I'll talk to him," said Annie with a determined lift to her chin.

He watched her as she got out and walked back to the entrance. He rolled down his car windows, shut off his engine, then turned in his seat so he could watch and hear. The man stirred at her approach, then suddenly stepped forward.

"Ma!" he cried in a high-pitched voice. "I thought you'd never get here!"

"You go away!" barked Annie. "I told you not to come here!"

"But Ma, I need a place to stay!" The man was swaying a little. "I'm sick, Ma!" He was speaking very loudly, probably in an attempt to get her to shush him by giving in.

"You're drunk. And you're not staying here!"

"I ain't drunk, Ma, and you got to let me in." The man reached for her arms. "You *got* to let me stay!" He began to shake her. "You hear me? I'm your *son*!"

"Let go, you're hurting me!"

Connor bailed out of the car and hurried up the sidewalk. He came up behind Annie and said firmly, "Is there a problem here?"

The man's whine vanished and he snarled, "This don't concern you!"

But Annie twisted out of his surprise-loosened grip, gasping, "How dare you hurt me!" Her sideways step left the two men directly confronting each other.

Connor, anger and concern making him feel large, said, "Leave her alone! Go on, get out of here!"

With no warning the drunk man struck Connor in the face with his fist.

Connor had spent most of his life in the merchant marine, and enough of that time in the mean districts of harbor towns. His conditioned response was to punch the drunk in the stomach as hard as he could.

"Ooff!" The man staggered back and sat down hard on the pavement.

Annie clapped both hands to her cheeks "Are you hurt?" she exclaimed.

Connor didn't know whom she was asking — possibly both of them. "Not badly," he said, though his left eye was watering and it felt as if his eyebrow had been torn off.

She looked at her son, sitting spraddle-legged on the walk in front of her door, his mouth moving like a goldfish's, unable to do more than make hicking sounds as he tried to regain his breath. "Is he hurt bad?"

"He's just had the wind knocked out of him. He'll be all right in a few minutes."

"Should we just leave him here?"

"Since he assaulted both of us, I'd say his next stop should be jail." His adrenaline ebbing, he softened his tone. "I think at least we should call the police. Is that all right with you?"

Annie's face puckered up, but she said, "I guess that would be the safest place for him." She sighed. "He's been in jail before, lots of times."

Cole looked up at her and held out both hands in a pleading gesture.

"No, Cole, it's way too late for that," she said. "Way too late."

■ ■ ■ ■

The next morning, the delicious smell of coffee woke Betsy. Since she didn't have an automatic coffeemaker with a timer on it, she knew Connor was in her kitchen. She wondered what time he'd gotten home last night. It must have been pretty late, since he'd gone into his own apartment rather than wake her.

She rolled onto her back and basked in the luxury of having someone else fix breakfast. In less than a minute there was a wobble on her mattress as Sophie jumped up for her morning cuddle.

Sophie wasn't the brightest cat in the world, but she had one virtue: She waited for signs of waking in her mistress before joining her in bed for a snuggle.

"Good morning, Sophie-Dophie," cooed Betsy, stroking the thick white fur with the tan and gray splotches on the head and back.

Sophie mewed back in her tiny voice, incongruous in an animal that weighted twenty-two pounds. Then she collapsed heavily against Betsy's side and began purring. Betsy stroked and tickled her for a few minutes, until the smell of bacon joined the scent of coffee, and she rolled out of bed.

"Mew!" objected Sophie.

"Sorry!" said Betsy.

A few minutes later Betsy walked into the kitchen and was startled to see a magnificent shiner around Connor's left eye.

"Oh my God, what happened to you?"

"Annie's son Cole was waiting for us when we got to her place."

"He *hit* you? Why?"

"He had taken his mother by the arms and was hurting her. I walked over and had the temerity to tell him to go away and not come back."

"Is Annie all right?"

"Yes, she's fine. He scared her more than hurt her."

"Did you hit him back?"

"Yes, of course." He seemed surprised she had to ask.

Betsy said, "A knock-out blow?"

"No. Long ago I got some good advice: 'Hit the soft parts with your hand, the hard parts with a utensil.' So I punched him in the stomach. He may have broken a knuckle hitting me, but my hand is whole this morning." He held it out, opening and closing it, smiling reminiscently.

Betsy paused a moment to adjust her attitude to this macho person occupying her kitchen, then came in for a hug. "I'm glad you were there for Annie. Where did Cole end up, or do you know?"

"He's in jail, charged with public drunkenness and assault. I figured it was best to get him on record for his behavior, and Annie agreed. She is going to apply for an order of protection against him. Now, are you ready for breakfast? I'm hungry as a hunter after my adventure of last night."

Betsy extracted more details of the event over bacon and soft-boiled eggs.

"How did Annie take all this? Is she sad? Angry? Pleased?"

"All of the above, plus embarrassed. Her ambition is to rise into the middle class, and in her opinion, middle-class people don't have altercations in the street with drunk relatives."

"Oh, if only she knew," sighed Betsy. "I hope Cole is properly ashamed of himself."

"Probably not. He didn't get his breath back until after I'd called the police, and before they arrived he tried to convince me it was all a misunderstanding, that I should help him persuade Annie to let him go upstairs with her and sleep it off. Annie, bless her heart, said no way was he ever going to see the inside of her apartment. The two of us stood firm, and by the time the police took him away, he was angry but she was pretty cheerful. I like her. She's brave and hard to keep down."

"Yes, she is." Betsy took a closer look at Connor's shiner. "I think maybe you should go to the doctor about that eye. It looks dreadful."

"No, it doesn't need stitches. I've had black eyes before; they heal by themselves."

"But you look like a pirate."

"No amount of medicine can cure that."

Betsy gave up. She got dressed, kissed him, and went down to open the shop.

TWENTY-FOUR

Right at ten, Annie called. She asked cautiously, "Have you seen Connor yet today?"

"Yes, and he told me all about last night. You both behaved beautifully!"

"I was scared, but Connor was a hero!" declared Annie. "Pow, right in the breadbasket!"

"Oh, Annie!" Betsy said, thinking Annie was being a little callous.

"Yeah, well, what can you do? He called me this morning."

"Connor?"

"No, Cole. I told him the police explained to me how to apply for a restraining order against him, and that I'd be doing that today. He wanted me to post his bail, and I told him no way. He told me it would be just a loan, I should help him because he sold his car for the price of a bus ticket to Minneapolis, but right then I hung up on him."

"This must be very difficult for you."

Annie sighed, her cheerfulness ebbing. "Oh, it is, it is. But lots of things are hard to do, especially if they're the right thing. My son has spent his whole life making that bed, now he has to lay down on it. I would like for you to tell Connor he's a real peach, and I will tell anyone who thinks to get up against him that they're making a big mistake. Pow, right in the breadbasket!" Annie's words were brave, but there were tears in her voice.

Betsy laughed, but she felt like crying, too. "I will, Annie. I think you're very brave and very tough, too. I want you to do something nice for yourself today, okay? And if you need anything, you let me know."

"You did the best thing for me, already, when you told Connor to drive me home last night. Thank you very much."

Godwin came in late — a new habit he'd developed since moving with Rafael into the gray clapboard condo right across the street. Being sixty seconds from work makes being on time harder for some people. But he got right to work.

Later that morning, he began marking down prices on some cross-stitch patterns going on sale. "I didn't think the fireworks were quite as good as last year, did you?" he asked Betsy.

"Hmmm?" she said. She was pulling yarn for a needlepoint canvas a customer had ordered.

"Fireworks," prompted Godwin. "Weren't you at the display last night?"

"Sure. I thought they had too many of those loud ones."

"And didn't you think the display wasn't quite as good as last year's?"

Betsy had spent the late evening snuggled under Connor's right arm. She would have been fine with sparklers tossed in the air. "I thought it was very nice," she said.

Godwin had gone to the event with Rafael, who was still depressed over his failure as a merchant, which dimmed the colors of everything for both of them, even fireworks.

Still, that meant Godwin wasn't going to have to choose to go into partnership with Rafael in a new enterprise, or stay with Betsy in her old one. In a little while he began to whistle.

"What is that tune?" asked Betsy. "You were whistling it the other day, too."

"It's the theme to *Sergeant Preston of the Yukon.*" Godwin deepened his voice and called dramatically, "On, King! On, you huskies!" And he made a noise with his mouth that sounded like a winter storm blowing across the arctic wastes. Godwin was, for reasons not even he could explain, a fan of old radio shows.

Betsy chuckled as she shook her head and continued pulling yarn.

An hour or so later, Betsy went to the basement of her building to locate a big poster she'd stored there, advertising DMC floss — she was going to hold a sale on the product.

She noticed the line strung up there, where she had hung the yarn Hailey had spun for Irene Potter. The yarn had been delivered to Irene, but the line still held up the knitted square that had been taken out of the pot of indigo. On the edge of the sink a small wooden bowl was half full of dried flowers.

The bowl had been full when Betsy first put it down in the basement. She had picked the red marigolds fresh from Hailey's garden. She had meant to ask Philadelphia if it was all right, but had forgotten. She had wanted to talk to Ruth Ladwig about making a dye from them, but she'd gotten sidetracked into investigating the Pierce-Marge love affair. Now they had dried and shrunken into crispness, their bright red color dulled. Were dried flowers still good for making a dye?

She would call Ruth and see what she had to say.

Ruth told her that she would be at the Science Museum in Saint Paul tomorrow, doing demos on dyeing to anyone who came by.

And yes, dye baths could be made from dried flowers as well as fresh.

And yes, Betsy could come by with some dried marigolds and Ruth would make a dye bath from them.

It was a bit of a struggle, but Betsy found a part-timer able to come in the next day. Around ten, Betsy set off for Saint Paul. With her, safely placed in a plastic bag, were the dried red marigolds.

She took I-94 East through Minneapolis to the Kellogg exit in Saint Paul, turned right, and went down a hill past the Basilica, around a bend, and turned right on Eagle Street, then left onto Chestnut, which fed directly into a multilevel underground parking garage.

She collected her parking ticket at the entrance and found a spot not far from the elevator.

Following Ruth's instructions, she took the elevator to the main floor of the museum, crossed the huge, light-filled lobby to the ticket counter, and got a pink cardboard bracelet Ruth had left for her.

She took the stairs down a floor, pausing to look over the landing into a cafeteria area far below, where some strange-fangled device suspended in the air played abstract marimba music one note at a time.

At the bottom of the stairs and around a corner was the entrance to a large room filled with displays, including miniature scenes hand carved in wood that were activated by cranks — a man in a bathtub scrubbing his back, for example, or a woman operating an old-fashioned typewriter. There also was a whale skeleton and an enormous grizzly bear standing on its hind legs. And sea-creature fossils. And there stood Ruth, in an apron, behind a low red counter set with cafe stools. Two pots, one small and one large, were already steaming on a gas stove set right near her.

"This place makes me wish I were a kid again!" said Betsy, looking at the outsize hanging loom across from them. "Hi, Ruth!"

"Hello, Betsy. Did you bring the flowers?"

"Yes, here they are. I picked all the blooms off the red marigold growing in Hailey's garden, but there weren't a lot. I hope there are enough."

Ruth inspected the plastic bag, weighing it in her hand, pressing with her fingers to test its density. "I think there are. We'll just make a small dye bath." She opened the bag and plucked a bloom from it, then sifted the remaining dried flowers through her fingers into the smaller pot. She stirred them with a wooden dowel to get them to sink into the simmering water.

Then she took a closer look at what she held in her fingers.

"What are you looking for?" asked Betsy.

"I want to see if these were fully developed before you picked them." She showed Betsy the bulge forming at the base of the flower. "See, here is where the seeds form." She used her thumbnail to break it open, but there were no seeds inside. "No, this is a young flower. Which is to be expected: You find seeds in the late fall."

She dropped the flower into the pot with the others and went into a cabinet, where she brought out two fabric squares about four inches in diameter. Slits had been cut along the bottom of each square, and slip-knotted through the slits were short lengths of white yarn.

"Hey," Betsy said, "those look like the squares Hailey brought to the dyeing demo in my shop!"

"That's because they are the same. I gave her a box of them to use in her demos."

"You were a good friend to her."

Ruth shrugged and gave her gray and silver hair a shake. "I did it with the encouragement of the museum. Hailey wrote to the curator." She turned, stirred the pot with the dowel, and checked her watch. "We'll give it five minutes."

"On balance," said Betsy after a bit, "was Hailey a positive or a negative presence in the world?"

Ruth thought. "Positive, I'd say. Though I didn't know the secrets of her heart. But what heart doesn't have secrets, and who knows the secrets of any other person's heart?" She smiled. "I guess I'm being more philosophical than usual today."

Betsy avoided an examination of her own conscience by posing another question. "Do you know what Hailey thought of Marge Schultz?"

"I know they used to be friends, but something happened, I'm not sure what. Hailey used to say how smart Marge was, how hardworking and independent. Knowing how Hailey was about men, I'd say Marge started talking about a man she liked and Hailey objected to it. Is that possible? I mean, I don't live in Excelsior, so I don't know the people out there."

"I'd say it's possible. Of course, anything's possible." Betsy shrugged.

"Now it's you getting philosophical," said Ruth with a smile.

"Did Hailey know Joanne McMurphy outside of Tai Chi classes?"

"Is that how they knew each other?" Ruth asked. "Hailey was uncomfortable about Joanne. She said she was getting crazier and crazier — but she generally added, 'Poor thing,' after saying so. She pointed Joanne out to me one time and said I shouldn't say anything to her because she was very touchy. The way she said it made me think maybe she'd said something to Joanne that set her off. What's her story, anyhow? Do you know?"

"She was in a car accident four years ago that damaged her brain. She has trouble controlling her emotions, especially anger."

"Ouch! 'Poor thing' for real!"

"How about Pierce McMurphy?" asked Betsy.

"I don't know him at all."

"Did Hailey?"

"I doubt it. She never went out of her way to strike up an acquaintance with a member of the male sex."

"Well, that's true. Do you think Hailey

was sincere about encouraging Randi More-ham to separate from her husband?"

"Very sincere. Vehement, even. She even tried that argument out on me. Once. Huh!" Another toss of her head made it clear what Ruth thought of Hailey's attempt.

"Do you think Randi's husband, Walter, knew about this?"

"I have no idea. Why, what have you found out?"

"Since Hailey's death, Randi's opinion of her husband has undergone a change, and they're now in couples counseling to see if they can work out their problems."

"Oh my. I bet your question is, did Walter figure out it was Hailey, not Randi, who wanted them divorced?"

"Yes, that's a very big question. He says he didn't know. But he would say that, wouldn't he?"

"Even if only to keep people from thinking he's an idiot, not able to tell that his wife was under the spell of someone else's opinion."

Betsy nodded. It did seem a little odd that Walter didn't realize his wife's turnaround from loving homemaker to wannabe divorcee wasn't a natural progression for her. Of course, if he was working crazy hours at a demanding job, maybe the marital friction they experienced was understandable.

Ruth poked at the simmering flowers. "I think this is ready."

She poured the mixture through a strainer into a glass bowl sitting on the counter beside the stove. Then she tapped the strainer on the edge of the counter to shake loose the last of the liquid, and dumped the wet marigolds into a waiting plastic bag.

She picked up the two squares with their hanging strands of yarn and said, "Ready? One square is wool, the other square is soy — I marked it with an S."

"Ready," Betsy said.

Ruth slid the two squares into the bowl and prodded them with the dowel to get them well into the dye bath, which was the color of tea.

Betsy went into her purse and got out the knitted square Ruth had lifted from the pot of indigo all those weeks ago. "Oh, I forgot to bring a pair of scissors!"

"I've got a pair that should work," said Ruth. She went into the short, cabinet-lined hallway off her dyeing area. From a drawer she retrieved a small pair of scissors, and brought them to Betsy.

Betsy snipped at a corner of the square and began raveling it.

Ruth poked at the squares in the bowl. "Hmmm, we're getting there," she said. She put the dowel down and came to look at what Betsy was doing. "There, see what I mean?" she said and touched strands of the yarn as it came undone. "Wherever the yarn crossed, the original color can be seen."

It was a strong red-orange.

And in another few minutes, when Ruth lifted the knitted square from the bath, the colors varied from yellow-orange to tan, to yellow, to cream, to — in the case of the tin-mordanted wool — a strong red-orange.

Betsy nodded and watched Ruth go to rinse off the squares. At last, she had a piece of the puzzle that seemed to illuminate things more than complicate them.

TWENTY-FIVE

There was a time when Sergeant Mike Malloy would have groaned when the desk sergeant called to say Ms. Betsy Devonshire was here to see him. But he had slowly and reluctantly realized that while she may only be an amateur sleuth, she was a singularly talented one.

Still, she was an amateur, and capable of messing up a case by moving an important piece of evidence, or warning a suspect of her suspicions, or precipitating an arrest before the case was ready.

She was currently working on proving the innocence of his main suspect in the murder of Hailey Brent. She had a history of being right, which was one of the reasons he had grown willing to deal with her. It was possible she had something tangible to offer him today. Like another viable suspect.

"All right, send her down," he said into the phone, and closed the folder he'd been working on.

He watched as Betsy paused a moment in the open door to his small office, a short, plump woman with curly blond hair, wearing a lightweight, short-sleeved gray pantsuit and gold earrings, each set with a round jade stone, and carrying a big, dark gray leather purse that matched her low-heeled sandals. She looked intelligent and self-assured, even a little excited. Maybe she did have something useful to offer.

He rose with the old-fashioned manners his father had taught him and indicated the hard wooden chair set beside his old metal desk. "Good afternoon, Betsy," he said. "Have a seat."

She sat down, holding her purse in her lap with both hands. "I know who murdered Hailey Brent, Mike," she announced.

Though he'd half expected something like this, he felt his pale eyebrows rise on his freckled face. "Who?" he asked bluntly.

"Marge Schultz."

He stared at her for several seconds, his face disbelieving. "I thought you were out to prove she *didn't* do it."

"That's what she asked me to do. And I tried to do it. But facts are facts."

Mike smiled and sat back in his chair,

prepared to listen. "All right, tell me the facts."

Betsy said, "It started a few years ago — I don't know precisely how many, but more than three, probably more than four. Hailey Brent had been growing herbs and flowers and making dyes from them since before that, for a long time. She was a spinner, too, spinning wool into yarn and coloring it, making soft, beautiful colors from her own dyes. I was one of her customers — her yarns were expensive but popular."

"You knit things from the yarn she sold you?" Mike was trying gamely to follow this meandering story. Was knitting one of the clues?

"No, I bought the yarn for resale, in my shop. And she sold to other shops as well." Betsy nodded sideways to show she'd slipped a little off target, then continued back on track. "She was a bright and talented dyer and had this attitude that, as an artist, she was above the rules of ordinary behavior."

"Hell, I know all about that. How she'd go over to Green Gaia when no one was around and clip flowers off the plants to make her dyes. Marge knew she was doing it, but said that it didn't happen often enough and that Hailey didn't take enough to bother her bottom line — or at any rate it didn't bother her enough to call the cops about it."

"But it did bother her. It's just that Hailey had a secret she was holding over Marge. In fact, I think her cutting blooms off Marge's flowers was a way of twitting Marge about it."

"You mean about Marge having an affair with Pierce McMurphy? Is that why you think Marge shot Hailey?" Mike would give a great deal to have solid evidence of that.

"No, I think it's possible Hailey didn't know about the affair. But it's also possible Marge told Pierce she did. That was my first theory."

Mike opened his mouth, then closed it again. "Why would she do that?" he asked.

"Because Marge wants Pierce to divorce Joanne and marry her, but he's stalling. Joanne's behavior has been getting worse lately, and Marge thinks she should be moved into a secure facility. And she told me Pierce agrees. If Joanne found out Pierce is being unfaithful to her with Marge, she might go over the edge and attack one or both of them. I was thinking Marge persuaded Pierce to fake that theft from his car and give her the gun so she could frighten Hailey into silence. Marge might have told

Pierce it went wrong and she accidentally shot Hailey."

Mike considered that. He, too, had wondered if the theft was faked. "But if the car burglary was a fake, why didn't Pierce shoot Hailey himself? Why give the gun to Marge?"

"Because it gave Pierce the opportunity to establish an ironclad alibi — which he has got, remember."

Mike wriggled in his chair. Ungentlemanly of Pierce. "Okay."

Betsy nodded. "But from what I've seen of Pierce, he doesn't seem the type to give a terrible job like murder to his mistress. And, anyway, if the problem was Joanne, the solution was to put her away, not kill Hailey. I think Marge stole the gun without Pierce's knowing it was her."

"Or," said Mike, "the burglary was real and Marge — if Marge murdered Hailey — got a gun somewhere else."

Betsy shook her head. "But where, Mike? I'm sure, since you've been looking hard at Marge, you've been checking to see if she bought a gun legally. Where would someone get a gun without leaving a record of its purchase?"

"It can be done. Crooks do it all the time," said Mike.

"But Marge isn't a crook. She wouldn't know who to talk to, where to go. No, I think Pierce's gun was used to kill Hailey."

"But how did Marge know about Pierce's gun?"

Betsy smiled. "How do I know that Jill Larson has a concealed carry license and packs heat at all times?"

Mike smothered a laugh. " 'Packs heat'? Listen to you! Why'd she tell you, is she trying to persuade you to get a concealed carry license, too?"

Betsy nodded. "Not a chance, thank you very much. But we're wandering from the topic again. I'm sure Marge and Pierce talked about their respective professions, and it's likely Pierce told her about his gun when she worried about him carrying estimates and blueprints into bad neighborhoods. He may even have bragged about the gun, or offered to let her try to shoot it with him."

Mike rubbed his lower face with one thin hand. "So if Hailey didn't know about the affair, and the crime wasn't to keep her from blabbing to Joanne, why did Marge Schultz murder Hailey Brent?"

"It was about the red marigolds."

"Red marigolds," Mike echoed. He had already found out that Marge was growing a new variety of marigolds, but so what?

"You see, Hailey is the one who first found them growing in her own garden. Or, more likely, one single plant with red blooms on it, a mutant. She might have mentioned it to Marge — she would go to the garden center for legitimate purposes sometimes; for instance, to see a plant in person after seeing it in a catalog. If she liked it, she'd order it from the catalog instead of buying it from Green Gaia, because the catalog price was lower. Like people sometimes come to Crewel World to look at a pattern or a new variety of floss or a pair of scissors — then order it online." Betsy's lips thinned. She didn't mind that kind of thing once in a while, but some people made a practice of it.

Mike nodded. His brother-in-law liked to tell the story of seeing a woman in a bookstore with a Kindle in her hand, perusing books on shelves then ordering them on her device.

But they were wandering from the point again.

Betsy said, "I know for a fact that Hailey Brent did not buy red marigolds from Green Gaia, and that they are not for sale anywhere else. But if you go by her house, you will see one blooming in her backyard."

"And?" Mike asked. Was there a point in here somewhere? But Betsy was looking very earnest. He reached for his notebook.

"Anyway, Marge found out about the new variety of marigold growing in Hailey's garden and sneaked over for a look." She raised a finger to indicate her next point was the important one. "Did you know there can be a great deal of money made from a new color of marigold? That you can actually patent it, so other suppliers have to pay money to carry it?"

"No, I didn't know that." Mike now knew where Betsy was going. "You're saying Marge stole the red marigold plant."

"No, she wouldn't dare do that. Hailey paid close attention to the plants in her garden, and she would have noticed if the strange red marigold suddenly went missing. Marge stole the seeds. All she needed was one bloom, picked in the late fall, when the seed bulb was fully developed. I think Marge took those seeds and planted them to see if it was a true mutation, and finding it was, propagated them."

"Propagated — ?"

"Grew more of them. Did whatever gardeners do to strengthen and ensure the new color — it's called line breeding when you do it with dogs, breeding sons and mothers, daughters and fathers, together. I guess you can do something similar with flowers. Marge is an experienced and talented gardener. She'd patented a new variety of aster and made enough money to expand and improve her garden center. Here was a chance to do it again — perhaps an even more lucrative chance."

"Didn't Hailey notice when she saw Marge putting out the new plants?"

"I think she didn't realize right away that the new plants originated in her garden. There was only one red marigold growing in Hailey's garden, after all. Perhaps a bird had carried the seed over the fence. But talking with an employee made her realize that Marge started growing red marigolds the season *after* Hailey saw one in her own garden."

"So why not acknowledge it?" asked Mike reasonably. "Share the wealth. Marge could have given Hailey some of the money."

"Because Marge needed it all. Pierce couldn't simply abandon Joanne; she needed to be put into a good, well-run facility — a very expensive proposition that would eat up most, if not all, of the settlement given her as a result of that car accident. Joanne and Pierce were living comfortably on that settlement. Marge felt she

331

needed to bring a great deal of money to her prospective marriage to Pierce to compensate for the funds potentially spent on Joanne's care."

Mike waited for more, but Betsy was done.

"Sounds kind of cold-blooded," he noted.

"No, I think there's plenty of heat between Pierce and Marge. But strip away the passion, and you're right, there are elements of commerce in it. Marge felt she needed to contribute to the new arrangement, in order to remove an argument against implementing it."

"So what can you offer as proof that this is what's going on?"

"Come on, Mike, I've got the only explanation that fits all the little oddments and curvatures of this thing!"

"Your reasoning is all you've got? It's an interesting story — it might even be true — but I need more than your active imagination."

"But there are all sorts of little things." Betsy spread her hands out, palms up. "And when you put them together, it shows me I'm right about what happened."

"Like what?"

"Well, when Ruth Ladwig and I looked around Hailey's dyeing setup —"

"Who's Ruth Ladwin?"

"She's a dyer, does demos over at the Science Museum. She and Hailey were friends."

Mike went back in his notebook and found the name. "Yeah, okay. So you and Ruth Ladwin —"

"Ladwig. Ruth Ladwig. L-A-D-W-I-G."

"Gotcha." Mike corrected the spelling. His notes reminded him that he had talked to Ms. Ladwig but gotten nothing useful from her.

"She was a friend of Hailey's. They talked methods, recipes, mordants, how to use bark and roots and flowers, and things like that."

"Yes, I know." Mike was starting to feel impatient. "Are you going to tell me she told you Hailey told her about Marge stealing the red marigolds?"

"I'm afraid not. But going through the dyeing setup in the basement, we found some pots still on the stove. We went down there with the permission of Hailey's daughter, of course."

"Of course."

"And there was some dyed yarn hanging on a line over the sink."

Mike tapped his pen on his desk and nodded. "I remember seeing the pots and the yarn."

"Good. But there were still some things in the pots. One big one held indigo dye, and there was yarn in it — and this, too." Betsy opened her big purse and pulled out what had probably once been a square made of knitted yarn. An uninteresting shade of brown with some spots of red-orange here and there on the loose part. It was about a third unraveled. She handed it to him.

"What is it?"

"Possibly a pot holder. More likely an experiment. It had been dyed that red-orange you can still see in spots, then dumped in the pot of indigo and overdyed blue — but blue and red-orange make brown. Except where the yarn crossed over itself. You can see the original color showing where I raveled it."

"Unraveled it, you mean."

"No, unravel means to knit it up again. Like from Shakespeare, 'Sleep knits up the raveled sleeve of care.' "

Mike Malloy looked slantwise at her, one eyebrow lifted.

"Well, it does," she murmured defensively.

"So she dyed it red-orange, and then put it in the pot of indigo to see what color she'd get," said Mike, handing it back.

"No, her murderer put it in the pot of indigo."

"Why?"

"Because . . ." Betsy dived into her purse again, and this time she pulled out a limp square of fabric with four thin strands of yarn in different soft colors hanging from the bottom of it. She handed it to Mike. "See, that one strand is the same red-orange color, or nearly, as the spots on the raveled square."

Mike laid the red-orange strand across the red-orange spot. They pretty much matched. "So?" he asked.

"That little red-orange piece of yarn was dyed a few hours ago over at the Science Museum using red marigolds to make the dye bath. I think Hailey dyed the pot holder with red marigold blooms and her killer saw it floating in a dye bath with wet red marigold blooms standing in a strainer beside it. I think she thought that Hailey had decided to stop hinting that Marge was a thief and was plotting to prove the red marigold variety was her own. Marge put the pot holder into the indigo dye bath, dumped the blooms in the garbage can, and took the liner away with her. I think that's why Ruth and I found the can empty, with no liner."

"But you don't think it's equally likely that Hailey emptied the garbage can herself."

"No, because there was another pot with

carrot tops floating in it. Hailey wouldn't have taken the liner out without first draining the second pot. And she would have put a fresh liner in the can."

Betsy, reading Mike's doubting mind, said, "I told you these were minor things!"

Yeah, but minor things could add up. Still, he wished there was something more, something solid, something he could sink his investigative teeth into.

"I'm sorry. What you're telling me is one way it *might have* happened. Your evidence is interesting, but too thin to convince a prosecutor or a jury. I need something more than this if I'm going to make an arrest."

"Like what?"

"A concrete piece of evidence. A note from Hailey demanding money. Or, say, the gun."

"If the killer had more than two active brain cells, any note has long since been destroyed, and that gun is at the bottom of Lake Minnetonka."

"Find me an eyewitness then, someone who saw something."

"I don't have one. But come on, Mike, it all fits together the way I'm telling it! Go dig up the red marigold in Hailey's backyard!"

"What would that prove this long after the

fact of the mutant's discovery? I admit, you've got a very pretty theory. I'm glad you brought it to me. I'm going to start looking at it from the angle you presented to me. Maybe I can come up with the proof you haven't found. Meanwhile —" He lifted his thin shoulders in a shrug and rubbed at his faded-red hair. "I'm sorry."

Betsy looked as if she was going to cry, then sucked it up. "All right," she said, and, deflated, left Mike in his little office.

She spent the rest of the day furiously cleaning to work off her frustration. Connor came by at one point, but when he saw her standing grimly in her kitchen amid stacks of pots and pans — she was cleaning out her cabinets — with a scarf pulled crookedly over her hair and a smudge on her nose, he wisely retreated.

He came back in the early evening, bringing white cartons of Chinese food, to find peace restored. Betsy was happy to see him, and even happier that he'd brought a hot meal for each of them, since she'd been thinking, without enthusiasm, about a tuna fish sandwich.

"Now," he said, dishing out the food in the dining nook, "what was that all about?"

She explained how she'd taken her well-thought-out theory to Sergeant Malloy, and how he'd decided it was not solid enough to warrant the immediate arrest of Marge Schultz.

"You haven't shared this theory with anyone else, have you?" he asked. "Godwin, for example?"

"No, of course not. I don't want Marge to be warned that we're onto her."

"Wise woman," he said, nodding. "Very wise. But now what?"

"I. Don't. Know." Confessing as much made her sad, and the food she'd been enjoying turned to cement in her stomach.

But Connor began to talk about her previous successes, mixing in humorous anecdotes about the good times they'd had together, and in a while she felt better.

After dinner they did the dishes together, which took about four minutes, and then went into the living room. Connor got out his knitting — he was working now on a bright yellow glove — and Betsy followed his example. She was trying her hand at a Fair Isle sweater, but this evening, still shaken by her failure to convince Mike Malloy of Marge's guilt, she couldn't concentrate on the complex pattern. She put it aside and got out the plaited weave scarf. In a few minutes she had settled into the pattern and relaxed.

As her mind cleared, she began to run the case through her memory. All those weeks ago — not really that many, it just seemed like a lot! — Marge had come into her shop, scared because Mike had asked her if she had murdered Hailey. Would Betsy please do for her what she had done for others, and prove she hadn't done it?

The audacity of that woman!

"Humph!" Betsy snorted. Connor glanced over and smiled.

Wearily, Betsy trod yet again the lengthy path of her investigation. But now, in sheer desperation, she wandered off the track, looking for a new insight. She remembered going through the upstairs of Hailey's house, the tiny, old-fashioned bathroom, the long crocheted topper on the old dresser. She remembered Amy Stromberg's pleasure at getting the Mark Parsons needlepoint canvas. She remembered the night Jill and Lars came over for Rock Cornish game hens and Scrabble. She remembered the mushroom omelet breakfast with Philadelphia at Antiquity Rose. She remembered the Fourth of July picnic, and Jill telling Marge she wanted a pink hydrangea and a blue hydrangea, one for each of her children.

Pink and blue. Aluminum to make blue.

She put her knitting down. "Connor," she said, "I think I finally can give Mike Malloy his solid piece of evidence."

TWENTY-SIX

Betsy called Mike Malloy. "I think I can tell you where to find your evidence," she said. "But it depends on your answer to one question about Pierce McMurphy's stolen gun."

But Malloy, after answering her question and hearing her latest idea, said, "I'd need a search warrant, and I can tell you right now, I wouldn't get it. There simply aren't grounds for it. Marge Schultz may be a suspect, but so are Pierce McMurphy, Joanne McMurphy, and Walter Moreham. The real killer may be nobody we suspect at present. Your reasoning is creative, and maybe even right, but I can just see myself trying to give a judge gardening lessons — won't happen, I'm sorry."

Betsy hung up, rubbed the tip of her nose with a forefinger, and thought hard. "I think we're going to have to go for it ourselves, Connor," she said.

"*Machree,* do you understand the rules of evidence? There has to be an unbroken line between the piece of evidence and the courtroom. You might go looking for that gun, you might even find it, but when you take it to Mike tomorrow, it's only your word that you found it where you say you found it. Plus, to get it you have to go trespassing, which weakens your case right from the start."

"Hmmmm," said Betsy, and called Jill.

The evening of the next day it was still daylight out, though it was after eight. Jill gave Betsy a quick lesson in using her video camera as they drove over to Green Gaia. Betsy had wanted Jill to use the camera but Jill wanted both hands free "just in case." Betsy did not want to ask, "In case what?"

"What if she's still there?" asked Connor from the driver's seat.

"I'll say I didn't know it was so late — daylight saving time keeps it daylight till nine — and that I had hoped to pick up those hydrangea plants," said Jill.

"And we're just along for the ride," offered Betsy.

"No, you're coming over to help me plant them — that's why there's a spade in the backseat."

"And then we'll have ice cream," said Connor, falsely bright. He wasn't a very chipper lawbreaker; he'd had his fill of explaining things to the police the night of July Fourth, when he'd driven Annie home.

He found a parking spot not far from the entrance to the garden center and they all sat in the car for a few minutes, watching for pedestrians and vehicle traffic, and getting a few last-minute instructions on the video camera.

"I got it, I got it," said Betsy at last. "Come on, we've got a hole to dig."

They bailed out and walked quickly into the center, noting the closed sign on the shop door, and made their way to the greenhouse and the big hydrangea bush by it.

Betsy started the camera, panning around to show the entrance, the tables with their potted plants, the sign for Green Gaia Gardens in fancy script over the shop door. She then trained it on the hydrangea bush, careful to cut off the heads of her coconspirators.

"Dig," Betsy murmured to Connor, and he pushed the pointed end of the spade into the earth near the shrub's roots. Jill stood nearby, her head constantly moving, keeping watch.

He began on the side away from the street, going down about two feet, then gradually widening the hole and extending its reach around the plant. He worked very quietly, taking small bites of the earth, which had been kept loose, unlike the path beside it, which was tramped down hard. A perimeter about a yard across had been marked with stones painted white to keep customers and employees at bay; he stayed inside it.

Betsy kept the camera running. As Connor dug and dug, her palms grew sweaty, though the evening was cool. Connor did not look as if he was sweating, though he was breathing more deeply than usual.

No results, no results. Was she wrong? No, she couldn't be wrong. Could he have missed it? He was being very careful, poking the blade into the soil several times before raising more of it.

What if they found nothing? Could they just replace the earth, make it look as if it had not been disturbed and quietly slip away?

Connor was more than halfway around when the blade of his implement struck something with an audible *tink.*

Jill, who had been looking toward the street, swung around, and they all exchanged an anticipatory look.

"Probably a stone," murmured Jill.

Betsy closed in on the trench with the camera and held her breath as Connor pushed the spade under and lifted the object. It lay in dirt and was encrusted with dirt, but it was clearly a semiautomatic pistol.

"What are you *doing*?" came a very loud woman's voice, high-pitched and obviously scared. "Stop it! Stop it!"

The trio whirled, but the woman was upon them, swinging a garden rake, its teeth sharp and heavy. Marge.

The end of the rake caught Connor on his shoulder and his spade flew up in the air, sending the gun flying amid a shower of earth. The impact made him shout and sent him reeling.

Marge was screaming and swinging in big arcs. "Thieves! Get out!" She was grunting with effort.

She smashed the camera out of Betsy's hands. Betsy's hands exploded in pain. She screamed.

Then a gun went off, its sound huge, and everyone froze.

"Drop the rake!" said Jill.

Betsy looked over and saw Jill standing bent-kneed, both of her hands wrapped around a snub-nosed revolver.

"Don't shoot, don't shoot!" cried Marge, and she threw the rake down.

There was a pause of several seconds. Then Marge said, "Wait, wait a minute! You're Jill Larson! What are you doing here?"

Betsy stooped and nursed her aching fingers. "Ow, ow, ow," she moaned.

"Betsy?" asked Marge.

"Ow, ow, *ow!*" replied Betsy.

Connor was by her side in an instant. "You're not shot, are you?"

"No, no, it's my fingers. She hit the camera with that rake and it hurt my fingers. Damn, damn, dammit! Where's the gun?" She looked around and saw it lying on the ground, a few yards away.

"Nobody move," said Jill, her revolver firmly in both hands. "Betsy, where's your cell phone?"

"In my shirt pocket."

"Take it out and dial 911. Say a shot has been fired and we're holding a person in custody."

"Wait a minute, wait a minute!" cried Marge. "What's going on? Holding a person in custody? I thought you were thieves!"

Betsy ignored her and placed the call, giving her name and location, and repeating Jill's message. "I'm sure they'll be right here," she said, on disconnecting.

"I want to know what's going on," repeated Marge. "Why are you digging up my hydrangea?"

"We're not digging up the hydrangea, we're digging up the gun you buried under it," said Betsy. "The gun you used to shoot Hailey."

"What are you talking about? What gun?"

"Pierce McMurphy's gun. Over there on the ground. It's got an aluminum frame. That's why your hydrangea changed from pink to blue."

Marge stared at her. "Aluminum frame?" She looked at Jill, at the gun in her hands. "A gun has an aluminum frame? But that wouldn't make a hydrangea change color!"

Betsy said, "Sure it would. At the Fourth of July picnic Annie told us about a neighbor who changed her hydrangeas from pink to blue by burying a set of aluminum measuring cups by the roots."

"No, no, that's an old wives' tale. Not enough aluminum will leach out of an aluminum object to change the pH of the soil. You dug up my hydrangea because of an old wives' tale?"

It was Betsy's turn to stare. "Then why did your beautiful pink hydrangea turn blue?"

With an exasperated air of stating the obvious, Marge replied, "Because I mixed up a batch of Color Me Blue in water and poured it on the roots."

"Why did you want to change the color of your hydrangea?"

"Because Como Flower Center in Saint Paul was going under — I knew that last fall — and I knew she had a truckload of potted hydrangeas on her hands. I thought, if she had a batch of them left over, I could get a good price on them. But I needed an angle. Lots of people know about my big pink hydrangea. I got this idea to change its color to blue. People would see it and want to know what happened, and maybe I could sell them a hydrangea they could work some magic on themselves."

She added in a tone of tired wonder, "And you thought it was an aluminum frame gun that did it."

"Yes. And we found the gun. Marge, look, we found Pierce McMurphy's gun!"

Marge half sat, half collapsed onto the ground, and covered her eyes with her hands. "Oh my God, done in by an old wives' tale!" She began to weep.

Connor said to Jill, "May I retrieve the gun?"

"Handle it carefully, okay?" She had taken

her finger off the trigger of her own gun and lowered it to her side with one hand.

"I will." Connor took the spade with him and scooped up the gun one-handed.

"Marge, why didn't you throw it in the lake?" asked Betsy.

"I tried to. I bought a ticket on the *Minnehaha,* but there were always people around, so I brought it home again. I thought it was safe to bury it under my one plant that wasn't for sale!"

There was the sound of an approaching siren.

"Marge, is this the gun that killed Hailey?" asked Jill, as Connor came back with the dirty gun balanced on the blade of the spade.

Marge nodded. "Yes," she whispered.

"Did you murder Hailey Brent?" The siren was rapidly coming closer. A second siren was heard, also approaching.

"Yes." She began to sob. "Oh, God, oh, God. Yes, yes."

Connor lifted his left arm just a little, experimentally, and winced.

"Are you hurt, Connor?" asked Betsy.

"She hit me a good one on the shoulder," he replied. "Nothing broken, I don't think, but it hurts."

"I guess being around me is dangerous to

your health."

"Yes, but always very interesting, *machree.*"

The siren grew very loud, and a flicker of red and blue lights began to bounce in the air.

"Things are about to get complicated," said Jill to them all. "Everyone just stay calm and very, very obedient."

TWENTY-SEVEN

"That's something you're supposed to think about before you decide to carry a gun," Jill had told Betsy over lunch a couple of days later. "It's not just deciding to carry it, it's deciding to be very reluctant to draw it. I could have been arrested on the spot; in fact, I still may face charges. If I do, I'll have to hire an attorney. We could lose our house defending me in a trial and I could still go to prison."

Betsy was aghast. "But Marge was trying very hard to hurt us, even kill us with that rake! How can the police not see that? I can't believe you might still be arrested! They know you wouldn't be careless. You used to be one of them — Lars still is!"

"All the more reason I'm supposed to be careful about pulling a weapon."

And another good reason, decided Betsy, not to apply for a concealed carry permit.

The Monday Bunch worried at its next

meeting, too; and about a week later, there were ecstatic expressions of happiness and relief when the news came that the police had decided not to file charges against Jill.

"Of all the silly nonsense I've ever heard," declared Bershada at the meeting, "the silliest was the notion that our Jill is a gun nut!"

Jill smiled but said nothing.

"I didn't even know you carried a gun," said Doris. "Since you stopped being a police officer, I thought you turned it in."

"I did," Jill said. "But I bought a new one, smaller, easier to conceal."

Emily said, "That must be why I never saw a bulge on you. Where did you keep it? In your bra?"

"No," said Jill, with a laugh. "There are places, and ways, to conceal a weapon. But let's not get into that, okay?"

Phil said, "So, is it okay now to talk about what happened at the garden center when all this went down?"

Connor had joined the Bunch at the table in Crewel World today. He looked at Jill, who looked at Betsy, who looked at him.

"You first," said Connor to Betsy.

But Betsy was tired of the story — and eager to hear the results of the template contest Crewel World had been running. Sitting on the table, under the Fair Isle sweater she was painstakingly knitting, was a long white envelope addressed to the shop with a return address of one of the three contest judges. It had come by registered mail, and Betsy's fingers fairly itched to open it. The envelope was nice and fat, so there was probably commentary on at least the winning patterns.

But she wanted to announce the winners on the Crewel World web site on the date promised, which wasn't until tomorrow. How could she open the envelope in front of the members of the Monday Bunch without telling them the results? Especially since some of them had entered the contest and so would know whether or not they won?

"Excuse me," she said, and took the envelope over to her desk to put it in a drawer that locked.

Then she came back and sat down. "Where were we?" she asked.

Bershada said in her driest voice, "You were going to tell us how you came to realize that the woman who asked you to prove Mike Malloy was wrong to suspect her of murder was, in fact, a murderer."

"It was a mistake," said Betsy.

Emily said, shocked, "You mean she *isn't* a murderer?"

"No, I mean it was a mistake that led me to the correct conclusion. Oh yes, Marge murdered Hailey, sure enough. And I figured it out, but I couldn't prove it. Then I made a mistake — or rather, Alice, you made a mistake."

"Me? What did I do?" The big woman wrinkled her forehead in a frown.

"You told me you knew someone who changed the color of a hydrangea from pink to blue by burying aluminum measuring cups under it. You believed that story — and so did I, when you told it to me. So when I remembered that Marge's hydrangea was turning blue, and that Lars told me Pierce McMurphy's stolen gun had an aluminum frame, I was sure Marge had buried the murder weapon under her hydrangea bush."

"But I thought she did bury it there," said Emily, still confused.

"Well, in fact, she did," said Betsy. "But that isn't the reason the flowers turned blue. Marge fed the plant a solution of aluminum sulfate to turn its blooms blue on purpose, as an advertising gimmick."

Alice said, in her deepest voice, "I will always believe that gun helped turn the flowers blue."

Phil made a faint scoffing noise, but Emily, blue eyes wide, nodded in agreement.

Doris, without pausing in the little rhythmic motions of punchneedle, turned to Connor. "How's your shoulder coming along?" she asked him.

Connor bent over the tricky thumb of the glove he was knitting, nodded to her. "Only a little stiff now. No permanent damage."

"I'm glad to hear that."

"We all are," said Bershada, to general agreement.

"Whatever possessed Marge?" asked Emily. "I don't mean just to murder someone — I suppose anyone can get scared enough or mad enough to murder. But to think that Pierce McMurphy would put his wife in a home just so he could marry Marge . . ." She shook her head. "Marge must have been crazy. Pierce *loved* Joanne."

"Then why was he boinking Marge?" asked Phil reasonably. He was frowning over an upper corner of his counted cross-stitch piece of wild geese in a field, where the sky was six different shades of gray and cream.

"Oh, *men*," said Bershada. "Didn't mean a thing to him."

Connor said, "Speaking as a representative of my sex, I object to that. Pierce was probably hungry for some give-and-take with a woman who wouldn't go off like an unreliable firework if he took a misstep.

Marge was comfortable, reliable, sexy, and intelligent. A very tasty side dish when the main dish has become complicated and difficult."

Bershada pushed her lips forward disapprovingly but didn't argue.

"Does she know?" asked Emily.

"Does who know what?" asked Alice, her crochet needle coming to a pause as she tried to follow that question.

"Does Joanne know that her husband was the cause of all this?"

Emily's question caused a minor uproar as the others tried to disagree, agree, or say it was more complicated than that, all at once.

"But didn't Pierce let Marge burgle his car?" asked Emily at last.

"We don't know that," said Jill.

"We don't?" Bershada's tone was dark.

"I suppose it will all come out at the trial," Phil pointed out.

"What do you think, Betsy?" asked Doris, deferring to her as resident sleuth.

"I don't know," confessed Betsy, lifting her shoulders high. "And I'm hoping Marge sticks to her confession and just pleads guilty in court."

"Amen," said Connor.

"It wouldn't have worked out even if she'd

gotten away with it," said Doris.

"What makes you say that?" asked Phil, looking at his wife in surprise.

"Because marriages that begin with affairs rarely succeed. He'd be carrying guilt — and she'd be feeling guilty twice over. Plus she'd always be wondering if someone would figure it out. Betsy did, after all — and, pardon me, Betsy, if you could do it, so could someone else."

But Betsy only said, "That's true."

Bershada said, "And when you marry a man who fooled around on his wife, you get a man who fools around on his wife."

"Well, yes," said Connor, "but these circumstances were a little unusual, don't you think?"

Jill said, "I do think we have to cut Pierce some slack."

Bershada said, "Unlike the man an old girlfriend of mine got engaged to. He divorced his wife for her, and one week before the wedding, he left her for her maid of honor. They got engaged, and a month before *their* wedding, he left her and went back to his wife."

"Sounds like he had a problem with commitment," said Emily, amused.

"He had a problem, all right," said Bershada.

"I think he just wanted a ride on a merry-go-round," said Phil.

"Would you have taken him back?" Jill asked Bershada.

"Yes, but I would have made sure he went to bed worried for a long time."

Connor said, "I read about a man who came home from work and heard talk and laughter coming from his kitchen. He walked in on his wife and his mistress sitting at the table drinking coffee together. They quickly shut up when he came in and sat there giving him the same look."

Doris asked, "What did he do?"

"Packed a bag and left town."

And on that note, the Bunch began to break up.

When the last of them had left and Connor had gone back upstairs, Betsy unlocked the drawer and took out the fat white envelope. She tore it open at one end and extracted the contents.

Taking three pages, the judges had written a sentence or two about each entry. They had come up with a one-to-fifty numerical scoring system that they used three times for each entry — Best Execution in red, Cleverest Use of Space in blue, Just Plain Wow in orange.

A separate note from the judges said they

had enjoyed judging the entries, and that choosing the winners had been very difficult — "It took three fistfights and two arm-wrestling matches to pick Best Execution."

Betsy got out her list matching the numbers that had been assigned to each entry to the actual names of the contestants.

The judges noted that Rafael's entry was very clever and made good use of space, but that an error in counting had given the central rectangle an extra row up and down.

Annie's entry was given middling grades for cleverness and use of space, and a low-middle grade for execution. The comments noted that the execution seemed to improve from left to right, "the mark of an ardent beginner."

Helen Foster's Tiger in a Cage won Cleverest Use of Space, Alix Jordan's Climbing Roses won Best Execution, and Susan Okkonen won Just Plain Wow. Susan was just one point lower than Alix in Best Execution — which was a good thing, as the prize was the same for each of the three categories, and what would Susan have done with two OttLites?

Mike Malloy sat at his desk, going over the files and notes he would turn over to the prosecutor. He shook his head. *Betsy isn't even Irish. Where does she get the dumb luck,* he asked himself, *of solving the case by way of a misunderstanding?*

Well, half the case. Mike was morally sure Pierce McMurphy had staged that car burglary in order to give Marge Schultz the gun. But Pierce was sticking to his theft story, and Marge said she often talked to Pierce about his deliveries and so knew where he'd be the day she followed him and broke into his car. She was taking the whole rap herself, even down to insisting that she and Pierce were just good friends. She claimed that the sole reason she killed Hailey was so she wouldn't have to share any of the credit — and money — she was going to get from the mutant marigold.

Now, instead, current plans were for Marge's two daughters to go ahead with the patent process and split the proceeds with Philadelphia and her brother, JR. Mike felt that decision, coming out of the horrible mess created by Marge, wasn't the worst possible.

Betsy was silent in bed that night. Sophie, aware that her mistress was not sleeping, lay close by her side, now and again reminding Betsy, with a gentle touch of her paw, that she wanted some more stroking.

Connor was deep asleep on Betsy's other side.

Had there been a miscarriage of justice here? Marge was claiming sole responsibility for the murder of Hailey — but was Pierce in some way responsible, too?

Betsy tickled Sophie's right ear. The cat purred softly.

Was Marge so besotted with love for Pierce that she was willing to go alone to prison for the rest of her life in order to protect him from the consequences of their shared crime?

That didn't seem to be an accurate description of Marge — or Pierce, for that matter. Betsy remembered how he'd insisted his wife apologize for scaring Betsy.

Or was that to forestall an assault charge against her?

Betsy recalled the look of love on his face when Joanne, entirely unwilling, nevertheless asked Betsy's pardon. And her basking in that look with a smile of her own. No, there was more than fear of an assault charge causing that loving exchange.

So how, loving his wife as he did, could Pierce collaborate with his mistress to murder a third party?

She could understand the mistress part. Most men, despite all the sexist jokes and macho posing, yearned to have a warm, loyal, and reliable relationship with a woman. Joanne could no longer provide all of that; sometimes, none of it. It must have seemed to Pierce that Marge could.

But loyalty went both ways, and Pierce was loyal to Joanne. Betsy closed her eyes and tried to recall as accurately as she could the conversation between Pierce and Marge on the other side of that tall wooden fence.

"We have to stay away from each other for now," Pierce had said, or something like that. Did that sound as if he knew, or suspected, that Marge was a murderer? Or was he merely anxious not to give Mike Malloy a reason to think she might be?

Ruth Ladwig had said it was impossible to see into the hearts of other people.

Betsy could feel herself starting to fall asleep. She wanted to solve this puzzle before she did.

She remembered the touching letter from Marge's daughter, Louise. Marge, Louise had written, was "married" to Green Gaia, and loved it more than even her daughter and granddaughter.

There it was, thought Betsy, as her limbs grew heavy and her eyes closed. The real reason for the murder was not to protect Pierce from a charge of infidelity, but to enrich Green Gaia. If it became known that Marge had cheated Hailey by refusing to share credit for the mutant marigold, her patent application might be turned down. Marge needed that money to keep Green Gaia up and growing. Her reputation shattered, she might never be able to patent another flower.

Pierce loved Marge, but he was not going to abandon his wife for her. Betsy could see Pierce's face, the way he looked that day in her shop, loving his wife.

A man whose love could not be destroyed by so terrible a fate visited on his wife would not connive at the murder of another person.

And Marge Schultz, clever and efficient, would do anything necessary to protect her occupation. She had broken into Pierce's car, had stolen the GPS device, the attaché case, and the gun. She had gotten rid of the cashier's check by stuffing it into the pocket of a coat later shoplifted. Foolish move; she should have burned it. The GPS device was probably dropped into a donation bin outside a Salvation Army building.

Satisfied at last by the conclusions she'd drawn, Betsy's finger stopped tickling her cat's ear, and she and Sophie fell asleep.

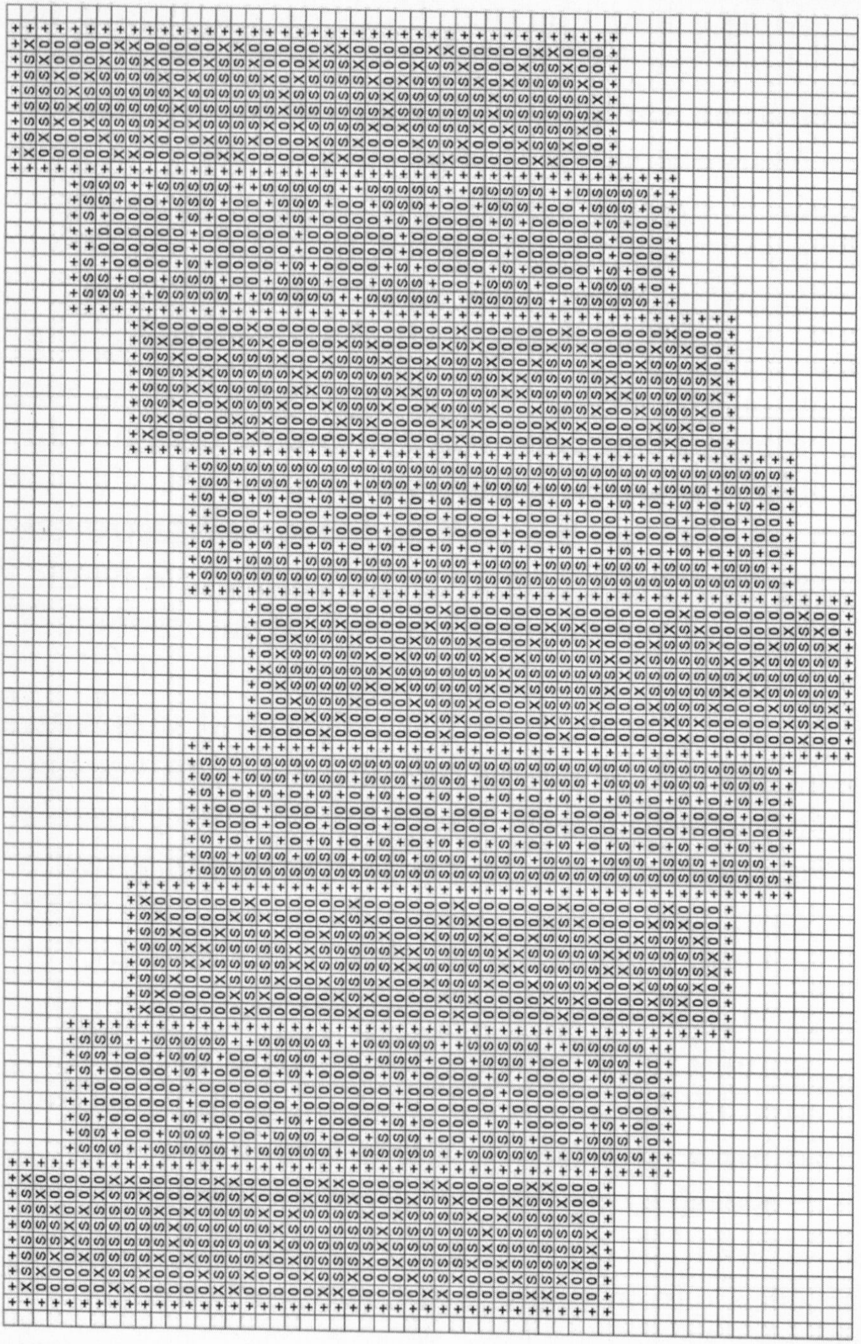

Mary Monica's Argyle Clock Towers

A Dusty Rose Original Pattern
Designed by Alixandra Jordan of
Dusty Rose Designs

Design size: 83w × 57h

Sample was stitched on white Aida 18 count using 3 strands of DMC cotton thread.

Note: Each section should be stitched one at a time, left to right and top to bottom.

Symbol, Number, Description
X, 168, Pewter — very light
S, 3844, Bright Turquoise — dark
0, 3846, Bright Turquoise — light
+, 310, Black

3/13